W9-BEK-959

PRAISE FOR

The Reason Is You

"A spot-on debut novel, Sharla Lovelace's prose is smart, witty, funny, with a hot, sexy edge that makes *The Reason Is You* an oh-so-tantalizing romantic journey, without any gooey gushiness oozing too-sweet sentiment. She takes us through the lives of Dani and a fascinating cast of characters—and lucky for readers, the line between our world and the mystical one is deliciously blurred. I could not put down this book, devoured it quickly, and can't wait to see what the author comes up with next." —Kathryn Magendie, author of *The Firefly Dance*

"*The Reason Is You* is a romantic story about love, ghosts, and second chances. But under all of that, it's a story about redemption. This novel is the definition of a page-turner."
—Therese Walsh, author of *The Last Will of Moira Leahy*

"A hauntingly beautiful story from a writer with a fresh new voice."
—Jodi Thomas, author of *Just Down the Road*

"Sharla Lovelace is going on my auto-buy list. Wow! I loved this book. *The Reason Is You* is an impressive debut novel about love and loss, family bonds and family secrets, redemption and starting over. Oh, yeah, and also ghosts! . . . I would highly recommend *The Reason Is You* to fans of romantic women's fiction." —*Novel Reflections*

"*The Reason Is You,* Sharla Lovelace's debut novel, transported me to a small town, complete with small-town drama, a slight Southern feel, and a whole lot of love-triangle action! It was easy to identify with Dani, our protagonist . . . The relationships within the story are complex and fleshed out, enabling the reader to be in the moment with the characters. Great debut, Ms. Lovelace!" —*That's What I'm Talking About*

"Wow, this book was amazing . . . An amazing tale of romance and love in both the lands of the living and the dead, and a tale of how strong family bonds can form when the going gets tough and there is no one else to turn to." —*The Phantom Paragrapher*

titles by Sharla Lovelace

THE REASON IS YOU
BEFORE AND EVER SINCE

Before
AND EVER
Since

SHARLA LOVELACE

BERKLEY SENSATION, NEW YORK

THE BERKLEY PUBLISHING GROUP
Published by the Penguin Group
Penguin Group (USA) Inc.
375 Hudson Street, New York, New York 10014, USA
Penguin Group (Canada), 90 Eglinton Avenue East, Suite 700, Toronto, Ontario M4P 2Y3, Canada
(a division of Pearson Penguin Canada Inc.) • Penguin Books Ltd., 80 Strand, London WC2R 0RL,
England • Penguin Group Ireland, 25 St. Stephen's Green, Dublin 2, Ireland (a division of Penguin
Books Ltd.) • Penguin Group (Australia), 250 Camberwell Road, Camberwell, Victoria 3124, Australia
(a division of Pearson Australia Group Pty. Ltd.) • Penguin Books India Pvt. Ltd., 11 Community
Centre, Panchsheel Park, New Delhi—110 017, India • Penguin Group (NZ), 67 Apollo Drive,
Rosedale, Auckland 0632, New Zealand (a division of Pearson New Zealand Ltd.) • Penguin Books
(South Africa) (Pty.) Ltd., 24 Sturdee Avenue, Rosebank, Johannesburg 2196, South Africa

Penguin Books Ltd., Registered Offices: 80 Strand, London WC2R 0RL, England

This book is an original publication of The Berkley Publishing Group.

This is a work of fiction. Names, characters, places, and incidents either are the product of the author's
imagination or are used fictitiously, and any resemblance to actual persons, living or dead, business
establishments, events, or locales is entirely coincidental. The publisher does not have any control over
and does not assume any responsibility for author or third-party websites or their content.

Copyright © 2012 by Sharla Lovelace Scroggs.
Excerpt from *The Reason Is You* by Sharla Lovelace copyright © 2012 by Sharla Lovelace Scroggs.
Cover illustration by Irene Lamprakou/Arcangel Images.
Cover design by Lesley Worrell.

All rights reserved.
No part of this book may be reproduced, scanned, or distributed in any printed or
electronic form without permission. Please do not participate in or encourage piracy of
copyrighted materials in violation of the author's rights. Purchase only authorized editions.
BERKLEY SENSATION® is a registered trademark of Penguin Group (USA) Inc.
The "B" design is a trademark of Penguin Group (USA) Inc.

ISBN 978-1-62090-598-2

PRINTED IN THE UNITED STATES OF AMERICA

To Mom and Dad, who are still with me every single day. Thank you for teaching me that the world we see is not all there is.

ACKNOWLEDGMENTS

Thanks again to my wonderful family and friends. You never know just how amazing your little circle is until it surrounds you with so much love and support. My husband, Troy, is my biggest fan, and I love you, sweetheart. My fantastic kids, Amanda and Ethan—you will never know how much your excitement has meant to me. And Amanda, the fact that you trolled the mall with bookmarks, and wanted to hurl the whole time—I love you for that!

A shout-out to the ladies of the St. Elizabeth's ACTS community. Your love and excitement for *The Reason Is You*'s release into the world was overwhelming. Your friendship reached a place in my heart that opened me up . . . and got me on my feet! LOL! You know what I'm talking about.

To my fab friends at the Book Club Babes group—my very first book club appearance will always be special to me. Love y'all!

To my Street Peeps, the fabulous people who donate their time to help me spread the word about my books, I love y'all. The biggest hurdle for a new author is getting known. And one person can reach only so far. Your enthusiasm and help are priceless!

Love again to my wondrous rock-star-super-agent-extraordinaire, Jessica Faust of BookEnds. I'm so lucky to have the best. And to my amazing editor, Wendy McCurdy, for once again guiding the way to a fantastic finished book, and for having the patience to answer five hundred and one newbie publishing questions along the way.

Huge thank-yous to all the reviewers and bloggers and individuals who have taken the time to leave reviews and even send me private e-mails telling me how much they loved my work. Writing is a solitary world sometimes, and those messages and reviews mean everything. When someone I don't even know takes time out of their day to share their personal experience with my story, I'm just in awe. It doesn't get better than that.

Enjoy!

CHAPTER

1

THERE IS A DISTINCT MOMENT WHEN YOU KNOW THAT YOUR DAY has gone down the toilet. Mine was before lunch, and after my fourth cup of coffee, when an unexpected knock on my front door brought me face-to-face with my ex-husband.

Not that he was a horrible troll, or lying in wait to machete me in a weak moment, but he just wasn't one to drop by and say hello. Which was good with me. Child support and visitations came to a legal end three years prior, so daddy pickups were off the table. I stood in the doorway, wondering who died as I ran a hand through my unbrushed hair and then crossed my arms over my chest to disguise the no-bra action I had going on.

He gave me a once-over and frowned. "Are you sick?"

I started to protest that not having to get dressed was a perk of working from home, that until someone wanted to look at a house, talking to potential clients on the phone didn't require me to brush my hair or put on shoes. But I didn't feel like having that long a conversation with him. So I fake-coughed into my hand.

"Little bit. What's up?"

He shrugged. "I was wondering how much she's selling it for."

I blinked a few times, thinking I'd missed something. "Um—she, who?"

He tilted his head with widened eyes like he was humoring me. "Your mother?"

I opened my mouth but then just air came out. Maybe it was the coffee. Maybe I needed to eat something or go for a walk. Use the treadmill that was collecting dust in a corner of my office.

I shook my head. "I—I give up, Kevin. What about my mother?"

"Her house, Emily," he said, impatience lacing his tone. "How much is she selling the house for?"

I laughed then, which I knew would piss him off. "Selling her house? What kind of crack are you smoking?"

My mother would sooner sell one of us than sell that house. She and my dad lived in it their whole married life. Raised two kids there, multiple dogs, a couple of birds, and I think there was even a brief stint with a ferret. She didn't leave after my dad died in the living room, and if anything could have shoved her out, it would have been that.

Kevin's dark blue eyes glazed over at my comment. He held his hands up in front of him and shook his head as he turned. "Never mind. I forgot how crazy y'all are."

"Whoa, whoa, wait," I said, still laughing. "What are you babbling about?"

He took the steps two at a time, and waved a hand behind

him. "Never mind, Em, I'll just call Dedra. Although why it's listed with her beats the shit out of me."

I felt my smile start to fade and stick at the confusion point. Something was off. Something didn't make sense. Starting with him saying that sentence.

"*Dedra?*" I said. "What are you talking about?" My tone combined with her name was enough to tweak his attention because it turned him around. His expression changed to wary and unsure.

"Your mom's house? Her name's on the sign." He looked uncomfortable and pointed randomly at the air behind him as if to prove it. "I had nothing to do with it. I passed it this morning on my way out."

Another leftover piece of a laugh kind of popped out, but with much less confidence. I shook my head as I turned and walked away, knowing he'd follow me in.

"That's crazy," I said. "Has to be a joke or something. I just had lunch with my mom last week. I mean, come on. Don't you think she'd have mentioned that? She talked about her garden."

I landed back on the squeaky swivel chair in my office as Kevin found a spot on the couch among scattered manila folders. He moved a few aside, turning one over to read the name.

"Eight-twenty-nine Montgomery—why does that sound familiar?" he asked.

"It's one street over from my mom's," I said, clicking through the links that would bring me to the multiple listing database. "And quit snooping, it's not listed yet."

"Oh, yeah. The Landry place," he said, and I ignored the snide change of tone.

"Yep."

"Bobby's finally unloading it, huh?"

I blinked and sighed and continued to ignore the shiny object he was dangling to get a rise out of me. "Guess so."

"About time," Kevin continued. "It's been one strong breeze away from blowing over for years."

"Oh, it's not that bad," I said, scoffing. "Just needs a little attention. Vacant houses get that way."

"Well, I don't blame him," he said. "Ben left him high and dry with that place when their mom died. Never even came back for the funeral."

The old dig that used to stab me barely felt like a pinprick. "You don't know that."

"And you do?"

I cut my eyes at him. "This town can make a lot of noise when it wants to. You believe everything you hear?"

Kevin tossed the file over with the others, and I was grateful for the change. I watched him take in the overflowing bookshelf, the three different-colored jackets hanging on the treadmill, the row of file boxes stacked against one wall.

"I assume there's a method, as usual?" he asked.

"Ha-ha, very cute."

In our eleven years of marriage, he never learned to appreciate my version of décor or organization. Kevin preferred empty space. Like moving-into-a-house-with-no-stuff kind of empty. No pictures, no decorations, no curtains, no coasters or vases or magazines. Give him a chair and a rug and a TV and he's good. In fact, the rug would probably be pushing it.

"So, dating anybody?" he asked.

I hit a button and gave him a look. "Really?"

His face went all innocent. "What?"

Kevin was a very good-looking man, as long as you never had to have a real conversation with him, or a life. The pretty wore thin with the constant perfection and micromanaging.

"You really want to know about my love life?"

He looked away with a smile. "I want you to be happy, Em."

I coughed again, this time for real. "So, what's the deal?" I asked, changing the subject as I waited for the zip code filter to update. "You looking to move again? Sherry want to simplify and rub elbows with the common folk?"

He gave me a look and leaned back, his brown leather jacket making noise against the wanna-be leather of my couch. "I'm thinking about buying some rental property."

"Ah, you want to be a land baron, now."

"It's easy money," he said with a shrug.

"Not with old houses like—"

My words died on my tongue as the page populated, and there it was. Three listings down. A familiar address and equally familiar picture of my mother's house. Listed by Dedra Powers.

"You've gotta be shitting me," I said under my breath, and I heard Kevin and his jacket sit forward.

"So, how much is it listed for?"

I tore my eyes from the screen to glare at him. "Seriously?"

He lifted a hand. "What?"

I swiveled around in my chair to find my phone and leapt up to grab it off the top of my treadmill, hitting speed dial number two. Three rings led to voice mail, and my mother's voice telling me how sorry she was that she couldn't answer my call.

"Mom!" I yelled, then bit my lip and let my mouth work for a second. "Mom?" I tried again. "Please call me."

I hung up and stared at the listing again as I hit speed dial numbers one and three, both of which went to voice mail as well. "Jesus, where is everybody today?" I muttered as I tossed the phone to the couch next to Kevin and smiled not-so-patiently at him.

"I've gotta go change clothes and—interrogate my mother," I said. "So—" I did a little hand flourish that I felt encouraged his exit.

"You didn't know."

"That's pretty clear," I said, not enjoying his smirk.

He stood up and leaned over to view the page on my laptop, which I then flipped closed.

"Ninety thousand," he said, narrowing his eyes in that financial thinker's expression of his, and I shook my head before another second could pass.

"No."

He blinked and met my eyes. "What do you mean?"

"I mean, no," I said. "I don't know what's going on with this, but regardless, you aren't buying it."

"Why not?"

My head was spinning. I wanted answers and I wanted Kevin to be gone so I could go find them.

"Because." He tilted his head again, and I made a sound of disgust. "God, you look like such a girl when you do that. Stop it."

"You aren't answering my question."

"And I'm not going to right now," I said, taking him by the arm and walking. "Come on. I have to leave. I have to get naked first. And unless Sherry-bom-berry is okay with that, you probably shouldn't be here when I do."

We made it to the door and I pushed him gently out. Just as

he turned back around. "Oh, I almost forgot. Do you know if Cassidy sent in any of those business school applications yet?"

I sighed as I slowly guided the door closed. "She's twenty-one, Kevin. She's across town and doesn't run her day by me anymore. Call her."

"I have, and she doesn't call me back."

Shocking. "Gotta go."

I FELT A DULL HEADACHE FORMING BEHIND MY EYES AS I rounded the block to a house I could find blindfolded and drunk—not that I knew that—and saw my sister's car snuggled right up behind my mom's. My gaze went from there to the FOR SALE sign looming gaudily on one side of the sidewalk and instantly went hot over the prospect that my sister, Holly, was in on it. Of course she would be. First to arrive, last to leave, always doing the right thing, always there for my mom, always the suck-up.

FOR SALE. By Realtor Dedra Powers.

I pulled up alongside the ditch and took a series of cleansing breaths on my way up the uneven sidewalk and concrete porch. *I will not raise my voice . . . I will not raise my voice . . .*

I'd called my daughter for backup, but I wasn't sure how fast she would get there. She kind of laughed when I told her that Nana had lost her mind. I don't think she truly got the urgency of the situation.

When I opened the heavy wooden door with the fifteen-pound metal door knocker, the knocker bounced loudly like it always did with the momentum, announcing door movement to the entire neighborhood. It announced it to Tandy, as well. The ancient dachshund with a smoker's bark and a long-lost sense of smell came in a blaze of glory, ready to take out my shins until she saw it was me and backtracked to her beanbag chair, uninterested.

I steeled myself for the confrontation when I saw my mom and sister sitting at the elongated bar that served as the dining room table, but faltered a little when they looked my way and I saw the anxiety in my sister's eyes.

My volatile words kind of died on my lips and came out instead as, "So, this is new."

My mom sighed, and my sister just shook her head. Suddenly, I had the impression maybe they hadn't been in on it together. Holly had that fired-up look going that her red hair just amplified.

"You didn't know, either, I take it?" Holly asked.

I smiled. "No, I just found out from my ex."

"Oh, shit," Holly said under her breath.

I zeroed in on Mom. "Yeah. Care to know how wrong that conversation was?"

"Sorry, girls, it was just easier to make this decision without the two of you breathing down my neck," my mother said.

My mouth dropped open. I had no words.

"Mom, this isn't like deciding to sell baskets instead of candles," Holly said, holding back her hair like she always did when she was upset. "This is your home."

"Exactly," my mother said, rising from her stool. "My home. My decision."

"Why?" I asked, watching her go through the motions of rinsing out her coffee cup and setting it back next to what was probably the first Mr. Coffee coffeemaker ever made. I remembered when my dad bought it for her and she balked and made a fuss, claiming that coffee percolated on the stove was a hundred times better.

"Why not?" she said, her back to us. "Maybe I'm tired of dealing with this old house, ever think of that?"

"This old house raised your family," I said, suddenly feeling weirdly defensive of buckled paneling and ancient shag carpet.

"All your memories, your life—" Holly began.

"The plumbing, the settling, the cracks, the piers that are crumbling under my room, the wiring that's held together with duct tape," she countered. "Who's here to deal with all that? You?" she said to me and then looked at Holly. "You?"

My phone rang from my pocket, and I dug it out. It was a text from a client, wanting to reschedule their walk-through until the maid came. Jesus.

"I've told you, Greg can help—" Holly said, but Mom cut her off.

"Oh, please," she said, flipping a hand. "Greg would spend more time analyzing a nail than pounding it. That man's too soft for real work."

I bit my lip as Holly's face went scarlet. She laughed sarcastically as she got up and carried her glass of tea with her to the den, which was really just an extension of the kitchen.

"Wow, Mom, don't hold back."

"And by the way," Mom said, turning her attention to me. I suddenly had a flash to when I hid my fifth-grade report card and received a similar expression. I tucked my phone back into my pocket. "*This old house* didn't raise anybody. The people paying the mortgage did."

"Okay then," I said, wanting to get back to the real topic at hand. "Why the big secret? Why suddenly sneak this out there without even telling us?"

I noticed then as I waved a hand around that things were already different. Holly had stopped to look in a box that sat on the ottoman in front of Mom's chair, and I saw for the first time that the wall of family pictures was—just a wall. I joined her as she fingered through the frames gently, as if touching them wasn't allowed.

"Yeah, Mom, why the rush?" Holly asked, not looking up from the black-and-white picture of our parents, young and kissing in front of the county courthouse the day they bought their marriage license.

"Oh, for pete's sake, there was no secret, there was no rush," Mom said, pulling a metal container of cookies from the cabinet and setting it on the bar. "What there is now is a whole bunch of hullabaloo, which is exactly what I wanted to avoid."

Holly abandoned the pictures and faced Mom square on. "Avoid? What—did you think we wouldn't notice someone else living here when we come over next month for your birthday? Were you just going to mail us a change of address card?"

"We're just saying you might have mentioned it—oh, like last week when we met for lunch at the chicken place?" I said, turning in a circle to see what else wasn't in its preordained place. "Speaking of which," I said, stopping to face her straight on. "Dedra Powers?"

It wasn't speaking of that, but it had to be said. My mother let out a heavy sigh that said I was wearing her out and turned back to the cabinets for a glass. "I need some tea."

"That's all you can say to that?" I asked.

"No, I'm gonna splash a little Captain Morgan in there, too. That better?" At my likely bug-eyed look, she continued, "What do you want me to say?"

I scoffed and even Holly, for once, looked put out on my behalf. "Maybe that you're aware your daughter is a Realtor?" I said, hands on my hips as my phone went off again.

"God, I know that," she said irritably. "But you would have taken over."

I nodded like a crazy woman. "Yes! That's the whole point, Mom. A Realtor takes over. *Your* Realtor will take over." I felt the sneer shaping my lips without my input. "Dedra Powers will take over."

"And not be all up in my business, telling me what to do and what not to do," she said, perching back on her stool with her iced tea.

"Yes, she will," I said, the sneer turning into a smile. Probably not a nice smile. "She will be more about your business than anyone could ever be, Mom. And what kind of charge do you think she got over you bringing the listing to her instead of me?"

Mom held her head up defiantly. "I told her that I wanted to keep it out of the family so you wouldn't be burdened with a freebie."

I just closed my eyes and mentally switched gears. The current ones were going in circles. I pulled my phone out again and read as I spoke, asking the question I could ask in my sleep. "Okay, Mom, how does the contract read? Please tell me there's a contingency on you finding a home first?"

"I'm not getting another home."

You could have heard crickets in that silence. Holly and I both stopped breathing as we stared at the woman we once thought so wise. I wondered if Holly's panic journey included what room she'd have to give up in her house. I, for one, saw my messy office go up in a frenzy of silk flowers, craft glue, and Tandy's beanbag chair. Aside from that, the fleeting seed of doubt about her state of mind was skipping around in there, too.

"I think I need some rum in my tea, too," Holly said quietly.

Mom pulled the bottle from a box in the pantry, since the alcohol was evidently already packed. She poured some in both their glasses, and then held it out for me. Not having a glass was beside the point.

"That's okay, I think I need to be sober for this," I said, holding up a finger.

"All right," Holly said, gulping down her happy tea and sucking in a deep breath like that would prepare her for war. "Explain."

Mom gave each of us a look and began, "Your Aunt Bernie has that big Winnebago—"

"Oh, dear God, tell me no—" Holly started.

"Mom, please say you're not selling this house to live on the road with Aunt Bernie," I said, finishing the thought.

Any sentence that began with *Your Aunt Bernie* was a preface to some kind of lunacy. Mom's sister, Bernice, had been widowed for ten years and had done the very same thing. Sold her three-bedroom house with a pool and lived out of a powder blue Winnebago, traveling the states and landing wherever the whim struck her. When it struck her to visit home, she'd take up half the street and you could almost hear the neighbors groan.

"Why not?" she asked.

"Jesus, this is ludicrous," I said under my breath, turning around to find some normalcy in the pictures next to the TV. They weren't packed yet. They still sat in the same place they'd always sat, nestled together on the table I'd tried to paint with watercolors when I was five. It still had a green spot at the bottom of one leg where the grain absorbed the pigment.

"Seriously?" Holly asked. "You need reasons why you need a real home? Not one with wheels and a Porta-Potty?"

My mom grabbed a cookie from the tin and broke it in two, then halved those as well before popping a bite into her mouth and holding one down for Tandy, who suddenly sprang to life again at the potential for a snack.

"You know what?" she asked around the cookie. "I've been puttering around this house by myself for a long time."

"We know, Mom," I said.

"I'm still talking," she said with a look that I knew too well and could instantly make me feel eight. "Now—I'm a grown damn woman. My kids are grown; hell, my grandkids are grown. I have no reason to lie around this house, baking cookies or planting flowers and waiting to die. And if I want to ride around in a big ugly tank eating Cheetos with my sister, then I can damn well do it. I don't need you two little mother hens telling me what I can and can't do."

"We're not doing that," I said, glancing at Holly, who looked dumbfounded.

"The hell you're not," Mom said. "You two say more with your actions than you think. You come flying over here to see what this crazy old woman is doing, selling your precious childhood home out from under you, but where are you when everything breaks, falls apart, leaks, or when the taxes come due? You act like I'm senile or something, like I don't know what I'm doing."

She held her glass out, pointing it at Holly. "You make fun of me for my little side businesses, *selling baskets instead of candles,* but it's those damn baskets that paid for those straight white teeth of yours, Little Miss All That. It was the scrapbooking classes and things you don't even know about that kept the electricity on when your dad's store went under." Then she shifted to me and I wanted to duck. "And you. You get all uppity over me going to another real estate agent, but did it ever dawn on you that maybe I just wanted to do things my way, by myself for a change?"

I felt like we'd just gotten grounded, like I was in that uncomfortable place of not knowing if I was supposed to answer the question or stay shut up. I waited for Holly to pipe up like she always did, claiming some type of injustice or unfair point, but she said nothing. It felt like a huge chunk of silence before she moved to the bar and set her glass down, then she plucked her purse from the floor and walked out the front door without a word. When the knocker banged against the door, I met Mom's gaze. The fire in her blue eyes had fizzled a little. I was sure she had imagined or at least hoped it would go smoother than it did, but the element of surprise was just a little over the top.

I walked over and picked up Holly's glass, filling it with sweet tea from the pitcher and sitting down.

"What do you need us to do?" I asked, realizing she was past the point of talking down. It was going to happen. I grimaced as my phone went off yet again from the same person who was e-mailing since I didn't answer my text and clearly didn't understand boundaries.

"For starters, turn that damn thing off."

"It's work."

"It can wait five minutes. Now for here, you can start going through your stuff that's still in your rooms," she said, tracing a circle of condensation on the bar. "Throw out what doesn't mean anything, keep what you want."

I looked at her, trying to understand this woman that had taken over my mother. "Don't *you* want anything?"

She shook her head. "I've already got boxes put away of the things I can't live without," she said. "It's time for y'all to sort through what's left."

"Put away where?" I asked. "What are you doing with all your stuff?" I gestured in a circle.

"I paid for a storage unit the other day," she said. "For the important things. Pictures and stuff."

I was gaping. I knew I was. Maybe it was a full moon and it had rendered ex-husbands and mothers stupid. Or the world was ending. Or . . .

"Are you dying?"

She coughed on the tea she'd just swallowed. "Holy crap, girl, I hope not. Where'd you get that?"

I was relieved at her surprise, but it didn't fix anything. "Well, last month you were worried about your gardenias, Mom. Planting banana peppers in the corner by the swing. Looking for Dad's secret box. Now, you've got the house up for sale, getting rid of everything important to you, hitting the road with crazy Aunt Bernie—are you bringing Tandy with you?"

She chuckled. "Of course." She leaned forward as the dog put her front feet up on Mom's leg. "Like I'd leave my baby girl behind." She looked up at me. "Scared I'd leave her with you?"

"She doesn't like me, Mom, it wouldn't be pretty. Actually she doesn't like anybody but you and Cass."

"Oh, she likes you just fine," she said, scratching Tandy's ear.

"No," I said, smiling at Tandy when she turned around to gloat. "I think she sees all the rest of us as competition."

Mom sighed and sat back up. "Well, us old girls will stick together." She leveled a gaze at me. "Emmie, I'm just tired of the same old ordinary. I don't want to get to the end and say I grew flowers in my old age. Maybe Bernie's way isn't stylish, but at least it's doing something."

I nodded. On anyone else, it made a new age–artsy kind of sense. On Frances Lattimer, it was like she was possessed by aliens.

"You know, you could have just gone on some trips with Aunt Bernie without selling the house."

"I know," she said. "But then I'd be worried about the house, or y'all would have to worry about it, and honestly I'm tired of all that. This house has more aches and pains than I do. And I do plan on finding that box before I go, by the way."

I rubbed my temples. "Oh, lord."

For as long as I could remember, my dad talked about going to faraway places. He and my mom planned trips that they never went on, but he always said he was tucking money aside for them. Somewhere. For someday. It was their game.

Then he died. And my mother spent the last decade looking for some elusive box of money. Because he said there was one.

"Oh, lord, nothing," she said. "Think what you want."

"So what about Dad's stuff upstairs?" I said. "Any of that part of the *things you can't live without*?"

She blinked away the sadness that appeared in her face. "I still have to deal with that. I'm talking about your things. All that stuff you conveniently forget is still here, tucked away in closets and the attic like your own little private storages?" She nodded with a knowing smirk. "You have houses they can go to now."

"Okay," I said, changing the subject. "Two things."

"What?"

"Don't sell it to Kevin."

She physically jerked back. "Kevin! What on earth?"

I held my hands up. "He came by my house wanting to know what the asking price was. He's looking for rental property."

"No way in hell."

I flicked one finger. "Done. Now, two—you could have gone to any of fifty different Realtors in the area," I said quietly. "Why Dedra?"

Mom smiled. "I've only had the house listed for two days and I've already called her"—she reached for a nearby pad and peered through her glasses—"eighteen times to ask questions and change my information."

I raised an eyebrow. "Why?"

"To be the client from hell," she said, bringing an unexpected laugh from me. "You know how I don't sleep, right? Well, I figure since I'm her client now, she doesn't need to, either."

I covered my mouth, marveling at the level of shit-stirring my used-to-be-gardener mother could conjure. It was her way of getting back at the woman Kevin had thrown our marriage away for. Or the one he got busted for, anyway. A little delayed, since that'd been ten years earlier, but hey, who was I to split hairs. Personally, I'd made peace with it long ago. Sort of. Watching him go through one bad choice after another definitely helped.

The door knocker banged, not as an opening but as an actual knock, and I did a double take as Tandy made a fire trail to the door and started raising hell. "Oh, I forgot I called Cassidy on the way here. Although I don't know why she'd knock."

"Actually, that may be the carpenter I called to come do some updates around here."

I paused in mid-rise. "You have somebody coming to do work?" It made it more real. Less of my mother having a mental break. My stomach did a little wiggle.

"Yeah, *my Realtor* told me there was a lot of work to be done," she said. "Figured I'd get on that right away so there are no hold-ups. Bernie's coming through in about a month, and I want to be ready."

I laughed. "A month? Mom, it may be several months before this sells. It may be that long before it's fit to sell. Maybe even a year."

"Oh, I know, but Bernie's ride has internet and fax and that video thingy where you can see people—I don't need to be here when it actually goes down."

I sighed. No, I would. With Dedra. Joy. I got up to answer the door. "So, who'd you call for all these fix-ups?" I yelled over the dog's ruckus.

"Some guy that had a sign on the grocery store bulletin board. I think he said he went to school with you?" she said as I opened the door. "Name's—"

"Ben," I said.

"Emily," he said with a guarded but incredibly sexy almost-smile.

Forget the toilet. My day went straight to hell.

CHAPTER

2

OH, NO. NO, NO, NO, NO. GOOSE BUMPS RAN THE LENGTH OF MY
body and back again. Ben Landry. As I stared into that face, I felt
the old hurt I thought I'd forgotten seep through my bones right
down through my feet, rooting me to the floor.

"You're back," I said, hearing the words and how my voice
suddenly went all croaky and hating how stupid that was.

But I was painfully aware that I had thrown on only a pair of
jeans and a sweatshirt, and otherwise still looked like I'd just
crawled out of bed. Additionally, after twenty-one years, I was
looking at probably the only person on the planet that ever really
knew me. And could turn my life upside down.

"Yes, I am," he said, his voice quiet.

"Mr. Landry," my mother said from behind me as she moved
me over from where I'd dropped anchor in the doorway. "Come
on in."

SHARLA LOVELACE

"Just Ben, ma'am," he said, shaking her hand and then gesturing toward where I stood with my heart slamming against my ribs. His dark eyes warmed with memory. My stomach threatened to send me back my four cups of coffee as I recalled the last time I'd seen him.

"Emily and I are old friends."

Old friends.

Ben was the boy that put snakes in the teachers' lounge and snuck into the girls' bathroom. That popped all the girls' training bras and spent at least two days each week in detention. That wore an old black jacket with chains on it when he rode his bike, so he'd look like a badass. He was the boy that lured me under my house when we were seven for my first kiss and into a closet in the eighth grade for another one. He was the mysterious, dangerous-looking dark-eyed guy in high school who could part a room like the Red Sea when he entered it, who always sat with his back to the wall and never let his guard down. Except with me.

"I don't remember seeing you around here," Mom said.

Ben grinned, an endearing expression that transformed him back into the twenty-one-year-old I'd last seen him as. Time may have dulled some of the edges, but it worked for him, God help me.

His once-long dark hair was cut short and close, and was more salt and pepper than just pepper. That's what softened him, I decided, the lighter hair. His face was virtually unchanged, except for tiny laugh lines at those amazing dark eyes. He stood with his hands in the pockets of brown Dockers and a tucked-in khaki shirt, oddly at ease with what I found to be awkward as hell.

"Well, I'm sure we met at some point," he said, smoothly

moving the conversation on as his eyes slowly took in the walls and beams and ceiling. It was as if he were already seeing the possibilities. "So, tell me what your ideas are for this place."

He followed her as she talked about the paneling that needed to go, the ceiling that needed Sheetrock, the insulation that was probably rotten, and the gaping cracks around the windows. Just for starters.

Fortunately for me, it gave me the opportunity I needed to release the breath I'd been holding and suck in a few more.

"Jesus Christ, Ben Landry," I muttered under my breath on a sprint to the bathroom. What I saw when I got there made me want to hurl. My hair was still straight on one side, kinked up and tangled on the other, and a zit waved from one pale cheek. "Shit."

I dug in Mom's drawers for a brush and a ponytail band and managed to find an old cover-up stick for the zit. I couldn't find any powder or mascara or blush, but at least I'd moved up a notch from scary to just unappealing. I couldn't remember if I'd put on deodorant, but I saw a bottle of cologne and spritzed my neck.

"Oh, God!" I groaned.

It smelled like old woman. Not old woman like my mom, because she was fairly young at heart and active. Old like the women with the beehive hairdos and the stripe of blue eye shadow reaching to their eyebrows.

I found a box of wet wipes under the sink and attacked my neck with one, but I was pretty sure the smell was still there along with the aroma of aloe.

"Damn it, just shoot me now," I said to my reflection.

I was Cassidy's age the last time I'd seen Ben. The night of my twenty-first birthday. Looking at myself there in the mirror, with my brownish blonde hair that was overdue for a color, and a face that didn't pull off the natural look with grace, I figured he was counting his blessings for leaving town. For leaving me. I gave my head a little shake as that little gem ran across my brain. That was ancient history. I pulled myself back to the present, and the giant white elephant at hand.

"What are you gonna do about this, Emily?" I said to myself. "What the living hell are you gonna do?" No answers came back, so I held my chin up as I left the bathroom.

When I rounded the corner, I leaned against the wall and watched them—okay, I watched him. Watched how he moved, how his eyes could take in the smallest details with one look, how he still stood with his arms crossed over his chest when focusing hard, how he still pointed at things with his first two fingers instead of one, and noticing all those little quirks again made my heart take off like a freight train.

They were standing by the TV, discussing the buckled paneling. He tugged on a loose section, revealing the original wainscot wood and a gap where a piece was missing. My mother was explaining what was under that paneling throughout the house when the sounds turned to echoes and there was a weird pitch in my ears, like a ringing. I shook my head, and everything faded to black for a split second as the sound of air rushed by. I sucked in a breath, panicking as I blinked the room back into view.

But it was different. And I couldn't move.

♊

The light was different, coming in the windows brighter—because there were no blinds, I realized. No curtains. Where did they go?

Where was the TV? The couch? The corner table? The walls—I stared at where my hand rested against wallpaper. Wallpaper? It had lines of tiny roses and went halfway down the wall, ending at wooden wainscoting.

"What the hell?" I asked, directing it to my mother.

But my mother wasn't there. Neither was Ben. I turned a full circle to look for them, but stopped when I caught sight of the kitchen. The cabinets were gone. The long attached wooden bar was gone. It was wide open, the sink and countertop with low cabinets the only thing under the kitchen window. It was empty—everything was empty. No fridge, no furniture, and the back door leading out of the kitchen to the garage was solid wood instead of the one with the window. I started to curse again, but then the sound fell away as I caught sight of the floor. My feet stood on wood.

I picked up one foot and tapped it against the hard surface. No shag carpet.

I'm dreaming, I thought. I've passed out, had a heart attack, an aneurysm, a stroke. I'm in la-la land somewhere waiting to be jolted back to life. As unlikely as that seemed, anything else was infinitely more bizarre. I tried to take a step toward the kitchen, but my foot wouldn't go that far. I turned in a circle again and laughed at this crazy dream where I could move only within my two-foot circle of existence.

Then there were voices to my left, and I jumped, wondering how to explain this. I wanted to giggle like a kid in hiding, but I didn't have to. And all giddy thoughts went out the un-curtained window as a young couple came in the front door. A door with no heavy knocker to announce itself. The guy led the girl by the hand, and they stared around them, beaming. Walking right past me as he pointed at a corner that would come to hold a built-in sewing bar for my mom, I inhaled the Old Spice cologne as he passed within inches of me, my eyes filling. They were the same as their photographs, but in living color.

"Daddy," I said.

But he didn't hear me. Of course he didn't—it was a dream. I was delusional and probably flopping on the floor and having a psychotic episode. I was probably drooling in front of Ben, and he was probably wondering if I was dying and if he caused it. But then—if I were dying, wouldn't I see myself on the ground? In the present day? Would I really be making up scenes from—I stopped to think when they bought the house—I think it was 1964? Would I be that creative?

I wanted to walk over to them as they circled around the den. I wanted to go stare into my father's young face and hug him till my arms fell off. To see him like this—to see both of them, actually, young and eager and in love, not yet affected by the weight of life. To see the man that would become larger than life in my eyes.

"I love you, Daddy," I said anyway, as I squatted to sit in my little circle. The floor felt cold under my hands. Whatever was going on—whatever this little trip was about—I was going to watch. I mean, how often do you get to experience dreams that realistic?

If I woke up, I could tell my mom about it. If I didn't, I'd be talking to my dad shortly anyway.

"I think the wallpaper's kinda weird," my mother said. My mother who looked twelve. "Too flowery."

"We can cover all that," my dad said, pointing at the lower half. "And take off the wainscot. Kind of old-fashioned. Everybody's putting that paneling up that looks like wood."

"I do like the layout, though," my mother said, walking to the kitchen. "I mean, it needs more cabinets, but I love how open it is."

He scooted up behind her and picked her up, making her laugh. "I'll build you some cabinets," he said into her neck. "I'll build you a table and a place for your sewing—"

"Oh, most definitely that," she said, her voice full of innuendo as she smiled. "So I can make little clothes after we make little babies."

He turned her around and held her close, face-to-face. "So where do you want to make the first one?"

"Oh, God, really?" I said, then clapped a hand over my mouth. Then I laughed, remembering they couldn't hear me, but still, too much information.

My mom laughed softly as she kissed him. "Maybe right here."

He looked down at their feet. "Right here? Do I need some chalk to mark the spot?"

She laughed again and pushed him away playfully. "I think we'll remember."

"Oh, no," he said in mock seriousness, pulling a coin from his pocket. "It's been foretold now." He got to his knees and scratched a small x in the wood with the coin. "Just like the Egyptians marked their dwellings."

"Oh, now we're Egyptians, are we?" she said, laughter in her voice. She sounded so happy and—positive. I couldn't remember my mother ever sounding like that. "And you're carving up my floor!"

He stood up and bowed deeply. "My love, I present you the place of our home's christening."

She cracked up laughing and stood on the x. "Can I bring a blanket for this christening, or are you going to just take me on the wood, splinters and all?"

He grinned and wiggled his eyebrows as he took her in his arms again. "I love you, Frances Lattimer."

"I love you, Charles Lattimer," she whispered back before they kissed again.

"I'm going to take you to Egypt to see those drawings one day," he said against her lips. "And anywhere else you want to go."

"Montana."

He laughed, a deep-throated sound that brought new tears to my eyes to hear again. "Montana? Okay then. Egypt and Montana it is." He kissed her forehead. "Let's go sign the papers."

She looked so giddy, I was reminded of children opening presents. She looked around, taking in the whole room as he led her out by the hand, and for one microsecond, she looked right at me. Or through me, most likely, but it took my breath away just the same.

"By the way, I think we need to get carpet when we can afford it," I heard her say as they opened the front door.

There was the strange ringing in my ears again, the rushing of air, and blackness that took over the room. I held my breath, waiting to wake up, wondering if I would be incapacitated or if they'd had to do CPR. I thought of Cassidy then, and hoped she hadn't witnessed whatever happened to me.

⌒⌒

I heard the warbled sound of voices as they came back, and I felt my body spasm as I sucked in a very audible breath and blinked the room back into focus.

Still standing.

And they were still talking in the same place by the TV. Or at least they were until they turned to stare at me.

"My God, what was that, Emily?" my mother said, frowning. "You sounded like you just ate your tongue."

I was dumbfounded. I wasn't dying or passed out, or even

asleep. I glanced down at my body and feet that stood on carpet again. I was fine. It was like no time had passed. How was that possible?

The room was back to normal, blue shag on the floor, blue drapes on the windows, same knickknacks covering the same shelves over the sewing bar. Same photographs in a box on the ottoman. Same dark worn paneling around the same dark worn cabinets.

I knew I was standing there like a gaping fish, but I had no words.

"Emily, what's the matter with you?" Mom asked, walking up to where I still stood rooted to the spot. She laid the back of her hand against my forehead. "You're all clammy."

Great, I thought, as Ben stood in the middle of the room watching us. I managed to look at everything but him, but I could feel his gaze.

"Whoa, honey, what's that you've got on?" Mom said, waving a hand in front of her nose. "My gosh, that's strong."

"I—I'm—"

What was I? A lunatic? The door knocker saved me from speech but added to my anxiety when Cassidy strolled in, scooping up a frantic Tandy on the way. The dog licked her face as Cassidy cooed at her.

"Hey," she said in her carefree lackadaisical way, swinging her hand wide at the room. Her wild blonde curls bounced around her face, always a stunning contrast to her dark eyes. "So, what's the big dilemma?"

I blinked, her ability to float through life pulling me from my stupor. "Did you miss the big sign outside?"

"No," she said, setting Tandy down and going straight to the cabinet for a glass, and then turning around, sniffing. "What's that smell?"

"The house is for sale," I said loudly. Probably too loudly, since everyone flinched.

"O-kay," Cassidy said to me before looking at Mom. "Nana, you're moving?"

"Nope," Mom said. "Hitting the road with your Aunt Bernie, doodlebug."

The sweet tea sloshed forward from the pitcher as Cassidy stopped, mid-pour, and the dog lapped that up from the floor like it was a gift just for her.

"Seriously?" she said, her voice breaking into a chuckle.

"Yes, ma'am," Mom said, wrapping Cassidy up in a hug. "Gonna see something outside Texas, for once."

I looked at Ben as he stood outside the conversation, still not one to invite himself unless it was to be cocky. I wished he'd take it a step further, or several steps actually. Like all the way upstairs. Or out the front door.

"But like—forever?" Cassidy asked, looking over at me with concerned confusion. "You aren't coming back?"

"Of course I will," Mom said, throwing me a wink. "We'll go park Big Blue at your mom's house when we come through."

"Please don't call it that," I said quietly.

"What?" Mom asked.

"Big Blue." My Aunt Bernie called the Winnebago that. Actually she referred to her ride way too affectionately sometimes, and it could get disturbing.

Mom waved me off. "Whatever. We'll park *it* somewhere."

Cassidy laughed. "Cool!"

"Oh, yes, cool," I said, snatching a random piece of cardboard that had come from a package of something. I fanned myself with it and stood off to the side to attract Ben's attention away from Cassidy.

"So—you're visiting to help your brother with the house, I assume?" I asked, hopeful.

"Your brother?" Mom asked. "Who's that?"

"Bobby Landry," he said. "He still lives on Canterbury."

Her face registered the name, and then something flickered through her eyes as she looked from Ben to me and back to him again. "Bobby and Ben. You're Carol Landry's son."

I saw the flash of pain go through his expression and then disappear again. "Yes, ma'am."

She put a hand on his arm. "Sorry about your mom, honey. I always liked Carol; she was a tough lady. Y'all selling the house, I saw?"

The corners of his mouth twitched into a small grin, but his eyes didn't join. "No. I mean, we were, but not anymore."

"Oh," I said.

He smiled full-on at that. "Don't hold back there, Em."

Em. The familiarity instantly brought a pang to my heart that surprised me. I closed my eyes and wished for that dream to come back. It was weirdly more normal there.

"No, no, I'm sorry, I'm just—"

Babbling. That's what I was doing. I held my hair off my neck and tried to shake the last hour off me. The trip through the past was messing with me, and the present was already complicated enough.

"We aren't selling it," he said, rubbing his eyes. "I'm buying him out and keeping it."

For a split second, I forgot about my potential journey to the loony bin, my mother's journey on Big Blue, and the fact that Ben's return was about to send my life into a tailspin. What I remembered was how much he despised that house and couldn't wait to leave it. The issues there with his father that he escaped so often by climbing my roof in the middle of the night.

"Why?" I found myself asking.

His closed expression softened for a beat, and he did the smallest of face movements that I recalled equaled an all-out shrug with him.

"Time to come home."

My whole body went warm as he said it and his eyes transported me back in time to a place that stabbed my heart and twisted.

"Ben, this is my granddaughter, Cassidy Lockwood," my mother said, her voice breaking the moment. She frowned at my rudeness, and I stiffened and envisioned my chest cracking open at the mention of my daughter.

I smiled. "Yes, my—" My mouth dried up, and I licked my lips. "Cassidy, this is an old friend of mine, Ben Landry."

"Nice to meet you," she said with her dazzling smile, shaking his hand.

"Nice grip," he said, making her laugh.

Ben excused himself to go look at a window, and I ran a hand over my face, feeling the nervous dampness.

"I don't remember seeing him before," Cass said, straddling a bar stool, looking so relaxed in her oversized sweater and crazy furry boots.

"He just got back in town," I said, focusing on each word, making sure none of them wobbled or shook so that her keen sense of observation wouldn't pick it up. "Been gone a long time."

"Well, that's cool that he's helping Nana. When's the last time you saw him?"

I shrugged and got up, feigning interest in the dishes in the sink. "Don't know."

But I gripped the sink discreetly and closed my eyes as the real answer burned across my brain like a firebrand.

The night we made you.

CHAPTER

3

I MANAGED TO EXTRICATE MYSELF FROM THE HOUSE WITH CASsidy in tow, and she wasn't happy about it. I didn't care. My anxiety had rendered my feet and fingers numb, and her whining was the least of my concern.

"Mom, come on," she said as I walked behind her to assure her exit. "What is your problem?"

"I need you to meet me at the store," I said, pulling that out of thin air.

She stopped and turned to face me before I could barrel into her. "Meet you at the store?" She raised an eyebrow at me, and I suddenly longed for the days when we didn't stand eye to eye and I could order her around. She laid a hand on my arm. "You like whole-grain bread and the ice cream in the big bucket, Mom. Are you okay?" She grimaced and backed up a step. "And why do you reek of Aunt Bernie?"

That explained it. "I'm fine. Where are you going, then?"

She huffed out a breath. "Well, I *wasn't* going anywhere, I was gonna hang with Nana a little since I haven't been over in a while, but that guy's here, so . . ."

"Yeah, they're busy," I said, knowing I was jumping on it too fast.

She nodded, looking at me like maybe I'd had a seizure. "Yeah. So I'll probably go grab a coffee and hang out with Josh a little before work."

Before my irritation could go on automatic pilot at the mention of lackluster, non-ambitious, motorcycle-riding Josh, I weighed the options and picked the lesser of two evils.

"So, how *is* the car-wash business?"

A smirk lifted one corner of her mouth. "Now I know you're not right."

I held my palms up. "Hey, you're always saying I don't give him a chance, so I'm just trying to be nice. Was thinking of putting some Suds-It-Up cards in my client welcome packets." Ugh—I wanted to slap myself.

"Uh-huh," she said, laughing. "Okay, well, I'll be sure to let him know."

"So, are you on the river tonight, or at the café?" I asked. Cassidy had two waitressing jobs. One at the trendy Dock Hollidays restaurant on the boardwalk that flanked the Neches River and its new marina and dock. The other at a gritty café in the old section of town.

"I'm at Dock's the next three days," she said. "Stacking up some shifts for extra money."

"Oh, wait," I said as she headed to her car. "Your dad wanted to know if you'd done anything with those school applications."

"No," she said, continuing to walk.

"He's been trying to call you," I said to her retreating back.

"I know," she said, waving two fingers.

I just smiled and watched her climb into her little white Volks-wagen Bug. "Slow down!" I yelled as she zipped out of her spot and sped around the corner like a roadrunner.

I closed my eyes as she disappeared from sight, and held both hands on either side of my head, wishing to somehow reverse the events of that morning so far. Ben was back. Mom was selling her house. I was having some kind of mental break.

Ben was back. It felt like karma had finally caught up with me.

I trudged to my car and leaned against it, knowing I only had one place to go.

HAVING A SISTER ONLY ONE YEAR OLDER PROVIDED SOME VERY sure realities growing up. We knew most of the same people. We knew most of the same gossip. And we nearly always had to share a car. While those things tied us together in some memorable moments we probably wouldn't have shared otherwise, Holly and I never really hit that bonding level. We existed in that loop of sibling tolerance that I assumed would morph into something deeper when we grew up.

It didn't. We'd had our moments of sisterhood, but they were easy to count. When our dad died, when our kids were born, and my twenty-first birthday.

I stood outside Holly's door with my finger hovering over the button. She was the only one I could talk to about it. But would she be that Holly? Or the pissy know-it-all that had just huffed out of Mom's house? I grimaced and poked the button, feeling my heartbeat speed up at just the thought of what I was about to say.

There was a dramatic exhalation as the door swung open, followed by the planting of hands on hips.

"Can you freaking believe she talked to us like that?" she said by way of greeting.

"I know," I said, thinking it funny that I'd felt the same way, all self-righteous, less than an hour before. And yet right then I couldn't have cared less.

She held the door open and stood aside so I could come in and commiserate on the audacity of our mother. I felt kind of guilty for not being pissed, as I folded a leg underneath myself in her oversized chair. And to be honest, my outrage had faded before the rest of the circus began, so it wasn't just distraction.

Holly landed on the floor in front of me, pulling a tasseled pillow into her lap. "So, what happened afterward?"

I took a deep breath and blew it out. "Ben Landry came over."

She stopped twisting the soft material in her hand. Her face registered confusion, like I'd pulled the wrong card in Trivial Pursuit and she had no answer.

"What?"

I opened my mouth to elaborate, but her husband, Greg, strolled downstairs on his way to the kitchen.

"Hey, Emily," he said with a lift of his hand out of his pocket.

"Hi, Greg," I said, forcing a smile. "I didn't see his car," I whispered through my teeth at Holly. You never wanted to show an ounce of troubled thought around him, as he tended to be *on the job* twenty-four-seven.

"It's in the shop," she whispered back.

"So, what do you think is up with your mother?" he asked.

I shook my head, keeping my happy face on. "Who knows?"

"Hmm," he said, continuing on. He got a bottled water and headed back upstairs. "I'll be on a conference call for the next hour, babe."

"Okay," she said with a warm smile. As soon as he was gone, her expression returned to normal. "He's like a lost puppy, having to be here. I'll be so damned glad when they get his car done and he's back at the office."

"So give him your car," I said, thinking that was logical.

She started. "Then I'd be stuck here."

I had to shake my head clear of her crazy. "Okay, so anyway."

"Now, what happened?" she asked.

"Mom hired a carpenter off a flyer she saw. And he came while I was there."

She blinked a couple of times and I saw the dawning begin. "Ben?"

I wished for a pillow to mangle, myself. I needed something in my hands. "Yes."

Holly gave a little shake of her head. "Okay, start over. Ben Landry—*your* Ben Landry?"

I shut my eyes, wanting to scream from that connotation. "That would be the one."

"He's back?"

"And living in his mom's old house," I said.

Holly narrowed her eyes. "I thought it was up for sale."

"Evidently not anymore," I said, getting up. "And now he's working for Mom."

"Oh, Jesus," Holly said. "What about Cass?"

"They've met," I said, turning around with a smile, but I felt the hysteria touching my skin. At her mouth drop, I continued. "She came over next. It was like a revolving door."

"Oh my God," Holly whispered, rising in one smooth move without the help of her hands. "Emily, what happened?"

I lifted my ponytail off my neck and fanned myself with it. "Nothing, really. Mom introduced them and they shook hands. I managed not to stroke out."

"This isn't good," Holly said, her face solemn.

A laugh bubbled up from my core. "You think?" I headed around the big open bar that separated the living room from the kitchen, needing something cold. I briefly considered just putting my head on ice in the freezer, but settled on a green tea instead.

"So, what are you gonna do?" Holly asked.

I slugged back the cold tea, wishing it could cool off all the heat in my brain as well. I set down the nearly empty bottle on the counter and she immediately moved it to a nearby coaster.

"I don't know. I—thought—after all this time, you know—" The fire burned my eyes, and I fought it, especially in front of Holly.

She laid a hand on my arm, a huge PDA for her. "I know, but remember there's really no reason for anyone to question it." She leaned against the perfectly polished granite. "He left. He doesn't know why you got married. And Kevin's never had reason to think otherwise, either."

I covered my face, feeling tears come. Remembering the panic of finding out I was pregnant at twenty-one, with no man in the picture. Remembering how Holly urged me to forgive my then-ex-boyfriend's indiscretions, on the chance it could be his, and start over. It could have been his. And my fear of doing everything alone drove me to let him believe that. But my heart knew it wasn't. Even before she was born and I saw her eyes and read her blood type written on the paperwork, I knew. But Ben was gone.

"Kevin loves her so much, Holly," I said into my hands. "She's always been his little girl. This would kill him."

Holly pulled my hands away and when I opened my eyes, the sister who'd been my rock all those years ago was there behind forty-three-year-old eyes.

"Then he won't ever know," she said. "He doesn't need to. Now what about Mom?"

I ARRIVED BACK AT MY HOUSE WITH A MIXED SIGH OF RELIEF and irritation, leaning against the door as I clicked it shut. The distinct sound of nothing blanketed me. No questions, no griping, no complaining.

I'd left Holly's house with a head shake after a couple of rounds of questioning Mom's sanity. I knew I should be used to it, but I'd actually needed her for once, and still she flipped right back into Shallow Holly, able to leap tall subjects in a single second.

And Mom's sanity was the least of my worries. Mine had a much bigger target on it. What the hell was that thing I saw? That whole cute little scene with my parents that easily went on for ten or fifteen minutes but yet not one minute had gone by when I snapped out of it. I couldn't tell Holly; she'd sic Greg and his never-ending therapist theories on me. While I might end up on a shrink's couch, it would never be his.

I couldn't tell Cassidy—no child should ever witness their parents lose their marbles. It upsets the natural balance.

Cassidy. From where I stood, I could see the huge framed shadow box on the wall—my Cass shrine, she'd called it when I first got it done. It had pieces of everything from her infancy to high school graduation, photos, toys, bits of blankets, part of a homecoming corsage, a dried rose her dad had given her at her First Communion.

Her dad. My stomach tightened at that, and I wrapped my arms around my middle like that would keep it all in. All the fear, the worry, the secret that I thought was so long past I'd almost forgotten about it. It burned like it hadn't in years. I dropped my head, marveling at how a day could go so wrong in just a few hours.

My doorbell singing right behind me pulled me out of my funk with a start, and I whirled around, hoping it wasn't Kevin again. There was no way I could look him in the eye right then. But when I checked out the side window, I wished it *was* him.

"Oh, shit," I whispered, backing up and staring at the door like it had betrayed me.

Ben. What the hell. Why would he be standing on the other side of my door?

"Oh, shit, oh, shit, oh, shit," I mumbled as I held my head together with my hands and paced. Logically, if I waited him out, he'd just leave. And come back another day. When Cassidy might be there. I covered my face for a second. "Shit, damn, hell."

Taking a deep breath and blowing it out, I opened the door just as he pushed the doorbell button again. "Hey."

The crooked smile that had gotten him laid all through high school tugged at one side of his mouth, making me clasp my hands together for solidarity.

"Hey, back."

I swallowed hard. "How did you know—"

"I asked your mother, and she gave me directions."

A nervous laugh came out. "My mother. Of course she did."

He looked unsure but still so calm. It was unnerving. "I hoped you wouldn't mind. Just wanted to see how you were doing." He backed up a step and his whole expression changed, going cloudy. "In hindsight, maybe it wasn't a great idea."

"No, no, it's fine," I said, waving a hand, thinking that none of it was fine. And Ben was wearing preppy clothes and using words like *hindsight*. Yeah, everything was on a big wiggle. "Sorry, I'm just having an off day. Found out from my ex-husband that my mother is selling her house, found out from *her* that she's hitting the road like a hippie, and—" I paused, thinking about my little flashback moment.

"And then I show up?"

I smiled, feeling like such a fake. "How've you been?"

He nodded just slightly. "Good. You?"

"Good."

He kept nodding, a hint of amusement in his eyes, and I wanted to crawl under my rug. I couldn't shake the awkwardness, and I felt like a silly kid. It was the strangest sensation, looking at him now. Older, seasoned, but so much the same. Once upon a time, there wasn't anything we couldn't talk about. Standing there then, I couldn't seem to make my mouth form words.

"Look, Emily, I just thought—" He stopped and held up his

hands. "Actually, I shouldn't have just dropped by like this; I don't know what I was thinking."

"Old habits," I said, and then blinked at my own words as they fell out of my mouth.

He gave a small chuckle before his expression went dark again. "Yeah," he said. "Guess so. See you around," he said as he turned around and walked to an old truck that didn't match his clothes.

I watched his back retreat with a sudden urge to call him back. I didn't, though. I wouldn't have been able to explain it if I did. I just—suddenly wanted to see his face again. The eyes that had once cried for me. The mouth that had once told me he loved me, right before he climbed off the roof and disappeared for over twenty years. Maybe that's what made me want him to turn around. Just to see what coming back looked like.

I shut the door and pressed my forehead against it, breathing deep and slow. When I finally turned around, my eyes landed on Cassidy's shadow box. The huge, gaudy reminder of why Ben needed to keep going and not come back.

BECAUSE I'M NOT THE SELF-CONFIDENT WOMAN OF STEEL THAT I'd like everyone to believe I am, I found a reason to go to my mother's house the next day. Not that there needed to be a concrete reason; I mean, I could just drop by for the heck of it. I just usually didn't. Going to my mom's house was never a quick cup of coffee. It was a guaranteed two pots of coffee and possibly dinner if the timing fell right. That wasn't always a bad thing, but I did have to go armed with that knowledge.

And since I did already have the request to start going through my old room to help clean things out—well—there you go.

The only thing that really bothered me about my driving need to get myself over there was that I was freakishly concerned with my hair. And my face. And my outfit, which needed to look flattering and yet immensely casual in a boxing-up-crap sort of way.

I needed Ben to see me looking like I hoped I looked every day, and not like the drooling, sweating swamp thing he got right off the bat. And there again was the thing prodding under my skin like a hot poker. Why did I care? What I really needed to be doing was running in the other direction. Finding out when he'd be there and when he'd be gone, then show up the opposite time to do all this work. That would be the smart thing to do. That would be the mature, grown-up thing to do. Unfortunately, the fact that I spent all the previous night staring at the ceiling told me that when it came to Ben Landry I was still the twenty-one-year-old girl that sat on a roof all day, waiting for him to come back. That girl was not mature. Or grown-up. She was still living in her parents' house because she kept blowing her paychecks on new shoes.

So when I found myself rounding the corner of my mother's block at ten thirty in the morning and there was no old truck parked out front, I was a little peeved. And then annoyed with myself for being such a tool.

I had rescheduled showings till the afternoon. Postponed a walk-through till the next day. Completely not me. All so I could do what? Strut through my mother's house? Find out what he'd been doing for twenty years? Show him what he could have had?

"Jesus, I'm pathetic," I muttered, parking and nearly stomping to the door.

Mom was nowhere to be seen, but the back door was open so I headed out through the attached garage and laundry room, to the backyard. It dawned on me for probably the first time ever that the laundry room wasn't in the house. I'd never looked at it from a Realtor's point of view before, it just always was what it was. My house.

"Mom?" I called out when I didn't see her.

"Over here," her voice called from around a verbena bush.

I pulled off a stray group of leaves from the nearest bush, and tossed it aside. I hated verbenas. Out of control, grew like freaking weeds, and all those dumb little red berries that the birds would eat and poop out on your car. Okay, maybe I had a tad bit of an attitude.

"What are you doing?" I asked as I found her on her hands and knees digging in the dirt. "Oh. Looking for it again?"

"Yeah, yeah, y'all laugh, but I know your father. He said he put money away, so then he put money away." She continued hacking at the clay-packed soil with a garden trowel.

"In the flower bed?" I asked, standing over her in my good suede boots, not about to get in that dirt unless the money started crawling out on its own.

"You never know," she said. "And this area is the next on my list."

"And after you sell, Mom? What are you gonna do, keep coming over and digging up the new owner's yard?"

She waved me off. "What are you doing over here this morning?"

I put my hands on my hips. "Didn't you ask me to come start cleaning my things out?"

She stopped and rocked back on her heels, moving gray

blonde hair out of her face with the back of a gloved hand so she could peer up at me. And down. And up again.

"Like that?"

I looked down at my black jeans, snug white long-sleeved sweater, and the aforementioned boots. Okay, maybe I missed the mark on the boxing-up-crap outfit.

"I—have an appointment later," I kind of lied. I did have an appointment later, just six hours later. "Thought I'd come get some things done first."

"Shouldn't have worn white," she said, going back to her hacking. "Lot of dust in those closets up there."

"Great," I said on a sigh.

"Why didn't you bring Cassidy? You could have gone down memory lane with her."

Oh, there were some lanes Cass never needed to travel, I thought.

"She's working a double shift at Dock Hollidays today," I said, which was miraculously not a lie. "Did she tell you she got waitress of the month?"

"No," Mom said, her voice clipped with the exertion of digging. "You dragged her out of here yesterday before she could even finish her tea."

"Oh," I mumbled. "Yeah. Sorry. Well, I'm gonna go—see what's up there," I said, pointing, although she wasn't looking at me to see it.

"Just stay out of Mr. Landry's way," she called back, stopping me in my boots. "He's coming to start working on the windows around noon."

I nodded, mentally thanking her for not making me ask.

Tandy met me at the back door, sniffing like I was an imposter, clearly miffed that she'd missed my entrance the first time. I stepped around her and reached for the bag of treats that always resided on top of the fridge.

I wasn't above bribing.

"Here, psycho," I cooed as she simultaneously growled and took the bacon treat under a chair to devour it.

I looked around the kitchen that had never changed in all my memories of it. The same ceramic plaques adorned the wall over the pantry—the ones we made in vacation Bible school of strawberries and praying hands. The same flowerpots sat on the ledge over the sink holding notes and forgotten jewelry instead of flowers. Handmade pot holders hung in the same place they'd hung for four decades. I could close my eyes and tell anyone who asked exactly where the large square CorningWare dish was kept—in the cabinet under the bar, on the far left, behind the glass lids. The silverware drawer above it was immaculate, but the drawer across from it held everything from playing cards to batteries to old cigarette trading stamps that had expired thirty years earlier but my mom wouldn't throw out because they reminded her of when she quit smoking. The electric stove with the drip marks down the front of the door from when Mom's vegetable soup boiled over and we never could get it all out of the tiny stainless-steel grooves. The perpetual dish towels that always draped from its handle. All of those things made it my mother's kitchen. I couldn't imagine them being gone, packed up in a storage building somewhere.

"Ugh," I said as I shook off a body shiver.

I thought of what I'd seen the day before in my weird little delirium. My parents, young and eager, coming into this empty house with its bare walls and no cabinets or towels or even the stove, for that matter. How they had seen it, so different from how it currently looked. And how the previous owners must have felt, taking their items out of it. All the things that made it home to them.

I trailed a finger along the bar as I headed to the stairway, glancing underneath at all the crap she had stored in those lower shelves, when the dizziness hit me. I stopped and gripped the bar, hearing the blood rush in my ears, and the timing couldn't have been worse. I heard the back door open, and as I struggled to suck in air I saw Ben walk in wearing old jeans and an open flannel shirt over a T-shirt, looking more like the version I remembered. The most random question rolled across my brain asking why he'd just walk in without knocking, and then the blackness came. I was aware of groping around in the air with my left hand, but I couldn't see it. And my breath felt caught in my chest. The spinning sensation as I blinked free a different scene made my stomach tighten up.

"Oh my God, it's doing it ag—"

༄

I was holding my breath, and I slowly released it, shaking my head to clear it. I was holding on to a wooden table instead of the bar, which wasn't there. Neither was Ben. I whirled in a circle, searching for where he went, and then realized I was back there again. In the house, but not in the way I knew it. I looked around and saw that it wasn't completely bare like last time, however. There were new cabinets, freshly hung and lighter in color than what I was familiar with.

46

"Oh, shit," I muttered under my breath. "Shit, shit." I took a deep breath and let it go, still gripping the table. It seemed like I needed to touch something tangible, even if that thing kept changing.

The stove was there, and I had the oddest longing to go see the front. To go see if the soup stain was there. I tested movement with my foot, but it just confirmed what I seemed to already know. I was confined to my little circle.

A little girl with red hair toddled past me, barely staying on her feet as she scooted along, nearly touching me. She held a bottle of juice tight in her grip and wore an outfit decorated in watermelons. I stared at her, kneeling to her level to see her face.

"Holly?" I whispered. I felt the goose bumps on my back, so I knew I was really feeling it.

She moved along, headed to the living room where toys littered the floor and random furniture filled the spaces this time. The corner table was there, adorned with only the red glass bull and matador, pushed back out of the baby's reach. I had to laugh to myself, knowing that those two pieces they picked up on their honeymoon would still be in that spot forty years later, only surrounded by pictures.

"Holly bug," called a voice I recognized as my mother's, only lighter, less gritty.

I turned to see a very pregnant version of the girl in my last dream—vision—whatever it was. She walked slowly out from the hallway in a large smock and pedal pushers, one hand on her belly.

"Holly bug," she repeated, and then laughed as the baby ran faster, like it was a game.

"Holy crap, that's me," I said, staring at her huge stomach. I'd always heard I was a big baby, and that she'd felt like she was carrying an elephant when she was pregnant with me, but I'd always *thought it was a joke. Looking at her there, about to topple over with a strong breeze, I'd say most definitely not.*

"Hang on there, speedy," she said, pushing locks of strawberry blonde hair behind her ears. "Mommy's a little slow on the take these days." She scooped Holly up in her arms with a laugh, making her giggle in that way that only babies can, when you want to make them do it again and again just to hear it.

I noticed the hardwood floors still uncovered by carpet, the carved scratch still there from the last time. The paneling on the walls, darkening the room, and the vinyl couch that I found myself vaguely remembering from my childhood. The chairs were different as well, just plain chairs instead of the recliners that would replace them later. On the chairs were stacks of Avon books and small sampler bags.

"Oh, lord, this was the beginning of it," I said, chuckling, and then slapping a hand to my forehead as I looked around. The beginning of what? This time wasn't as fun as the last one, since then I'd thought I was dying and thus made sense. This time was just downright freaking creepy. Especially how I kept thinking I was really looking at the past. There was no way. That crap was for science fiction movies and bad dreams. And I already knew it wasn't that, either.

Mom held Holly facing forward, and they went to look out the back window while she sang to her, rocking from foot to foot. I wanted to go sit on the floor by them and just watch. I wanted it so badly I almost couldn't stand it.

The back door opened, catching my eye, and in he walked. My dad, young and smiling for his girls, in blue jeans and a button-down shirt that had come untucked on one side. He held an arm out to wrap them up. Holly giggled as he nibbled her neck, but I noticed his eyes were tired as he hugged them both.

"Hey, little bit," he said, kneeling to kiss my mom's belly.

My breath caught in my chest at the words he'd called me ever since I could remember.

"How'd you do today?" my mom asked, while he got back to his feet.

Dad rubbed his face and raked fingers through his dark hair before taking Holly from Mom's arms. "Slow," he said. "I think I sold a handsaw and some sandpaper."

I figured the timing in my head around Holly's age and grudgingly accepted that in this movie I kept falling into, he must have just opened the hardware store with Uncle Tommy. He looked beat, but yet had that spark in his eyes that he would get when he believed in something and was excited. Kind of made me proud and sad at the same time, to know how he started it from nothing and would end up losing it two decades later to his brother's gambling debts.

He hung Holly upside down to make her giggle, and Mom righted her back up. Dad went to sit in one of the chairs but stopped when he saw the stacks of catalogs.

"What's this?"

"Avon," Mom said. "It's sales. Makeup and perfume and stuff. I just have to pass out some catalogs to the other ladies in the neighborhood, and—"

"Frannie, I told you I would take care of the family," Dad interrupted, and the look on his face said it wasn't a new conversation. He sank onto the couch with Holly on his knee.

"Baby, it doesn't hurt anything for me to make some money. It's groceries. It's toys. Every little bit helps—and it's something to do."

She gestured toward the drooling, pink-cheeked little girl bouncing on his knee. "I put her in the stroller and we go talk to people."

His expression was stern, but she didn't falter, and I had to smile. She was tough like that even then. They looked at each other over Holly's bouncing head until he sighed and shook his head.

"I don't like it," he said. "Makes me look like I can't take care of my family."

Mom knelt in front of him awkwardly, holding on to his knees. Holly leaned forward and wrapped her little arms around her neck.

"It doesn't mean that at all, Charles," she said, stroking his knee-caps with her thumbs. "The hardware store will take off, but it's going to take a while."

He nodded. "I know."

"And you have to be there to make that happen, so I want to do what I can." She tilted her head. "And you know I'm not one to sit around and knit."

He broke into a reluctant smile and chuckled silently, running a long lock of her hair through his fingers. "Baby, I promise you, it won't always be like this."

"I know," she whispered, leaning into his hand and smiling.

"I mean it; it won't always be this hard. We'll get where it's comfortable and then we'll go on vacations with the kids. Take them all the places we've talked about."

Mom laughed. "I saw that you marked up that map my dad gave you."

"Yep," he said, tickling Holly so that she wiggled and squealed. "Bought a box of thumbtacks, too. For when we actually go there."

I thought of the poster upstairs in my dad's office. The one of the world and all the places he circled in red that they wanted to visit. My mom wouldn't take it down after he died, insisted that it stay *there behind his desk. My heart felt heavy and I wished I could change the fact that there were no thumbtacks in the poster. The only vacations we took were to go camping at the lake two hours from home.*

"It'll all be okay," she said. "I have faith in you, baby. You and Tommy will make this a success, I know you will."

His eyes lit up. "We will. It's just the hard part right now. The late hours, the advertising. But that's okay. Because you know if something's hard to get—"

"—Then it's gonna be the good stuff," I whispered along with him, having heard that my whole life.

"You watch, Holly bug," he said, holding her in his arms. "Daddy's gonna show you the world."

My eyes filled with tears, and I wished more than anything to make this crazy scene be prophetic in some way and give my dad that. To change the outcome.

But I couldn't think about that anymore, because the sounds were coming back, rushing past my ears, making everything wobbly. The blackness came, and with it the inability to inhale, and I sucked in as hard as I could, blinking furiously.

❧

I was back. Breathing like I'd run a mile. Still holding on to the bar. And Ben Landry was holding on to me.

One hand was in my hair and one was on my upper arm, and the expression on his face all up close to mine was panicked. If I wouldn't have been so unbelievably terrified, it would have been endearing.

"Emily, look at me," he was saying, his face very close to mine.

"I—I am," I said, clearing my throat of the mud that had

landed there. I remembered the last time, and how it appeared that no significant time had passed. "What—um—did I pass out or anything?" I asked. "How long have you been here?"

His eyebrows raised. "I just walked in the door," he said, jutting his head behind him. "You saw me."

I frowned. "Just now?"

He paused, looking at me funny. Great. "Yeah. Emily, what's wrong?"

"Nothing," I said, pulling free from his hands, realizing even through the craziness that I didn't want to, and knowing I couldn't cave to that. I put shaky hands over my face for a minute and took slower breaths, trying to calm my breathing. "I just—"

I just what? Kept going back in time? I laughed, which probably wasn't the greatest thing to do, because it only served to make me look more in need of a padded room.

"How long was I—um—whatever I was?"

He blinked a couple of times, as if unsure how to answer me. "I don't really know what you mean. I mean, you just kind of spaced out and looked upset, but it's like you—I don't know." He shook his head and backed up a step.

"Like I what?"

"Like you were somewhere else," he said, making my stomach hurt a little. "I talked to you and it was like you didn't hear me. Then all of a sudden, you sucked in like you were choking."

I licked my lips and pretended to inspect a nearby coaster. "So, how long?"

He did a tiny face shrug. "Maybe ten—fifteen seconds."

"Seconds?" I asked loudly.

He backed up again. "Yeah. Roughly."

I held my hair back and tried to breathe normal, tried to appear normal, tried to look like the together woman I'd dressed myself to be. I had to shake it off. Something weird was happening, but I couldn't deal with it in front of him. It would have to wait.

"Okay," I said, feeling very off balance. "Um—I'm good. What are you working on today?"

He looked taken aback by my abruptness, and honestly I couldn't blame him. I'd think I was pretty damn rude if it were me. I'd be pointing out my bitchiness right about then. But he didn't. He just let his eyes glaze over like I remembered they could do, and he nodded.

"I'm working on the windows today," he said, a sharper edge to his voice. "And was thinking about looking under the carpet, see what the wood looks like."

I inhaled as slowly as I could, considering my heart was still on a race. "Okay, well, I won't keep you." He stared for a couple of beats, and then averted his eyes and gave the slightest shake of his head as he moved around me. "And, um, thank you," I added, not meeting his eyes.

"For what?" he asked, his voice distant as he knelt down to pick lightly at a place in the center where the carpet seam was already separating.

"For—worrying about me, I guess." I tried laughing, but it sounded off.

"Whatever," he said quietly. He pulled back about a six-foot section of carpet that just basically lifted itself. "This isn't even attached anymore," he said, peering under it. "The padding is nearly gone. Look here." He swiped a hand over it to reveal the wood. "Wood's still in decent shape. At least here, anyway."

I didn't see the wood, the floor, the padding, or the carpet. All I saw was the faint scratch of an x in the wood, next to his hand.

CHAPTER

4

IT WAS REAL.

There was no way for me to know about that scratch. I knelt opposite him and traced a finger over it, trying to wrap my mind around something too impossible to fathom.

"How?" I whispered my thought, not realizing it was out loud.

"What?" Ben asked.

I met his gaze, startled, and cleared my throat to get myself together. So much for a better impression this time. I was just a more stylish nut job.

His eyes searched mine, and my first instinct was to spill it all. In that one second, he was my Ben again. The guy that once upon a time I could tell anything. The guy I had no secrets from. Except that now I did.

"Nothing," I said, scooping my hair back, my eyes falling to the scratch in the wood again.

Ben let the carpet fall back down but stayed on one knee.

When I chanced a look at his face again, his intensity nearly made me jump.

"What's wrong?" I asked, even though I already knew. In that earlier moment, he'd gone back there, too. To the days where we knew no taboo subjects, no boundaries, no hidden anythings.

"Exactly my question." He shook his head and got to his feet, raising me with him before I could protest. I could still feel the heat from his hands when he let go of my arms. "You don't want to be friends, Emily? Okay, whatever. It makes you uncomfortable. I get it."

The sudden barrage had the words pinging off my brain, and all I could do was blink.

"If I'd known it was gonna be a problem, I wouldn't have taken the job." he continued, walking away from me, narrowing his eyes as he studied the back windows.

"What?" I said, my head spinning. "Who said it was a problem?"

He threw a look back at me before turning back to run a finger along a gap between the frame and the wall. "It's all over you, Em."

I felt my mouth drop open as the rush of heat washed over me. "All over me?" I let the old hurt transform into anger, realizing in a flash of clarity that doing that was my best course of action. It would solve everything. "No, what's all over me right now is that you have a hell of a lot of nerve."

That turned him around, and he fixed me with a look that broke free of the glazed scowl. "*I* have a lot of nerve," he repeated.

A sarcastic chuckle found its way out of my mouth. "Yes, you." It was like the door had been thrown open, and everything was spilling past lines we hadn't even defined yet. "You come back here after all these years, and then get pissed off at me for not falling right back into where we left off."

There was a smile and a bitter laugh from him as he took a few steps toward me, accompanied by an even harsher look. "I never asked for *where we left off*, Emily," he said quietly, acid lacing the words. "That's ancient history. I just thought that twenty years later we were grown-up enough to have a cup of coffee."

I stared at him, unable to process the logic that he would be bitter with *me*. For what? For him saying things he didn't mean?

"A cup of coffee," I echoed. "Really?" I swiped under my eyes that I knew were misty from the anger seething in me. "You know, I imagined a lot of conversations with you the first few years after you left. Pictured what we'd say." I laughed, trying to make it sound bitter, like his. "Not once was it *let's go have a cup of coffee.*"

Ben opened his mouth, then closed it tight, the muscles in his jaw twitching as his eyes got darker than normal. Distant. Then gone. "You're right," he said, his voice just above whispering.

He bent to pick up a box I hadn't seen him bring in, and he carried it to the window, pulling out a caulk gun and various tubes.

He was done. I needed to be, as well. So then, why, as I turned and trudged up the stairs, did I feel the need to beat the damn horse? Ben's reaction hadn't been logical, but it wasn't supposed to matter if he was acting logically. Or if he was pissed off. Or if he liked me or didn't like me. It wasn't supposed to be any kind of driving factor. I wasn't supposed to care. I had a family to protect, not an old—whatever he was—to figure out.

And my mother's house was talking to me. That was enough drama for a lifetime.

PROBABLY, THE SAVING GRACE FOR HOLLY AND ME GROWING UP was that we never had to share a room. It was a good thing that Mom and Dad looked for something more than the potential for a sewing center when they house shopped, because Holly and I were way too different to have survived sharing.

I sat on the edge of the now-queen-sized bed that resided in my old room. It was just a double when I lived there, but had since been upgraded for guest room purposes. Actually, for Aunt Bernie's purposes. I tried really hard not to think about the sulky, brooding man downstairs and how my chest still hurt every time I looked at him. About the real live scratch on the floor that fell straight out of my head. And about what the hell was going on in the rest of my head. Or in this house.

All of those things—they needed to go. I needed all my wits about me just to keep the average, ordinary, comparatively normal drama of my daughter finding out who her father really was under wraps.

I let my gaze travel the room, seeing it differently now that it was going away. Seeing it through my Realtor eyes, past the bookshelves full of books no one had read in years, and the random knickknack décor that had replaced my obsession with heavy metal rock stars years earlier. Instead, I noticed the crack that ran from the window to the ceiling. The tiny gaps around the window that light peeped through. The heater vents at the floor that fronted outdated and probably not-to-code-anymore ductwork.

While a part of me groaned at all that needed to be done, and how long that meant Ben would be around making my life complicated, a tiny immature part of me also wanted that. To delay things. To make it too difficult to sell the house I knew every crack and crevice and sound of. To keep that door knocker knocking, and keep being able to walk in at any time and see all the pieces of our lives that still settled there all absorbed into the surfaces. And on the shallower end—to keep the woman who'd been caught naked with my husband from getting the sale.

I got up and went to the window. Holly hadn't been around for me on that front. Not when I'd decided enough was enough. She was always about forgiveness. About how love endures and all that crap. Where was *his* love for me when he was banging other women in his office, in his car, and in Dedra's case—in my bed? No, that was it. Holly didn't agree with me, and that was okay. It wasn't the first time. I filed for divorce the next week. I got the house. He got the bed.

I peeked through the wooden slats of the blinds that didn't used to be there. Once upon a time, my window just had red curtains and looked out onto a view no one cared for. No one but me.

The view from my window was of the roof over the garage. Nothing pretty like Holly's view of the backyard with its begonias and sunflowers and wisteria growing over a wooden arbor. I couldn't care less about wisteria. My rooftop access was like manna from heaven.

I raised the blinds as far as they would go so I could see out, and I smiled to see that it really hadn't changed. The big oak next to the garage still towered over the house, low-lying branches reaching across the garage section and blanketing that whole area

in a shimmering wall of leaves. Like a personal cave just for me—
for most of the year, anyway.

I pried my fingertips between the wood of the window and
that of the sill, and wiggled until it moved. One inch up, however, and I felt it. The spinning, the ringing, the feeling of being
sucked away into blackness.

"Oh, shit," I said, sinking to the floor. The sound of my own
voice sounded oddly far away, and all I could feel was the cold of
the wall against my palm.

◦◦◦

*I was there in my room—although an odd version of it. It was both
familiar and not, and I recognized the bedspread with a start. It was
the one I'd gotten for my eighth birthday, that looked like multicol-
ored shredded yarn had been smashed together. I loved that bedspread, and had been secretly sad to replace it when I was fifteen.
Somewhere there was a book with a snipped off piece of it hidden
inside for a keepsake.*

*"Oh my God," I said softly, still staying snug to the wall, like that
was safer.*

*That thought made me chuckle that anything tangible would
really be safer in that situation. I reached out tentatively with my left
hand to see if the same rules applied as before. It wasn't so much a
stopping point as it was just a feeling that I couldn't move any
farther.*

*It didn't matter. Once I watched my eleven-year-old self fly
through the door and pounce on that bed, I was paralyzed anyway.*

*It was the freakiest kind of bizarre. I held my breath as I watched
mini-me kick off the black sneakers I remembered decorating with
puff paint smiley faces.*

"Come on," she called out, and the craziness continued with Holly coming in.

She strolled in with all her twelve-year-old maturity, arms crossed and eyes looking down with disdain on whatever I was doing. The usual.

Her hair was redder, mine was blonder, and neither of us appeared to have an ounce of body fat. I remembered we were long and lanky, but I didn't remember looking quite so awkward.

Mini-me pulled her socks off as well and bounced to the window, right at me. I held my breath as she sat on the window box on her knees, opening the window and leaning out to suck in the fresh night air. Six inches closer and I could have touched her—me—her. I could see the brand-new burn on the inside of her right calf, the one that came from riding on the back of Uncle Tommy's motorcycle and accidentally letting my leg fall against the hot engine. I pulled up my jeans leg above where my boot was and fingered the scar left there.

"Can you hear me?" I asked her. She didn't blink. "If you can," I continued, "don't cheat on the social studies test. Mrs. Cartwright is watching."

What the heck, it was worth a shot.

"I'm telling you, it's not that scary, you're being a big baby," mini-me said to Holly.

"I'm not scared, it's just stupid," Holly said, keeping her arms crossed and jutting one hip out to look older. "Mom and Dad would board up that window forever if they knew you were climbing out of it every night."

"And I didn't invite them in, now did I?"

Holly huffed. "Well, I'm not going to go climb around on the roof in the dark," she said, landing on the bed and crossing her legs. "That's retarded."

Mini-me rolled her eyes and shook her head, turning back to the window. "You're such a stump, Holly, I swear."

"Oh, please," Holly said with a laugh, twisting the ends of her hair around her fingers. "You just want to see if that crazy boy comes back."

I sucked in a breath at the same time mini-me whirled around. I remembered this.

"I do not!"

"Bullshit," Holly said. "You've been glued to that roof ever since that psycho showed up the other night."

"He's not a psycho," mini-me said, her nose scrunching up in anger. "Don't talk about him like that or I'll tell Dad you're cussing."

"And I'll tell him you're sneaking out at night."

Mini-me's face got all sarcastic and it was so much like Cassidy's that I laughed out loud. "Oh, sneaking out?" she said, pointing out the window. "A whole ten feet?"

"You know good and well they'd ground you for a month, Emmie, so don't act all tough with me," Holly said, still playing with her hair.

"Whatever," mini-me said, seeming to realize she'd lost her leverage. She sat flat on the window box with her arms around her knees. "And I've been going on the roof since the third grade, long before Ben ever came over, so shut up."

"Why would anybody do that?" she asked. "Climb around on other people's property, climb around on their roof? He's gonna get shot one day doing things like that."

Mini-me gave her a look. "You may as well be a hundred and one years old, Holly. You sound like an old woman."

Holly shot her the finger, which mini-me promptly returned before turning back to the window. "Sorry I ever invited you. Go back to your crocheting, old lady."

"Whatever," Holly shot back. "Go visit your freaky boyfriend."

"He's not my boyfriend, he's my friend, and you'd better shut up or I'll tell him you have the hots for his brother."

Holly's face flushed pink, and she scooped her hair back. "I do not!"

Mini-me laughed, and so did I as I remembered how she really did have a major crush on Bobby Landry, who never even gave her a second glance.

"Yeah, you do, I heard you and Katy Pritchard talking about him."

"Oh, you don't know anything!" Holly stormed from the room, her face as red as her hair.

Mini-me snickered, and then stalled as she watched the door for a moment in case Mom or Dad showed up with guns blazing. As she looped one skinny leg through the window, I recalled the Landry brothers as kids and how they always caught the girls' attention with their long dark hair and guarded eyes.

I watched myself disappear into the darkness, toward the curtain of the big oak tree, where I knew I'd sit till the sound of the breeze made me sleepy. I peered out to see if I'd get a glimpse of young Ben, but somehow I remembered that he didn't come again for a while. I remembered he'd gotten punished after getting caught sneaking back into his house that first time. His punishment hadn't been grounding, though. His dad had a different theory on punishment. One that frequently required long sleeves in the summertime. Ben learned how to be craftier after that.

I didn't have long to ponder the memory of that first visit, when he'd climbed the big tree to my roof with a bag of his drawings, begging me to keep them so his dad wouldn't tear them up.

By the time my mind wrapped itself around that memory, the ringing filled my ears and the blackness of the night washed over me *until the room's brightness dimmed to nothing. I felt the tightness around my chest, squeezing the air from my lungs.*

Instead of freaking out that time, I focused on the wall against my hand, and waited for the light and rush of air. True to form, it came within seconds, snapping the tightness around me as if it were a rope. I sucked in sharply and opened my eyes.

∂∾

I was back. Sitting on the floor next to the window box. Thinking that there was some sort of point to the madness. There had to be.

I WAS AT THE GROCERY STORE, TRYING TO TRULY CARE ABOUT the organic choices that were so inconveniently stocked on the top shelf. As opposed to the saturated fat and preserved-for-the-next-eighty-years crap that always rested at eye level. I wanted to care about being healthy like Holly did. I wanted to eat right and drink half my body weight in water and burn up my treadmill melting away that little pooch that my jeans managed to flatten but did a parade wave when I was naked.

Not that too many people were seeing me naked lately. Or anyone, actually. Not that there wasn't the occasional potential for opportunity—there was the guy from the video store that seemed overly friendly, but then I got to thinking about how often I saw him there, and if he was there as much as I was, then he really was kind of sad. And then that was depressing, so I changed video stores.

And there was Chris at the office where I had to show up once a week for the roundtable meeting so the powers that be could see what we had in the works and that we weren't just sitting at home playing solitaire. He asked me on some form of date every single week. I went to lunch once, and realized that while Chris was nice, and certainly persistent, his fascination with his clothing was a little off base. Everything was perfectly pressed and pristine, but in addition to that, he wore only blue. Light blue shirts, dark blue pants, navy blue suits, midnight blue shoes. It took fifteen kinds of willpower not to buy him a red tie and watch him implode.

I'd only had three real relationships in the ten years since my divorce, and all of them ended on a fizzle. Once the initial hot factor wore thin, there wasn't enough to fall back on. I hadn't found love again. Not like before. And I was good with that. I'd learned to love my own company and relished not having to answer to anyone or clean piss off the floor. The only shining prize I'd received from a man was Cassidy, and she was the light of my life.

So, as I gazed upon the choices before me, I pulled my hoodie jacket tighter around my body and grabbed the eye-level crap. Who would care if I got ugly and fat? Kevin? Certainly not. He would celebrate. Ben? I wasn't going there.

My cell buzzed in my pocket, and I dug it out, noting it was the light of my life.

"Hey, doodlebug."

"Hey, what do you think about having a birthday party for Nana early?" she asked.

I stopped walking. "Her birthday isn't until next month."

"I know, but if Aunt Bernie comes before then, she may be on the road and we won't get a chance to celebrate with her."

My girl. She loved her Nana. They were cut from the same

cloth. Same love of history, same itch to see strange places, same love of ornery dogs.

"Okay, that's fine," I said, turning and nearly ramming carts with a woman who looked like queen of the soccer moms. Seriously. She even had the mommy version of the uniform on. "Sorry," I said to her, smiling. She probably thought I looked like queen of the couch potatoes.

"Where are you?" Cassidy asked.

"The grocery store."

"Again? Didn't you just go there?"

I cursed my bad lying. "Oh, I forgot a few things." I pushed my cart faster, wanting to get done and get home. "So, anyway, that's fine if you want to do th—" I choked back the last word as I rounded an aisle into the produce, and there stood Ben. Fondling peaches.

"What's the matter?" Cassidy asked.

"Nothing," I said under my breath, jumping backward and tugging my cart with me.

"So, you're good with the party, Miss Anti-Party?"

"Absolutely," I said, doing a U-turn and heading the opposite way. "As long as all I have to do is show up."

"That's cool, I'll get with Aunt Holly," she said. "She likes that stuff."

"Well, right now she doesn't like Nana much," I said, laughing. "But maybe that will change."

I dead-ended at the meat section, thinking I could stay there, then had a panicked thought that he *was* a man and would probably buy meat.

"Shit," I said under my breath, forgetting Cassidy was still chattering.

She stopped. "What?"

"Oh, nothing, baby, I just—can't find the sea salt."

I darted across the endcaps till I found what was sure to be a safe aisle, and jumped in there with the tampons and sanitary pads. And then flattened myself as best I could to all the pink packaging, just in case he tended to look down each aisle.

"Did she tell you that Josh and I are going over there for lunch tomorrow?" Cassidy said.

"What? She who?"

"Nana," she said dramatically. "She called and invited us over."

My mind ticked off all the various reasons why there was no worse idea than that.

"Um—"

"And if you don't have anything to do and can be nice, you can come, too," she said.

Oh, I did have things to do. I had tons of things to do, but there was no way in hell I was missing it. My mother hadn't invited me, but what was family good for if you couldn't crash a party.

"I'll see," I said, glancing around to see if anyone saw me talking to the tampons. "I thought you had to work."

"Not till two."

"And Josh?"

"Not till the next day."

Of course. We said our good-byes and I strongly considered stalking the registers from afar to make sure he left. Then again, if I'd just hurried up, I would have been gone by then.

As if on cue, he passed my aisle, slowly pushing his cart as he studied a piece of paper in his hand. I stopped and froze in place, holding my breath, not blinking or breathing till he passed. Then I ran for the registers like the chickenshit I was, not caring that I'd only grabbed four of my thirty-something needed items. They'd be there tomorrow. Or no—the day after tomorrow, because I had a lunch date with karma.

I quick-scanned the registers for the fastest choice and picked one with an elderly man with only a pack of toilet paper and a box of candy under his arm. I'd be out of there in minutes, as compared to all the other lines sporting three and four people each, with mountains overflowing their carts.

I did a little shuffle move, waiting for my turn, looking behind me every five seconds. Why the hell was I so paranoid? Why was I hiding in *my* grocery store, in *my* town? He should be hiding from me. And no sooner had that thought crossed my brain when he rounded the corner, and I ducked.

Pretending to closely inspect the latest celebrity gossip on the rack, I silently begged the checker to hurry the hell up.

"Price check on four!" she called into a microphone, holding up the box of candy.

"It's five ninety-nine," the elderly man said.

"I have to check, sir," the pink-cheeked checker said, pulling out a reference card to prove it.

Great. I picked a newbie with anal retention.

"I actually saw it, too, and it was five ninety-five," I said, nodding from my bent-over stance.

The girl looked at me with giant eyes. "He said five ninety-nine."

I blinked. "That's what I said."

"No, you said five ninety-five," the man said.

"That's why we check it," the girl said, nodding.

"For four pennies? Seriously?" I said. I really actually kind of hissed it. "Don't y'all scan everything now, anyway?"

The girl scowled at me. "The scanners are down," she said.

The man just kind of shrugged, and I gave him a weary look. Of course the old man didn't care. All he had planned for the day was to sit on the toilet and eat chocolate caramels.

Finally, a greasy-haired stock boy ambled up, holding a hand out for the box. The old man looked almost physically pained to watch it leave with the boy, as if he'd taken great measures to select that very box and didn't trust the boy not to switch it.

I was still very much bent over when legs stopped behind me. Somehow I knew who they belonged to before I ever looked up.

"You okay?" Ben asked, not sounding particularly sincere.

I slowly lowered my stoop to a crouch, pretending fascination with a tabloid.

"I'm fine, how are you?" I asked, hoping I sounded as uninterested as he did.

He reached over me and plucked the tabloid out of the rack, giving off an aroma of warm soap when he did so.

"The end of the world, huh?" he read off the headline. "Nostradamus's prediction keep you up at night?"

I saw the humor in his eyes, but I refused to play. "Lots of things keep me up at night," I said, rising to my feet and hoping to pull off dignified. I smiled, looking at his handbasket. "You're all about the mac and cheese, I see?"

He tilted his head in a small shrug. "Don't have much time for cooking lately, have to go for fast and filling."

I nodded, noting the stock boy finally returning with the vitally important four-cent price difference, and I got to move ahead. The checker glared at me and tapped in the prices of my four items, slinging them behind her.

"So, you cook?" I asked over my shoulder.

"Sure," he said, setting his basket on the counter. "My mother taught us never to be dependent on a woman."

I felt the jab and turned to try to understand it. He had a hell of a nerve saying something like that to me. "Ever get married, Ben?" I asked quietly.

The dark eyes went darker. "No."

"Then I guess you learned well."

I felt the heat on the back of my neck as I grabbed my bags and turned toward the exit. A younger piece of me ached inside. The rest of me that knew the score ran like hell.

CHAPTER

5

I RESCHEDULED MY LIFE AROUND HIM—AGAIN. BEN DIDN'T realize it, but just his presence was jacking with my life, my job, my family, my sanity. I hadn't cleaned a thing or washed a dish in three days, I hadn't updated my listings, watered my thirsty herb garden, or met with a single new client since Ben had arrived on my mother's porch. Every phone call I received, I put to voice mail. Every e-mail for showings, I scheduled for another day or deferred to another Realtor.

There was an argument to be made that I didn't need to put off any of those things for him. He hadn't given *me* a second thought when he ditched me after professing his love and getting into my pants. Why was I giving him any thoughts at all?

Keeping me up at night—ugh, his attitude reminded me of how he used to be with everyone else. Girls at school hated him for his arrogance but were drawn to his good looks long enough to get a taste of him. Guys gave him a wide berth and ignored him, because those who were cocky enough to try to knock the top off that arrogance got the shit beat out of them. There was no winning against Ben or Bobby Landry. They were too well trained in the art of fighting dirty.

But with me, he was different. No show, no pompous attitude. He was real with me, a normal guy, with normal thoughts and conversations, and a not-so-normal home life. We didn't hang out together at school, or even after graduation, since I went to the local college and he worked in a lumberyard. But at night, we'd catch up. The girls he dated probably never knew about me because they weren't around long enough to get that invested. Kevin, on the other hand, couldn't stand him.

He hated that Ben and I were friends and never lost an opportunity to tell me. Partially because he didn't trust Ben with his lothario ways. Also, I heard through the grapevine once that Ben had a talk with him after one of his straying flings. I never asked about that, but I believed it. Ben was protective of me.

Well—until he wasn't.

So, I stood outside my mother's house again, looking from Ben's truck to Cassidy's little bug and cursing my life. Knowing him, he would probably keep himself completely out of the picture, but I couldn't take that gamble. I had to make sure that he and Cass didn't spend too much time together.

I could hear the chatter as I took the garage route and approached the back door. Actually it sounded more animated than chatter, and when I opened the door, I was greeted with Tandy rushing me like a pit bull and the view of Josh and Ben competing in an arm wrestling match there at the bar. Cassidy and Mom were cheering them on over the perpetual droning of the TV, as if it were a sporting event.

So much for knowing him.

I closed the door behind me, held a foot out to keep the dog down, then stood in stunned silence while the two men—and that was a loose term for Josh—grinned at each other and refused to blink. Looking at Ben, I was reminded of his earlier fighting days. Even at forty-two years old, and evenly matched by the looks of where their arms were, he looked almost relaxed. His face wasn't red with exertion, no veins bulged at his throat or temples. He still knew how to psyche out an opponent and play that mental game.

Fair-haired, pale-skinned Josh, on the other hand, looked as if he might erupt at any moment. His ears were turning purple.

"Go, baby, you've got this," Cassidy said, her hands on Josh's shoulders.

I saw Ben glance up at her like he wanted to laugh, then he shook his head almost imperceptibly. I could hear my heart in my ears as he looked at her. I wanted to tell him not to look at her, not to laugh with her, to go back to hammering something or gluing something or whatever it was he was doing before Josh probably dared him into this. I would have just about given my right pinkie finger for him to leave the house completely. Leave before he looked too closely and saw what seemed so blinking-neon-sign blatantly obvious to me. Maybe it was just because I was looking for it, maybe it was because I knew, but it was crystal clear to me the very second they laid that tiny slimy screaming human on my chest. She was all him.

Her hair changed to golden, but everything else about her features and even her skin tone was closer to his than to mine.

I looked over at the appetizer spread my mother had set out, trying to calm my nerves with a sense of normal. But there was nothing normal about that table. She had a freaking food array set up as if she were entertaining the mayor. Cassidy let go of Josh long enough to reach for two cake balls she popped into her mouth at the same time.

"My lord, Mom, who else is coming?" I asked.

"Actually, I didn't even know you were coming," she said with a wink. "Just something I decided to play around with."

I looked at her—at Ben—back at her. "You're going to cook, now?"

I plucked a rolled something-or-other-that-looked-like-turkey off a plate and topped it with a Wheat Thin. My mother stopped cheering and moved to rearrange the plate I'd evidently just tainted.

"It's just food," she said, adding a ladle to the cheese dip.

I raised my eyebrows and attempted a chuckle around my turkey-something. "Mom, *just food* is usually potato chips in a bowl. And why a ladle?"

"Why not?" she asked.

"Because since when do we step up from just finding a really large chip?"

"Oh, for pete's sake," she said, her eyebrows furrowing, "You act like I fed you out of pig troughs. It won't kill you to step it up a little."

"Damn," Josh said, making me turn around.

Ben had finally finished Josh off with a flourish and shook his hand, laughing. "Thanks for the invite, bud, that was fun. Haven't done that in a long time."

"What, won? Or just wrestled?" Josh said, smiling through what I'm sure was an ego hit, being taken by a man twice his age.

"Both," Ben said. He slapped Josh on the shoulder and got up. "Need to get back to it."

He gave me the briefest of looks before turning away. I felt the weight of it like it was dropped from the moon.

"No, come on, Ben, why don't you eat lunch with us," Cassidy said, reaching out to tug his sleeve. "We have enough food here to feed China. I mean seriously."

Some funky noise escaped my throat and everyone turned to me.

"Are you choking on your own spit again, Emily?" my mother said, which would have been infinitely better than the horror I already had going on.

I tried laughing, but it felt crazy, so I just shook my head. "No, I'm fine. Um—Cass, I'm sure *Mr. Landry* is on a schedule."

"Nonsense," my mother exclaimed, looking at me with that parental flash of eternal disappointment. "There's a ton of food, and he's an old friend of *yours*," she emphasized for that extra punch. "Of course he's eating with us."

Ben looked like he wanted to leave and never return. "Really, I'm fine, I need to—"

"Sit down, young man," Mom said, making the corner to the cabinet to pull out glasses.

Ben pulled out his stool and obeyed, and if it weren't for the turmoil going on in my head, that would have been humorous. Cassidy went to help put ice in the glasses, and Josh was given a handful of silverware to dole out. I stood there like a lump, not quite knowing what to do with myself.

"What are these things?" Cassidy asked, leaning to point at a tray of yellow spongy-looking balls on a green platter. She picked one up gingerly and sniffed it, pushing a crazy blonde curl out of her face with the other hand.

"Cheese puffs," Mom said. Tandy morphed at her side as she spoke the words, as if that were an order for her to beg. Of course Mom complied, pinching off a piece for her.

I picked up my plate and put things on it blindly, not even seeing the food. My appetite was gone, my stomach was a swirling mess, and all I could do was go through the motions.

"We could call Holly," I suggested, suddenly feeling a need for an ally. "She might be able to get off work for lunch."

"Holly isn't speaking to me, remember?" Mom said as she hovered over everything like a honeybee.

"Why not?" Cassidy asked.

"Because I didn't ask her permission to sell the house," Mom said.

She said it all snarky, but I knew that it was really eating at her. Holly was always the sweet one and the one to do no wrong. Holly's marriage and pregnancies came in the correct order. Her college education went the whole four years instead of just two and a half, because her grades got her scholarships and mine didn't. Her kids went off to fancy colleges, mine was a waitress. But I'd take Cassidy's brain over her two snobs any day. Cass was smart as a whip; she just hated formal education.

But Holly being off the map was odd. She would normally be the one making sure everyone had the same number of ice cubes, enough napkins, enough tea—and that's when I realized I'd found something to do.

I made my way around to grab the pot, which Mom grabbed at the same time.

"I've got this, Emmie," she said. "Go eat."

"No, I've got it," I said, pulling back. "You go eat; you've worked hard on all this."

"And ate a lifetime's worth while I did it," she said, shooing me.

"Please, I beg you, let me make the freaking tea," I muttered under my breath so no one else would hear. Mom's eyebrows raised and she let go of the pot. "Thank you."

The fire I turned on under the little red pot was nothing on what my blood was doing. I could feel the heat tickling my hair. But it was okay as long as I didn't have to sit there at the same table with the man that—my heart stopped as I looked up on that thought and found him staring at me, hard, his arms crossed and leaning on the bar. I dropped the teabags and gasped as I had to dig them out of the burner before they caught fire. I darted a look around to see if anyone noticed through Mom and Cassidy's gabbing and the increasing volume of the TV in the background. No one except Ben, of course. And his face gave away nothing.

Josh had swiped the TV remote off a nearby stool. I watched him hold it down by his leg and click the volume up two more notches on whatever Fox News had to say, as he feigned interest in a barbecued weenie. Now there was an interesting twist. Carwashing Josh interested in world news. I also noticed that the knickknacks and pictures on top of the TV and table were now gone. It was really disappearing. Our life there was slowly being packed away.

Okay, I thought, as I soaked the teabags and everyone had sort of settled in somewhere with a plate. Mom was standing over hers, but that was pretty normal for her. Cassidy was busy stealing food off Josh's plate, and I needed to calm the hell down.

Yes, I'd been dealt a freaky hand lately. The new "home movies" were just a bit over the top, but I was clearly meant to figure something out. Just hopefully not during lunch. And Ben coming back was something I couldn't control. He didn't look to be going anywhere, so I was going to have to learn how to coexist with him. With him and Cassidy. I clutched at my middle on that one.

Ben, thankfully, had stopped watching me and seemed very interested in the food. He was pulling the cheese puffs apart and studying them. The stuffed pork loin I hadn't even noticed before, he appeared to be analyzing before he savored each bite.

"Mrs. Lattimer, how'd you make this?" he asked, holding up another slice of the pork loin that had cream cheese and jalapeños oozing from its middle.

Mom beamed. I wanted to know that answer myself, since we certainly never got food like that. We had roast and rice and gravy or baked chicken with mashed potatoes. Sometimes spaghetti. Sometimes sandwiches. Sometimes milk hash on toast. Most definitely nothing got stuffed or puffed. And I'm pretty sure that Mom had never bought cream cheese before in her life.

"Let me show you," Mom said, pulling a book out of a drawer, one that was laden with Post-it notes and flags. She turned to a page and showed him, and he read with interest as she copied it onto a neon green Post-it note.

Another interesting twist. Not only was he just basically *not dependent on a woman*, but he also had a culinary eye beyond mac and cheese.

"So, Ben, where'd you go when you left here?" Cassidy asked.

I was pretty proud of myself for getting the tea inside the pitcher on that one, and I refused to turn around. I wanted to know, too, but every time Cass talked to him directly my fingers and toes went numb.

There was a pause, and I didn't know if the heat on my back was from his eyes or my own anxiety. "Lots of different places at first," he said slowly.

"So you traveled around?" Cassidy asked. "I want to travel so bad; I want to see stuff like Aunt Bernie does." I did turn around on that, and she laughed at my expression. "I do! She just goes where she wants to go. I want to do that—except not when I'm sixty."

"We'll do it," Josh said, giving Cass a squeeze. "We'll go anywhere you want to go."

Not washing cars, he wasn't. I let out a sigh and pushed the negative away.

"I hope you get to, doodlebug," Mom said, and there was a lacing of sadness in her voice. I realized at that second how familiar those words were to her. "Don't wait for someday."

"My Paw-Paw had a poster that he circled all the places he wanted to go," Cassidy said to Josh.

"Good lord, girl, you remember that?" Mom said. "You were barely eight years old when your Paw-Paw died."

"Yeah! We'd go look at the stars and then talk about Japan and Greece and Alaska, and then he'd give me peppermints."

I laughed in spite of the headache tapping on my skull and headed back around to where my plate awaited. "I remember those same talks. Except without the peppermints."

"So did you go anywhere interesting like that, Ben?" Cass asked him, making me grip my fork a little harder. I really needed her to stop calling him Ben.

He chuckled and stabbed at some food. "I don't think so. My adventures were much more—raw Americana than that."

"Really?" Josh said, perking up. "See that's just the kind of trips I want to take. Down and gritty. See things like they really are, not the touristy version."

Ben didn't say anything at first, just nodded very minimally and then set his fork down and wiped his mouth. He looked at Josh and then Cassidy, and I had to fight the urge to jump in front of her. His mouth opened to say something, then closed again, and he just kind of shook his head at his own thought and smiled at my mother.

"Thank you for lunch, Mrs. Lattimer, and for the recipe." He held up the note. "It was amazing and you have a gift."

My mom looked happy enough to burst, but Cassidy said, "What, you're leaving?"

"No, I'm going upstairs to work on the windows, but I appreciate the company." He slapped Josh on the shoulder again, with a little less gusto than before. "Had a good time wrestling with you, bud."

"Yeah, you, too," Josh said, looking a little off-kilter.

Ben got up and washed off his plate and headed back around the bar. I didn't look up. I felt like I'd survived the first event in a triathlon. With many more to come.

My dad's office was always intriguing to me. Papers stacked to look important, colored pens in a cup by an ancient solid-metal crank-type calculator that weighed five tons. I'd spend hours when I was little, typing numbers in and cranking the handle so that the numbers would print on the paper. I think it came from his mother or grandmother, and he preferred it with its old paper and could-crush-a-skull potential to using anything new. He'd pay bills and do the books for the hardware store he ran with his brother, read the newspaper—basically the room was what a "man cave" would be today, with less technology.

But he always had the most interesting things sitting around. A big wooden duck that his dad had made for him when he was young and went on his first duck hunt. Random drawings of tools that my uncle Tommy had done right after they opened the hardware store. Old tins that didn't hold anything anymore but sported sayings about tobacco or soft drinks or coffee. A whole corner of Gulf Oil memorabilia that he collected later in life when the company was no more. And a big, beautiful telescope.

The telescope always reminded me of the ones you see in movies that reside in old sailors' houses, up in some high room looking out a window. It was brushed brass and huge and seemed almost alive, like it couldn't wait to look at things with us. I remember thinking that my dad had to be really important to own such a thing. We'd aim it out his window and find all the constellations and planets we could find.

It was still there. Every time I came in his office in the thirteen years since he died, I was struck by how sad it was. Still sitting up there in its same spot, framed and tucked into the bay window. Like it was waiting for us, ready to discover something, ready to be loved, but just left alone instead with the lights turned out. I'd asked my mother a hundred times if I could take it home, but she always put me off. Just like his office remained decorated with the tins and the duck. We went through the papers for anything important, but the calculator, the telescope, the books, and everything else—all remained there. Including his desk calendar, with the yellowed page turned to May 7, 1998, the day he died. I think my mother was afraid we'd lose more of him if any of it moved. So there it all stayed, dusty and sad. Along with the faded poster of the world that was tacked up to the wainscot planks that they never got around to replacing with that horrid fake paneling.

The poster with the red circles drawn that actually weren't red anymore but more of a putrid orange. I traced a finger around one and felt the dust on it. I remembered the talks like Cassidy had described. The countless hours staring at all the places outside my little world and listening to him describe where he and my mother would visit one day. I looked at them—the Grand Canyon, Hawaii, New York, Alaska, then Greece and Australia and Japan and Egypt. I walked behind his desk and pulled out the top drawer, and there they were. The box of thumbtacks he bought, unused except for the four he had holding the poster up. Three actually, one appeared to be missing.

I typed in 1 . . . 2 . . . 3 . . . 4 . . . on the calculator and pulled the crank, making the little metal typefaces lurch into action like they'd forgotten how. Just the sound of it gave me goose bumps and brought tears to my eyes.

"I miss you, Daddy," I said, running my fingers over his desk, leaving trails in the dust that had settled there.

It hit me then, what was making this sale so difficult. What probably had Holly balking. My dad was there. He was everywhere, on the walls, in the cabinets he made, and especially in that room with all his things just where they were supposed to be.

I heard a noise and looked up from my reverie to see Ben walk in and stop short.

"Sorry," he said. "I didn't think anyone was in here."

I shook my head, although something in me didn't want him in there. Like it would take some of my dad's presence away. I guessed that's how my mother felt about us in there.

"It's okay."

"I can come back." He turned toward the door.

"No, it's okay," I repeated. "Really."

His eyes traveled the room, taking in every detail as usual. "Your dad's office?"

"Yeah," I said, sitting on the desk.

He met my eyes. "I was sorry to hear about it—when he died, I mean."

"You knew?"

He did a mini-shrug. "Bobby told me."

I just nodded through the silence that followed, squeezing my other hand to keep from asking the questions that wanted out. I was afraid that if I put voice to them, I would never be able to close those gates.

He gestured toward the window with a caulk gun. "I need to get over there to seal up around the window," he said. "Can we move the telescope?"

I did a head jerk back to the ancient piece of equipment I once thought was made of gold. Move it? Was that legal? Was it even possible? I'd never seen it moved from its sacred place there by the window.

"Uh—I guess so," I said.

"Will you get in trouble?"

I slung a look at him and couldn't read his eyes to see if he was joking. "It's just really old," I said. "We need to be careful."

An old familiar smile tugged at his mouth, and for a second—just a second—I found myself missing that. "I'm not gonna throw it across the room, Em."

I couldn't help but smile, but I hugged my arms around myself and looked away.

"Come on, come help me."

He and I stood on either side of it and each supported the scope and legs to lift it. It was bulky, but lighter than I expected. I guess in my mind, it should have been anchored to the floor.

We shuffled to an open area off to the side and set it down, finding ourselves nearly nose to nose. The slow way we both straightened up, with his eyes boring into mine, made my skin tingle like I was some hormonal teenager. The pull nearly took my breath clean out of me. Then his expression went from soft to demanding, as if then *he* wanted to say something but wouldn't, and I stepped back a step to catch my breath.

Instead, we both blinked the moment past. He moved to what suddenly felt like an old, boring empty window. Without the telescope flocking the front, there was nothing special about it.

Ben set about caulking the seams, hitting a slow, precise speed. I watched him for a second, his expression hard and focused, and I felt a tiny pang of the old hurt nick my heart. We were once so in sync with each other's thoughts, so tuned in. And now we had nothing to say.

"Your daughter—she's nice," he finally said right as I got up to leave. His voice was low, and once I got past the initial panic over him talking about Cassidy, I realized he'd been trying to think of something to say, too. "Reminds me of you back then."

I licked my lips. "Thank you."

He paused in his caulking trip down the side of the window and looked back at me, then let the gun hang by his side.

"Thank you?" he said, eyebrows raised.

"What?"

He faced me and leaned against the wall, propping one foot up. "What's happened to you, Em? You used to be so full of life." He gestured toward me with the caulk gun. "Now look at you, arms crossed so tight you look like you'll break if you laugh."

My jaw dropped, and I felt the heat of indignation wash over me. *Break if I laugh?* I'd show him just how full of life I could really be. Or was he right?

"Where's the crazy, fearless girl that used to climb out on a roof every night just to *stargaze*? That would shimmy down a tree to go swimming at the docks at midnight?"

It was everything I could do to keep a straight face and not flinch. "She's got a bad knee now," I said, attempting light, but I didn't feel it.

"No, she's downstairs," he said, ignoring me and pointing at the floor. "You have roof access at your house?"

I blinked twice at the connotation. "No."

"Be glad. Because she'd be there. With that idiot she's hanging on."

I had to quit talking about Cassidy or my head was going to start spinning around.

"Don't act like you know us, Ben," I said softly. "You left."

There. There it was.

"Yeah," he said on a bitter laugh. "So it's just me being back here on this side of the window that's got you like this?" he asked, walking toward me. "Or did Kevin drain the life out of you?"

That actually struck me and a laugh came up on its own. A

full-body one that started as a giggle and then took over, probably because it diffused the topic and let me breathe. For that moment, Ben lost his haughty rant composure and smiled.

"There it is," he said. "In your eyes. I knew you were still in there somewhere."

I forced myself to look away, and he was too close for comfort. "I've always been here, Ben. I just grew up since you left."

"Bullshit."

I gave him a look. "Excuse me?"

"Everybody grows up. You have a chip on your shoulder about something."

I chuckled again. "You think?"

He narrowed his eyes, and it amazed me that he actually looked confused by that. He shook his head. "About what?"

About what? Unbelievable. But instead of flashing in anger like I always thought I would, I smiled and crossed my arms again—tight, so I wouldn't fucking break—and gave a little laugh.

"You know what? Nothing," I said. I walked around him to the door. "Let me know if you need anything."

CHAPTER

6

WHEN I WAS MARRIED TO KEVIN, BASIC MAINTENANCE AROUND the house was fairly easy. The house was clean because there was very little in it; the yard was easy to maintain because there was essentially just grass there. In retrospect, that could have been his reasoning all along.

After our divorce, I did what most divorcees do—go ass opposite on everything. I cluttered up the house with stuff, subscribed to every magazine I could find, and redesigned my backyard.

I rescued a great swing from the garbageman three blocks from my house one day. It was old with peeling paint and a broken armrest. Always wanting a swing, I maneuvered the thing home by way of a guy that kept calling to ask me out. I wasn't ready for the guy, but I thought maybe that would push me into having lunch with him if I felt obligated. Anyway, I sanded down the swing, fixed the armrest by way of that same guy, bought a frame and some chain, and painted the whole thing fire-engine red.

Because everything looks better in red.

The guy didn't last but a few weeks, but the swing persevered. One of my favorite stress relievers was to sit in it with a tall glass of sweet tea at sunset or a steaming cup of coffee at sunup, with hummingbirds whizzing by my head like fighter jets.

That swing was the only part of the new-yard marvel that I could lay claim to. The rest—the bushes, the special little trees with the knobby leaves that I couldn't remember the name of, the ivy, the flowers that seemed to bloom from different places at different times of year, the rocks and the Pavestones and the fountain and the little statues of cherubic children—all that was my mom and Holly. Even the arbor over the stone table and the flowers on either side of my hot red swing—that was their doing. My dad could kill cactus, and I inherited his thumb.

It being a Saturday, I had to sort of get semi-ready and then do whatever needed doing while waiting for inevitable phone calls. I was more likely to have to work than the rest of the working world, because Saturdays are when people have time to go looking.

That day's *whatever* was sitting in my wonderful red swing with a hot mug of coffee that turned into the tall glass of tea an hour later. It wasn't too cold out, it wasn't muggy; it was one of those days I was really hoping the phone wouldn't ring. I didn't even want to go to my mom's house. I wasn't in the mood for packing or memory lane or somebody else's memory lane. Or Ben. Especially Ben.

I heard the side gate open, and I waved at Holly as she came in with her arms wrapped around a new statue.

"What on earth?" I said, rising to help.

She waved me off with one hand, so I figured it wasn't too heavy and sat back down.

"They had these on sale two-for-one at that gardening place. I knew it would look fantastic over there next to the arbor."

She pointed the way as she carried it there, plopped it down, and fussed with it till it was angled just right. It was of a man picking grapes, so the grapevine she had growing on my arbor looked really cool hanging down around him.

"Think he'll scare the birds away from the grapes?" I asked.

Holly shook her head and wiped her hands on her jeans. "Nah. More likely, they'll just have another place to sit and poop while they eat the grapes."

I chuckled and held a hand up. "Well, as long as it's useful."

"I just couldn't resist."

"You're right, it does look good there," I said. "Where'd you put yours?"

Holly's yard made mine look like a dump. She had hers set up like a Roman courtyard. "In that corner off the patio next to the stone fireplace where the vines are hanging off that beam," she answered, her voice lilting up as if it were a question.

I nodded. She sat on the swing with me and we pushed it lightly with our toes, having exhausted any real conversation. Or actually, just waiting for the real reason Holly bought me a statue and carted it over to my backyard.

"So, how's it going with lover boy?" she asked, leaning away from me with a small grin.

I elbowed her. "Cute." I did a neck roll. "He thinks Cass is nice and like me when I was her age."

"She is."

"I wish she'd quit going over there."

"Well, she probably wants to visit with Mom before she takes off for the wild, wild West," Holly said snarkily.

And—there it was.

I sighed. "Yeah, I know. But it's giving me an ulcer."

"Are you going over there today?" she asked.

"I guess. Was kind of hoping to ignore it today, but I'll probably end up there." I looked at her. "Why?"

She shook her head and gazed out at the pretty picture she'd made with the statue. "Just wondering."

"Yeah, I still have to finish my room, and I was thinking there's probably a ton of crap in the attic. Mom doesn't need to be climbing around up there."

"I can't believe she's actually doing this," Holly said, crossing her arms.

I looked at her profile. The perfect white skin that showed tiny lines around her eyes. The perfect red hair that no one ever saw messy. The pale blue eyes that were always so set and serious. Holly always did things the way they were supposed to be done. She always followed the rules. Always stayed in the lines.

She would never sell a rock-solid foundation to live on wheels. She would never climb out a window and sneak down to the river to go swimming or drink a beer. Or crawl up in the tree over the house to disappear. Or have sex on the garage roof.

Holly lived safe. Stiff. With her arms crossed. My stomach burned as I saw her with different eyes and thought of Ben's words. Was I becoming my sister?

"She appears to be," I said, not really hearing my own voice as that thought bounced around.

"Do you know what the tax ramifications will be if she doesn't buy another house?" Holly asked.

A little laugh came out. "Yeah, actually, I do know a little about that."

She cut her eyes at me and sighed impatiently. "I know you do. Does she?"

"I don't know, but she's a big girl, Holly. You're not her mother. She'll figure it all out. She can put it in a trust or investment and be just fine."

"And everything they worked for their whole life was for nothing."

"That's not our call," I said, and then gave her a double take. "Is that really what's got you so bugged on this? Mom's tax issues?"

"Doesn't it bother you?" she asked, reaching for her hair. That told me she was more eaten up than she let on.

"Sentimentally, yeah," I said, pushing off with a toe again. "But not for the reasons you're saying. There are a lot of memories there."

"Exactly."

I stared at the statue, wishing so badly that I could tell her what had been happening at the house. "Lately, even more than I realized."

"And how can she just walk away from that?" Holly said, twisting furiously at her hair. "Dad would be mortified."

I frowned in her direction. "Why do you say that?"

"Because he worked himself to death for that house. So they wouldn't lose it when the store went under."

I blinked at her adamant tone. I'd never heard her so opinionated about it before. "Okay," I said. "He also wanted nothing more than to travel. So I think he'd be happy for her."

Holly got up so fast, I had to grab on to the swing to steady it back out. "You think he'd be happy that she's going to drive around the country with another crazy old woman in a gas-guzzling unreliable piece of shit? He had a cow when we didn't check our oil every three thousand miles, and we were still living at home!"

I had to laugh at that; she did have a point. "I know."

"And calling that thing Big Blue—" Holly shook her head. "*All the time.* Like it's a person or a man in her life or something. Makes my skin crawl."

My cell did its little chime thing, telling me I had an e-mail. "Hey, I'm just saying it's not for us to get all mad about."

"Well, you can be okay with it all you want," she said as I typed back to a client that I'd meet them in thirty. "I'm not."

I glanced up at her as I hit send. "No secret there." I got up and brushed my pants off. "I've gotta go change and meet a client over in Garwood Estates to show a house. I'll probably go to Mom's afterward if you want to meet me there."

Holly sighed and smoothed her hair, visibly attempting to regain her famous self-control. "Call me when you're on your way," she said calmly. "I'll see what I'm doing then."

GARWOOD ESTATES WAS THE NEWEST ADDITION IN TOWN, ALL shiny and polished with the best of everything. In ten years, after the baby trees grew up and offered some shade, I could see the appeal, but it was a bit too new and sunny to me. I preferred some charm and character to a home. But I suppose every house had to start somewhere. Everything was new once upon a time.

As I walked through the house at 459 Lance Street, waiting on the couple to show up, I scrunched my nose at the wood laminate flooring that echoed under my heels. For what the prices ran in that addition, they could have put in actual wood floors. The ceiling in the entryway was easily thirty feet up, which to me was a waste of utilities to heat and cool the place. That space could have been lofted and made into a sitting area or playroom or recreation area and been really interesting. And the stone fireplace, while gorgeous—was faux fronted. And electric.

Okay, I was nitpicking, I knew that, but where was the charm there? I knew many people who loved the convenience of fake fireplaces—just flick a switch and voila! Personally, I want some wood. I want some aroma. I want some sparks and embers and I want to get in there with the poker and mess around with the wood while it's burning.

I heard the knock and put on my sales face, leading the eager-faced couple around the house, pointing out the built-in appliances that gleamed from their ordained places. No stains tainted their fronts. No tiles were chipped in the immaculate cooktop island. No grout was discolored anywhere in the almost three-thousand-square-foot masterpiece.

"It's so beautiful," the lady breathed to her husband. "I'm almost afraid to touch anything."

The man nodded, his eyes taking in the crown molding that laced every room. "I know, it's kind of hard to imagine actually living here." He looked at me and laughed. "Our two kids would have this place destroyed in a week."

"I don't even know if my furniture is worthy," the woman said, laughing, too. She nudged her husband. "We'd have to buy new. Ours is too grungy."

I thought of my mother's house and its banged-up appliances and worn-out carpet that would likely come out. The old wood floors underneath. The solid wood bar with the handmade cabinets. The old Formica bathroom counters. The gas heaters in the walls and the wainscot wood paneling still upstairs in my dad's office because they never got that far in their redo.

"I know what you're saying," I said. "If you're more interested in an older home, I have some nice ones I can show you next week. Just need to arrange it with the owners."

The couple exchanged glances. "Yeah, let's do that," the husband said. "Gives us some options on which way to go."

I smiled. "Sounds good."

It was beginning.

When I made it to Mom's house twenty minutes later, Holly was already there, which surprised me because I forgot to call her. To my additional joy, Ben was there as well.

"Damn it," I said to the steering wheel as I pulled in. "Can't he take a day off?"

I went in the front door, deciding that when the house did sell, I was taking the knocker with me. I filled my lungs for inner strength as I entered, not expecting to be accosted by fumes.

"Jesus, what the—"

And then I saw what. As I walked past the stairway, I was stunned. From the kitchen, all the way through to the den, the old paneling was gone. I had to blink to adjust my vision to the brightness coming in the windows. The windows with no curtains. Or TV in front of them. Or tables next to them. Or furniture facing them. The room was empty except for the plastic across the carpet and Ben standing in it rolling paint on the wall.

Holly sat at the bar watching in silence, and Mom was at the sink chopping a mountain of potatoes.

"What the hell?"

Even Tandy stayed in her bed and didn't bother to come growl at me. It was like even she was traumatized.

"Hey, sweetheart," Mom said without turning around. "What do you think of the new color?"

"Really?" I said, feeling a little like Holly for a second. "That's not my first thought."

Mom looked back over her shoulder. "What?" she said, looking confused as she held a knife with little bits of raw potato stuck to it.

I pointed. "Where is—everything?"

"In the storage building," Mom said, going back to her chopping as if that made perfect sense. "I told y'all I got one."

I shook my head, thinking that there were no more words. I nudged Holly, who hadn't even twitched.

"You could have warned me."

"I—sort of forgot everything when I got here. Sorry."

She looked defeated, and I felt bad for her. I looked at the bare, bright room being doused in a shade of taupe that was actually pretty. But it no longer resembled the room where we used to have blanket forts and slumber parties.

Ben had already painted the ceiling, and two of the walls, and was going at the third like we weren't even there.

"How did—I mean, there was—actual furniture in here," I said. "Yesterday."

"Yes," my mother said as she calmly diced five million little potato cubes. "Ben and Cassidy and Josh came and the four of us got everything brought over there last night."

My eyebrows shot up. No one saw it. Ben was like a freaking hologram, painting ten feet away like he couldn't even hear us. Holly stared straight ahead.

"Ben and Cassidy and Josh," I repeated, landing on a bar stool next to Holly, forcing her to look at me. "All working together." I smiled. "How nice."

"Yep," Mom said. "Josh had a trailer."

"Really?" I licked my suddenly dry lips. "Why didn't you call me?"

Mom turned around again. "Because we had enough people."

"Mmm." I nodded and tried to let it go at that, but my need to keep going at all costs overcame. "Everything go okay?"

Mom frowned. "Yes, Mommy, she drank all her milk, too." She turned back around as I gave her a look. "My gosh, and you talk about Kevin being a hoverer."

"How *is* Kevin?" Ben asked, coming out of silent mode on his way back to the garage. I saw the sarcasm in his face as he spoke his name.

"Kevin's just fine," said Kevin as he strode through the back door.

"Oh, crap," I muttered under my breath. I heard Holly snicker next to me.

Ben swung around, the surprise flickering for just a second before he masked it. He offered Kevin his free hand. "Lockwood. Good to see you, man."

Kevin looked dumbfounded as he put his hand out on autopilot. "Landry." His eyes went to me as if I'd put Ben there myself. "My God, where'd you come from?" Then he caught sight of the room. "Holy cow."

Ben let his hand go to grab a rag off a stool. "Just about ran you over with a paint roller. Wasn't expecting anyone to just walk in."

Kevin chuckled. "Well, you know how it is with family. We don't knock."

"You're not family anymore," my mother chimed in from the sink. "Go back to knocking."

He didn't lose his grin, he was accustomed to her callousness with him. "Frances, good to see you." He gave me a once-over. "Emily, you're looking nicer than the last time I saw you."

I looked down at my heels and blouse and snug black pencil skirt, and back up to see Ben's eyes make the same slow trip.

"I'd say you look *really* nice," Ben said, with such emphasis on the words that my face and ears felt as if they caught fire before he made it back to my eyes.

I didn't know if that'd truly been for my benefit or to piss Kevin off, but he achieved it anyway. Kevin's jaw tightened as he stepped forward. I threw Ben a look that I hoped said to grow up, as Kevin puffed up and turned to Holly by way of what I suppose was neutral ground.

"I wanted to talk to y'all about the house," he said, pulling up a stool.

My mother turned, knife still in hand. "There's no *y'all* in the equation, Kevin, just me."

I bit my lip to keep from laughing and I noticed Holly's face kind of came to life to enjoy it, too.

"Well then," Kevin began, then turned around as if noticing Ben was still there. "Do you mind excusing us for a second?"

Mom tossed the knife in the sink and walked forward wiping her hands on a kitchen towel. "Ben's fine right where he is," she said, bringing what only I knew was the hint of a smile to Ben's lips as he painted carefully around the corners of an outlet. "He has a reason to be here. Cass isn't here, so what's yours?"

Kevin gave her a patient smile anyway. "I want to buy your house."

"I have a couple that might be interested," I blurted out, raising my hand like I was in middle school. "I'm gonna show it to them next week."

Mom ignored me. "I'm not selling to you, Kevin," she said with a pat on his shoulder and a wink. "You're Cassidy's dad and I love you for that, but you aren't getting my house."

"You don't know my bid."

She shrugged. "Don't care."

He tilted his head. "You might."

"You're a womanizing prick, Kev," my mom said, causing my jaw to drop. "No."

Ben even took the silence of the moment to walk outside. I assumed to have a good laugh. Honestly, in my opinion, what he did wasn't that much better.

"You know what?" I said, getting up before Kevin had to try to save face. "I'm gonna go upstairs. Maybe go up in the attic."

"Dressed like that?" Mom asked, already blowing Kevin off.

"I have a pair of sweatpants in the car."

I went out through the garage, where Ben was leaning over a five-gallon bucket of paint, stirring it with a flat piece of wood. Next to him on a makeshift table were two other small cans of paint with little wooden stir sticks poking out.

"Why do you do that?" I asked.

"What?" he responded, not looking up.

"Bait him like that," I said, picking my way carefully around the random tools and pieces of discarded wood on the floor. "Is it on purpose, or does he just bring out the twelve-year-old in you?"

I felt, rather than saw the smile. "Little of both, probably."

"Why?" I repeated as I got closer, my three-inch heels playing hell with all the power cords.

"Because he's the same condescending asshole now that he was then."

"And—"

I was about to tell him that I agreed with him and he didn't need to bait Kevin anymore. But then I remembered that there wouldn't be a reason anyway since he'd left me and made all those petty arguments between them go away. The thoughts jumped over each other, distracting me long enough to step on a block of wood that turned under my foot.

"Oh—shi—" I exclaimed as I lurched sideways and the spike of my heel snapped off.

My left hand flailed out for support, met with one of the little stir sticks instead, and flipped it out of the can and across Ben's face. The paint splattered across his left cheek and nose, and slung streaks into my hair as I continued my sideways direction right into his arms.

"Whoa!" he said as I landed hard against him. "Are you okay?"

I gasped and then looked up just inches from his face, suddenly recalling the last time I was held so tightly against his body. I even was acutely aware of where his hands were and one of them was fairly south. Not that that had been by his choice. But then the sight of the paint across his face and in his eyebrows broke the moment and I clamped my lips shut as the laughter shook me.

"I'm—" I laughed again, trying to stop. "I'm so sorry."

He let go with one hand to wipe a blob off his nose, and while I tried to stem the funny that just kept bubbling up in me, he smeared it along my cheek.

"Oh!" I said, laughing. "Not cool!"

I looked down at my clothes as he set me back on my feet, but he didn't back up for more space. Instead he picked a dripping clump of paint from my hair and smiled slowly, while we were still so close I could feel him breathe. His expression was playful and achingly reminiscent of the old days.

"*Now* you look really good," he said, slowly backing up and not breaking eye contact with me until he bent to pick up my broken heel.

"Ha-ha," I said, still chuckling. "Sorry about that."

He shook his head. "No big deal. Hand me your shoe, I'll fix it while you're here."

I handed it to him and walked lopsided out of the garage as he laughed and did damage repair on himself. The farther away I got, the more my heart constricted and I could feel the chemistry pulling me back. That had been a moment. Like the ones we used to have when we were best friends and thought the same and talked the same and were falling in love and didn't know it. For that dumb little second in time, there was no tension or secrets or resentment.

But as I tugged the sweatpants out of my backseat, I felt the familiar heaviness seep back in. The oppressing weight that reminded me that it was only me that fell in love back then. It was me that fell for the line and some tears and ended up hurt like I'd never been or would ever be again. Not even when my marriage ended. That left me angry and humiliated, but nothing like the deep hole that Ben left me with.

It was when I was face-to-face with him that it got all blurry. Like no time had passed and we were supposed to be friends. Except that he'd walked away from that.

I headed back through the garage holding my pants and wearing a pair of flip-flops I'd found on the floorboard. He handed me my shoe and set down a bottle of some really strong-smelling glue.

"Let it set good for twenty-four hours, and it should be okay."

I sniffed it and wrinkled my nose. "Thanks."

He pushed a piece of hair from my face, the unexpected brush of his fingers against my temple causing me to catch my breath. His eyes met mine as I did that and showed a flicker of something old.

"You were about to get paint in your eyes," he said softly.

I laughed nervously as his fingers came back goopy, trying to disguise and shut down my reaction to his touch, but he'd already seen it. And to be honest, I was having trouble fighting the pull.

The sound of the back door shutting made me jump, and I turned to see Kevin standing there with another old expression I recognized.

"Jesus, get a room."

CHAPTER

7

I glared at him. "Grow up, Kevin. My God, we had a little paint dilemma here, if you couldn't tell."

I held my arms wide to demonstrate the Jackson Pollock masterpiece I'd become. Kevin ignored me, narrowing his eyes at Ben, who'd gone back to cleaning himself up.

"If you're gonna hit on my ex-wife, Landry," he began, and my stomach dropped. "Have the decency to not do it in her mother's garage, with me here."

"Kevin!" I said, fighting the overwhelming urge to stab him in the eye with the heel of my shoe.

But Ben just laughed. His face was relaxed when I looked, but there was the old game. That thing behind the smile when all would go dark and unreadable in his eyes.

"Lockwood, I've never thought about throwing paint around as foreplay, but maybe you're on to something." He winked at me and one side of his mouth curved up in his playful way.

I looked at him and just shook my head. "Really?"

"And by the way, when I decide to hit on *your ex-wife*," he continued in a low voice as Kevin passed us. "You can get a front-row seat for all I care."

"Okay," I said, clapping my hands together as I slung my sweatpants over one shoulder. The dick swinging was getting a little over the top, and yet my girly mind honed in on the *when* in Ben's sentence like it was crack. "We need to go in and clean up. Kevin, please go home."

I looked at him in all his blue-eyed blondness and back at Ben and was reminded of fifty-five million similar altercations at every locker area we'd ever had. Landry, Lattimer, and Lockwood sealed the deal that we would always be together. And it usually looked just like what I was standing in the middle of.

"Kevin," I repeated, getting his gaze back to me. "Please."

When he finally got in his glares and left, I turned to Ben.

"Just can't help yourself?"

He looked my way for just long enough. Enough to see the darkness still there. "Guess not."

"Why?"

It fell out of my mouth before I could think out whether it should. He was on his way to the back door and turned around, a look of disbelief on his face.

"You're seriously asking me that question?"

Suddenly I was seriously confused, for the second go-around. Every time we circled that cage, it felt like we were on different playing fields. He didn't understand what I meant. I didn't understand what he meant. Whatever it was, I couldn't pull anything out of my head to justify the long look he was giving me.

"Let's just go clean up, Em, okay?" he said quietly, reaching for the doorknob.

I followed him in, met by Tandy, who finally crawled out of bed and growled at us.

"Little late, there," I said to her. "Why didn't you chew on his ankles?"

Holly gasped. "Oh my lord, what did Kevin do to y'all?"

I looked up and laughed, wishing we still had that moment where Ben would be laughing with me, but he had moved back behind the walls. He did smile on the way to the bathroom and splayed his hands.

"I was a bit of a klutz," I said, holding up my shoe.

"You've got my den in your hair," my mother said, holding out a piece. "And it's about the same color."

I huffed at that. "My hair is not taupe."

"Kind of is," she replied, nodding.

"It is not!"

"You need highlights," Holly said quietly, and I felt my mouth fall open.

Ben came back out a few minutes later, most of the paint scrubbed from his face but still some streaks in his hair.

"Ben, don't you think Emily's hair is the same color as the paint?" my mother said, laughing.

I closed my eyes. "Mom, are there any boundaries with you?" I had to laugh anyway. It was too sad if I didn't. When I opened them, he was closer than I thought and looking at me with awe as I laughed. A smile crept upon his lips as if he didn't want it to, and then he gave a micro-shake of his head. Suddenly there was warmth in his eyes again, as if he couldn't hold it back.

He touched the dried paint smear on my face, and I held my breath. "I think as long as she laughs, her hair could be green for all I care."

He let his finger trail down my cheek and then went back out the door, leaving me stuck in place under the light fixture and right on top of the spot where Holly was evidently conceived.

Holly's eyebrows shot up, Mom pulled out a stool and sat, and both of them stared at me.

"What in holy hell did I miss?" Mom said.

"So, what is with all the potatoes?" I asked Holly after I'd somehow extricated myself from that conversation—only because Mom realized she didn't have mustard and had to make a run for it. Holly and I hightailed it up to the attic before she decided we needed to run for it with her. "Why does she have five hundred potatoes down there?"

"Something about potato salad for some barbecue stand out on the interstate," Holly said, as we stood up there and just looked around, overwhelmed. This was after she got everything she wanted. Boxes were everywhere. Old furniture, toys, plastic tubs marked with pieces of masking tape advertising *Holly First Grade* or *Emily Girl Scout Stuff*.

"Of course," I said.

"I don't know," she said, "I was still in shock at the time so the words kind of bounced off me."

"So, are y'all okay now?" I asked, looking at her in the odd light from the tiny dirty window mixed with the two bare bulbs overhead. "I mean about selling the house and all that?"

She shrugged and halfheartedly peeked into a box. "Not much I can do about it. She's just—I don't know. It's like she's throwing everything away."

"Throwing what away?"

"Us, I guess. Dad." She looked up and gave a little smile like she knew that was crazy. "I know that sounds stupid, but it feels like that. Like she's stripping away all the things that made this home so she won't miss it."

I sat on a nearby wooden trunk. "Maybe you're right. Maybe that is what she's doing, but I think there are reasons."

She raised her eyebrows. "Like?"

"I don't know." Suddenly I was too worn out to try to analyze my mother's problems. "Maybe it's not all that complicated. Maybe she's just tired, and wants to play for a while."

Holly laughed at that. "Speaking of playing, what's with you and Ben painting each other?"

"Oh my God," I groaned, covering my face with my hands.

"And *her hair can be green as long as she laughs*?" Holly nearly squealed. "You can bluff Mom on that maybe, but not me."

"I don't know, Holly." I dropped my hands and shook my head. "That's the honest truth."

"Are you—?" she asked, looking at me with raised eyebrows instead of finishing the sentence.

"No!" I said, giving her a look. "Are you crazy?" I got up from my stool and went to find something to dig into, as just the thought of getting physical with Ben made me sweat. "I'm avoiding him at every turn. Problem is, he's *at* every freaking turn."

Holly tilted her head. "Looks to me like he still has a thing for you."

I shook my head. "He's—confusing. I don't know that he ever *did* have a thing for me. That could have all been a lie."

She made a sarcastic noise. "Actions don't lie, Em. Anyone could see the chemistry y'all had." She widened her eyes. "Still do."

I thought of his expression in the garage, his touch on my cheek, and felt goose bumps trickle down my spine. "Half the time he's trying to get me to be like old times, and then the other half it's like he's pissed off at me. At me! I mean, really?"

"Have you talked about it?" she asked, closing a box back up. "About why he left."

"No. It's the giant walrus we dance around."

"Why?"

"I don't know." I saw a bicycle tire poking out around the back of a box, and I started pulling some boxes out of the way. "Probably because I don't want it to lead to Cassidy?"

"That would be the first thing I would've asked," she said. "Where the hell did your sorry ass go, and why?"

"Well, I'm chickenshit like that," I muttered as I put my back into a particularly heavy box.

"You avoid confrontation."

I cut my eyes her direction.

"Okay, Greg."

She held up her palms. "Whatever, just saying."

"Look over here," I said, pulling the bike out.

It was a blue and purple English Racer with white stripes, and a glittery purple seat.

"Oh, my—I can't believe it," she said, her face breaking into a huge grin. "My bike! Wow, I can't believe it's still up here." She looked around. "Is yours here, too?"

I sighed. "No, I sold mine to Tina Blake, remember? For money to go to the festival."

Holly laughed. "Oh, yeah. And then she moved or something? God, they were so pissed off at you."

I shrugged. "Oh, well, I was an entrepreneur."

"You came by it honestly," she said, a strong hint of sarcasm lacing her voice. "Oh, look." She pointed at three hand-painted stars along the main bar, with the words *Love, Daddy*, and smiled in memory. "Daddy painted these on here just for me. Our three favorite stars from Orion's Belt."

"I remember that," I said.

She looked back up at me, her eyes a little misty. "Daddy may have not taken Mom on the trips they wanted, but he was there for us. He was there for what mattered. Making the memories in this house."

I nodded, but not so much to agree with Holly, but for something to do to disguise whatever I looked like when the past decided to suck me backward. Because the ringing, the sound of air rushing by, the tightening of my chest as the blackness closed in—all that was happening. Again.

I TRIED TO FOCUS ON HOLLY, ON FINDING A PLACE TO SIT SO I didn't fall over—although I never had before. I tried not to flail around as everything went dark, thinking I probably *had* done that before.

"Emily?" I could hear Holly saying. "You okay? You look—" I never got to hear how I looked because I blinked my vision free to see a much emptier attic.

I stood next to a support beam, wondering why I was there. I'd come to realize that each of my traipses backward had some sort of purpose, even if I didn't understand it yet. And each time, I stayed in the room—even the very spot I stood in. I couldn't imagine what could have happened in the attic that I needed to see.

Oddly enough, I was calm. I didn't know why. It still wasn't normal, but maybe since I'd been there and done that a few times, I had a fairly good feeling that I wasn't going to die.

There was no one there. Just me and the dust and much fewer boxes than what would be there decades later. As I turned in my customary circle of allowed movement, I saw Holly's bike. I chuckled as I looked upon the shiny bright and perfect purple-and-blue spectacle, and realized Holly's fourteenth birthday must have been close.

The familiar sound of clomping footsteps reached my ears, and I sat down cross-legged to await whomever was coming up the creaky pull-down stairway.

My mom's head poked up first, her blonde curls tied up in a silver scarf that glittered in the light when she pulled the chain at the top of the stairs. Behind her was my Uncle Tommy.

"What on earth could this be?" I whispered, and then shook my head at myself. Just once, I wanted to yell at the top of my lungs at someone to see if they would hear me. I didn't know what I'd do if they did, but it would be cool to try.

Tommy looked so young, I noticed. Younger and healthier than I'd ever remembered. He didn't have the sweaty, creepy look with the dark circles under his eyes that I always associated with him.

He lugged a large box in front of him. "I appreciate this, Frannie," he said with some effort. "I promise it's just till I get my feet under me again and get a new place. I'll come get all this stuff." He set down the box with a thud as my mom watched with her hands on her hips.

"I know," she said, her voice quiet, like it wasn't the first rodeo. Knowing how many times Uncle Tommy was evicted or kicked out of wherever he was lucky enough to land for a while, it probably wasn't. "How many more boxes do you have in your truck?"

"Five or six."

My mom just nodded. "Okay, let's go." She glanced around the dark walls. "We can slide them up against the sides here so they'll be easy for you to find."

"Thank you," he said again, putting a hand on her arm. "You know how he gets about stuff like this, I just didn't want to sit through another lecture—"

"Another lecture?" Mom said. "Tommy, he has the right to get pissed."

Uncle Tommy sighed and visibly deflated. "I know."

"Do you?" Mom asked. "You say that, but you keep doing this anyway. Throwing money at blinking lights like it'll reproduce, and expecting everyone to float you when it doesn't."

"Frannie, the economy is bad right now, I'm just trying to get us some more capital for inventory."

My mom's face screwed up. "Capital for inventory? Tommy, the capital comes from sales, not a roulette wheel. When there are no sales, you don't buy more."

"Okay, okay," he said, looking away.

"No, it's not okay," she said. "Not anymore." She leaned over so he had to look at her. "This isn't a game. It's your dream, yours and

Charles's. It's our livelihood, or it was supposed to be. It was supposed to feed our family, but lately it's only been feeding your bookies."

"Fran—"

"Don't Frannie me," she said, cutting him off. "I'm tired. I've resorted to cleaning houses four days a week while the girls are in school."

He blinked. "I didn't know that."

Wow, neither did I. That was one side business I never knew about.

"Charles doesn't, either," she said, shocking me even further. "He thinks it's magic, I guess, that the lights stay on. I suppose he thinks my trinkets and candles pay that well, I don't know. He'd be mortified if he knew I was scrubbing people's toilets, but how the hell else am I supposed to pay the bills with the pennies left after he pays yours?"

For once, Uncle Tommy didn't have anything to say. He just rubbed at his face and looked around like the dusty room would give him the answer.

"Stop gambling, Uncle Tommy," I called out, my voice sounding brash in the small area.

Neither of them blinked, or twitched, or even looked around curiously. No one heard me. Tommy shuffled back down the stairs to get more boxes, and Mom made her way over to Holly's new bike as she waited on him.

"Damn it," she said, picking up a tiny box I hadn't seen next to the bike and running two fingers over the bar. A bar still empty of painted words. "Charles, you said you'd do this," she said under her breath.

She opened the box and pulled out a tube of white paint, a napkin, and a tiny pointed brush and walked back to the door to grab *the flashlight that hung on a hook just inside. Propping it underneath her arm, she came back and aimed it at the bar in front of her. She squeezed a little blob of white paint onto the napkin, dipped the tip of the brush in it, and made three carefully shaped dots. Dad and Holly's favorite three stars. I watched in horrified awe as she then precisely painted the words* Love, Daddy.

My eyes filled with tears as I witnessed it, feeling as if so many things were not as I thought they'd been. Not that that one act meant everything else was different, but it opened up the possibility.

As she finished up the last touches, I heard the heavy steps again, but more than that, I heard the ringing again. Knowing what was coming, and wanting very much to leave that scene, I closed my eyes and waited for the pressure and the noise and the blackness.

❧

It came, hurling me back, pushing on my chest, shoving the air back through my lungs with a vengeance. I sucked in a gasp, staring straight into Holly's face.

"What the hell?" she said.

I took a few seconds. Probably more than a few—but I needed to get my wits back about me. Get my breath back in me.

"Um—sorry, I just spaced out for a minute," I said, hoping it was just a minute.

"You think?"

"Why?" I said, leery of her answer.

"Because it was like someone unplugged you and plugged you back in," she said, giving me another once-over. "Weirdest thing I ever saw you do."

There was a second or two there where I debated maybe telling her. Sharing it with someone would be so liberating. Being able to talk about it—especially with her—tell her some of the family scenes I'd witnessed. That would be awesome. But equally as awesome would be having that person believe me, and Holly wouldn't be that person. That would be too outside the box for her, and I'd lose whatever small bit of credibility I had. And Greg would be humping my leg.

"Hmm, sorry," I said instead.

She looked me in the eye, still unsure, but her thoughts were interrupted by Tandy raising hell downstairs like a parade of cats had invaded her doggie door.

"Helloooo?" came a voice from below.

Holly and I both head-jerked to the attic opening, momentarily thrown by what sounded like—

"Hello?" the voice repeated, abrasive and loud, like a parrot that's been smoking too long. "Anybody here?"

I looked at Holly, whose jaw dropped like mine. Tandy's rage was not to be calmed, and the combination of the dog's barking and an old woman griping was almost too much.

"Are you kidding me?" Holly said.

I closed my eyes and let out a breath. "Shit, shit, shit."

"Think we can stay up here and pretend we didn't hear her?" Holly said, snickering.

"England heard her," I said. "And the stairs are down."

"Y'all up there?" she yelled, and I winced.

"God, her voice hurts me," I whispered.

"We need to go down," Holly whispered back. "If she comes up here, it'll be memory lane for days. We'll have to come back and get this stuff later."

I got up, realizing I was still sitting cross-legged like in my vision. We headed to the opening, pulled the chain to blanket the attic in darkness, plodded down those stairs, and made it to the top of the regular stairway. All so we could gaze down at the crazy scene of Aunt Bernie holding Tandy at bay with an umbrella.

"Why is she here already?" Holly said through her teeth like a ventriloquist.

I thought of what I'd heard my mother say in the vision, about having to scrounge and scrimp to pay bills because of hard times or having to bail out Uncle Tommy. Of having to clean other people's houses in addition to her other side jobs, just to pay the bills and keep the roof over our heads when the hardware store wasn't doing it anymore.

"I guess Mom's ready to go," I said.

CHAPTER

8

"Well, get down here!" Aunt Bernie called out from below, looking up at us in all her green glory. She'd always been a firm believer in matching accessories, and it was clear that nothing had changed on that front. She wore green pants with a matching vest over a cream-colored blouse. Green flats on her feet. Green purse, earrings, bracelets, eye shadow, fingernails. Not joking. "I'm not climbing up there till I have to. Come down here and give me a hug."

We obeyed, like we were six, coming down and hugging her neck.

"Where's your mother?" she asked.

"She had to go run an errand," I said. "Was she expecting you today?" Because we sure the hell weren't.

Aunt Bernie flopped a color-coordinated hand my way. "Oh, I told her it'd be sometime this month, but I never really know where I'm gonna be when." She laughed, a sound that felt like it could peel the paint off the wall. "That's the beauty of life with Big Blue."

Holly nodded and clamped her mouth shut.

The front door opened and I turned to see Ben struggling to haul two big suitcases in. With a scowl on his face that the next city could have felt.

"Um—why are you bringing stuff in?" I asked, as Aunt Bernie turned in a whirl of green to intercept them.

"I'm gonna land in one of the rooms like usual," she said, which was precisely what I hoped she wouldn't say. "Gives me a chance to stretch a little. You can bring them upstairs, hon," she said to Ben, apparently oblivious to the glower. "I don't care which room."

"Holly's," I said quickly, ignoring her stare into the side of my head. "Here, I'll help—" I began, reaching for one of them.

"I've got it," he said through his teeth. "Just which way?"

"To the right, across from the bathroom," I said, scooting out of his way. I imagined being a bellhop wasn't part of what he signed up for.

Holly elbowed me hard. "Really?" she hissed, as Aunt Bernie peeked out the front door.

"I have a bunch of things still to do in my room," I whispered. Actually I was thinking about the flashbacks, and what might still come to pass in that room, and I didn't want an audience.

"So do I," she said.

"Sorry."

"So what the holy hell happened to you, Emily Ann?" Aunt Bernie asked, shutting the door with a force that brought the knocker in twice.

"What?"

She pointed at my head. "You and that worker guy both look like you've been shooting those paintball guns my nephews like to mess around with." She lifted what was now a dried hunk of hair and paint. "You've got dreadlocks, honey girl."

Great. "Oh, there was a little incident in the garage," I said and looked up as Ben made his way slowly back down the stairs. "And he's not a worker here, he's—" Ben stopped walking and locked eyes with me, amusement playing across his face. "An old friend of mine," I said, letting a smile creep up where it wanted to.

"Oh, sorry," she said, guffawing. "Didn't mean to put you to work, honey."

Ben waited a couple of beats before pulling his eyes away from me. Enough to send my stomach on a crazy ride that I wanted to kick myself for.

"It's all right," he said, pulling the smile that melted the pants off many a girl once upon a time.

Disturbingly, even Aunt Bernie reacted to it. "Well, aren't you sweet?" She leaned on one hip. "So, how do you and Emily know each other?"

I saw the thoughts whiz through his eyes. *We did the wild thing on her roof once.* "We went to school together."

"Really? I wouldn't have thought you were that old."

Holly snickered and headed off to the kitchen, as I fixed my aunt with the best kiss-my-ass look I could muster.

"So, you're going to have a travel buddy, huh?" I said. "Are you excited?"

"I'm tickled shitless," she said, making me laugh. "I get so tired of doing everything by myself."

She walked to the kitchen, so we followed her, and by *we* I mean me, because Ben quickly passed us up to jump back into his painting regimen and avoid the family reunion. I so didn't blame him. I so wished I could avoid it, too.

"I mean, I have my friends all over the place that I stop and see," she continued. "But it always seems like when I run across the most interesting things, I'm alone." She slapped a hand on the bar, making Holly jump and turn around. "Nobody to share the fun with."

"Well, I guess you and Mom will be—sharing all the time, now," Holly said with a smile that didn't go anywhere past her lips. "How long before y'all take off?"

Aunt Bernie shrugged. "That's up to her. To whenever she's comfortable leaving all this with you."

"Oh, well, it's only been a week since she told us," I said. "There's still so much to do, so that may be—" Tandy took up a rant again, after coming in her doggie door from the backyard and finding the intruder still there. "You realize she's coming with you, right?"

Aunt Bernie did a flippity thing with her eyes. "That's the rumor," she said thickly. "I keep hoping one of you will miss this thing and insist on keeping her."

"Oh, dear lord, no," I said. "We have a mutual love/hate relationship, leaning more on the dark side."

"Don't even think about me," Holly pitched in, standing in front of the fridge and eyeing the food like she would actually take something. I knew better. "I have two cats and a betta, and that's all we need."

I heard voices in the garage right then, and the back door opened for Mom, followed by Cassidy. My heart thunked, as it always did when Cass and Ben shared oxygen.

"Bernie!" Mom exclaimed, setting down a surprising load of

bags, considering she'd gone to the store for mustard. "I didn't know you'd be here today. I would have planned dinner or something."

Aunt Bernie nodded toward the sink and its potato-ness. "What are you doing?"

Mom glanced behind her and waved a hand at it. "Oh, that's for an order I'm making. Four pans of potato salad."

Aunt Bernie put her hands on her hips. "Of course you are. Well, why don't I make us up some soup or gumbo or something?"

My mouth instantly watered, knowing that in spite of Bernie's irritating ways, she could make any food into something orgasmic.

"You still work, right?" I asked Cass as she made the round for hugs. I was so thankful that Ben was on the other side of the living room and out of her reach because if she would have hugged him I think I'd have had a coronary.

She made a snarky face. "Nice to see you, too, Mom. And what the heck happened to you?" She backed up and glanced down at her clothes in worry.

"Oh, it's dry, goofy," I said, pulling her back to squeeze her tight. "Just had a little run-in with some paint, no big deal," I said, darting a look toward where Ben was painting. "It all comes out. And I love you, baby girl, I just worry when you seem to be here all the time." With Ben. Who was also there every flipping day. I wanted to schedule the work so that they'd be on opposite ends of the house, maybe make a spreadsheet? But then they'd probably spend the day laughing together over it.

Cassidy jutted her head toward Aunt Bernie. "I'm trying to spend as much time as I can with Nana before she hits the road, which evidently may be soon? I had her come pick me up." She shoved at my shoulder. "You can bring me home."

"Aw, I feel special."

"This is little Cassidy?" Bernie said, filling the room with her voice as usual.

Cass turned and gave her a mock glare. "You just saw me last year."

"Nah, it was the year before that," Aunt Bernie said, her mouth stretched wide in a grin. "You were definitely less grown-up." She patted Cass's cheek. "But you've always been a stunner. Even as a baby—you know, I think even your hospital picture was cute?"

Cassidy laughed. "Nobody's hospital picture is good; every one I've ever seen looks like an alien."

"Not yours," Aunt Bernie said, shaking her head. "I remember seeing those eyes and thinking where on earth did she get those?"

Holly grabbed a lighter like it was the most fascinating thing she'd ever seen. "Let's light some candles," she said, her smile brilliant. I glanced at Ben rolling paint and grabbed a nearby jar of cinnamon vanilla and shoved it at her. "We need something to mask the paint smell."

"Here you go."

Cassidy laughed, looking at each of us like we'd gone off the grid a little. "All better now?"

"Much," I said, pinching her cheek so she could flutter her eyelashes and think me crazy. Whatever. Anything to change that subject.

"So where are some of the places you've been, Aunt Bernie?" Cassidy asked.

"Oh, goodness, girl, everywhere," she responded. "Big Blue has brought me to every mainland state and a few places in Canada. Other than that, I've visited Honduras, Cancun, and Fiji."

"London," Mom said, stirring her giant bowl.

Aunt Bernie pointed. "There, too. Went there with your Uncle Frank."

Cassidy's eyes took on that wanderlust look of hers. "Do you have pictures?"

"Hmph," my mom said, a smile on her lips.

Aunt Bernie did her slap-down move again, making Holly jump for a second time, even though she was watching. "Do I have pictures?" Aunt Bernie laughed so loud, my ears rang with it. "Little girl, I've got albums upon albums."

Cass's eyes lit up, and I knew she'd found her mother lode. "Oh my God, I have to see." She bit at her lower lip. "Can I bring Josh over tomorrow and sit and look at them?"

Aunt Bernie tilted her head. "And who is Josh?"

"He's my boyfriend," Cass said with a smile that brought a glow from her ankles on up, and made me want to dig my eyeballs out. "And he feels the same way I do about travel. We both want to see everything." She said this while bouncing on her toes like a kid waiting for a carnival ride.

Aunt Bernie chuckled, and I marveled how even that was loud. "Well, you bring him on over; they are all tucked away in Big Blue and we can sit in there and travel by photo."

"Cool," she said, a huge grin on her face. "Ben, you never told me where all you went," she then called out to him, bringing him into the conversation. His back was to us, but I could tell by the slight drop in his shoulders that he would have rather painted himself into that wall.

"Nowhere exciting, really," he said, continuing to cut in the paint around the window, slow and perfectly steady. I could never be that steady. My lines always looked like I was drunk.

"Oh, come on," Cassidy said, relentless. "You had to go somewhere marginally cool."

"Cass, let him be," I said, trying to be light but feeling anything but. Holly caught my eye over the bar, where she sat tensely, watching Aunt Bernie put different things in an iron skillet that had rarely seen use. Probably nothing healthy.

"What?" Cassidy said, her easygoing mannerisms making me think of flower children in the seventies sometimes. "He said he traveled." She focused on his back. "So did you end up staying anywhere? Did you just keep moving all the time like Aunt Bernie? Were you looking for the deep meaning in life?" she added, deepening her voice with a laugh to follow.

Ben turned around, a small smile on his face that I knew was just for show. The rest of his body language was tight and closed. "Well, that would be somewhat, not really, and I stopped looking for meaning a long time ago."

I felt the goose bumps do a slow burn down my back, spreading around to my arms.

She laughed, a deep husky laugh I was always envious of. "So you just don't want to say."

He widened his eyes in mock play. "So, why haven't you gone to school? Is it fear of failure? Disinterest? What are your long-term goals?"

The room was quiet as she stared at him for a long moment and then let a slow smile tug at her lips. "Touché," she said softly.

He winked at her and turned back around, leaving the rest

of us to chuckle silently. Outwardly anyway. For me, I just saw two peas of the same pod face off on a subject they didn't even know they had in common.

"So," Aunt Bernie said, making us all turn around with a start. "What's up with your dad, little missy?" She said this with her head half in my mom's condiment cabinet.

Cassidy's eyebrows lifted and she looked my way as if I could decipher the question. "Um?"

"Kevin's fine," I said, my mouth feeling dusty. I went to the fridge and stole a Coke. "He was just here, actually. A little bit ago."

"Really? I'm so sorry I missed him," Aunt Bernie said, dumping more into the skillet. "Always thought that boy was so cute."

I could feel Ben's thoughts zooming through the room and I refused to turn around.

Cassidy's eyes got wide with sarcasm. "Ah, that's the perfection I smelled when I came in."

"That's not nice," I said.

"I know," she said, popping a cracker in her mouth from a platter that had morphed from nowhere. "Sue me. Oh my God, these are to die for."

I frowned, peering at them. "What are they?"

"Just crackers," Mom said, turning back to her potato salad. It dawned on me then how quiet she'd been through the whole traveling conversation. She had nothing to contribute. Neither did I, and neither did Holly, but I guess she felt like she should, next to her sister. I could understand that.

"These are not just crackers," Cass said.

"You mix ranch dressing seasoning with olive oil and toss them in it and sprinkle some red pepper. Better if they dry."

"Oh, no," Cass mumbled around a mouthful. "No way these are drying. They'll never make it that long." She swallowed and grabbed three more. "Nana, did I tell you about the sopapilla cobbler I learned to make?"

"No, you didn't."

"No, you didn't," I echoed, smiling at her.

"Well, surprise, surprise, *Nana*," she said, with exaggerated eyes at me.

"Huh, that sounds good," Aunt Bernie said, turning around. "What's that about?"

"That's about a zillion calories in sugar and butter," Cass said, bringing a chuckle from the other three women as she described the process.

It struck me as I watched her there, how grown-up she'd become while I talked to her about growing up. I was always being a mom. There she was amongst older women, talking about cooking and holding her own.

I snatched one of the to-die-for crackers and took a bite. "Oh, man," I mumbled, not really thinking it was out loud.

"I'm telling you," Cass said, reaching for two more. "I'm going to buy four boxes of crackers and do this to every one of them. I'm gonna gain fifty pounds."

"Cass, you're a stick," Holly said. "I think you're okay eating a few crackers. Just balance it with a piece of fruit."

Coming from another stick, I thought. Holly cut up an apple she'd managed to snag after two more forays through the fridge.

"I don't want fruit," Cassidy said, holding her crackers to her like someone was going to take them away. The sight made me laugh.

"Well, if you eat that much starch, you're going to—"

Holly's health rant was cut short by Mom cramming a cracker

into her mouth. "For once," Mom said. "Don't pick it apart. Just enjoy it."

Holly chewed in silence, giving her a defiant look.

"So how'd you hook up this gig with the barbecue place?" I asked my mom.

She shrugged. "I was there, noticed they didn't have it on the menu, and told them that no self-respecting Texas barbecue place leaves off potato salad."

"So you volunteered," Holly said, discreetly reaching for another cracker.

"Why not?" she said. "I enjoy it."

"Since when?" I asked.

Mom shook her head as she checked the potatoes for softness. "There you go again, the poor little children that lived on gruel."

"I heard there was occasionally water, too," Cassidy said with a chuckle.

"Not free-flowing," I said. "We were just allowed to lick the ice cubes sometimes."

Holly snickered and Mom poked her in the ribs. I laughed, too, but looked at Mom a little differently after what I'd seen. She'd devised all these side jobs over her lifetime to bring money into the house, and somewhere along the way it had defined her.

Ben gathered up some of his paintbrushes and held them in one hand as he headed toward the back door, stopping to nod at us. "I'm gonna head home for a little bit, go grab some lunch."

"You live here in town?" Aunt Bernie asked, starting what looked like a roux in my mom's skillet.

"Yes, ma'am, just down the road," he said.

"Then you need to eat gumbo with us tonight," she said.

Shit. I swear Ben was eating there more than I did.

"No, ma'am, I have to decline, but thank you," he said, making me give him a double take. *I have to decline*? Such properness.

"Doing something fun?" Cassidy said, looking antsy on her stool. She never was one for staying in one place for long. "Maybe I'll go hang with you."

I coughed up my Coke and it headed straight up my nose, making my eyes water. I reached for a paper towel, thinking of all the glamorous ways Ben had seen me so far.

"My goodness, Emmie," Mom said.

"Sorry," I sputtered.

Ben laughed. "Afraid not, Cassidy. Just spending a little family time of my own."

"If you're seeing Bobby, can I bring you some paperwork by?" I asked, trying to talk through the burn in my throat. "Y'all need to sign the papers to negate the contract, and if you can take care of that tonight, I can get that processed."

Ben nodded. "No problem. When do you want to come?"

A knock on the front door led to its opening and a head poking around the corner. "Hello?" Dedra Powers. "Can I come in?"

I swiveled my head to my mother. "Really?"

"Oh, yeah. Forgot she was coming by," she said sheepishly.

I looked at Ben. "Right now would be perfect."

I STOPPED AT MY HOUSE TO PICK UP THE PAPERWORK AND change my clothes. And find a hat. My hair was going to need a sandblaster later, but for the moment hiding it under a cute little cap was better.

I'd been through the house with Bobby's wife when they listed it, and while that was a little surreal going through it with

126

her when I'd never even been there with Ben, it was just like hundreds of other vacant houses I'd walked through and noted and cataloged. With no furniture or anything to make a house personal, it's hard to visualize the people that did.

I never knew Ben's family. I knew Bobby about as well as anyone could, as he was even more private than Ben. He was two years older than me, so he barely registered my existence as Ben's friend in high school. Later, he kept to himself, and I hadn't even known he had a wife until after Kevin and I had been married for five or six years. We ran into them with their son at a Disney movie. Even then, he was polite but guarded, guiding them along as if lingering would warrant too much conversation. At the time, I had agreed since Cass was with us and I suddenly popped out of my denial bubble and remembered that he would be her uncle. It had been all I could do not to shove her under my coat.

His wife, Karen, had met me to do the walk-through of his mother's house, and I felt like she had become very like him. The way couples together over many years sometimes do, melding their characteristics. She was quiet and careful with her words, redirecting with a small smile when a question needed diversion. Then again, maybe she had always been that way, since I hadn't known her previously. Karen seemed very sincere, however; and when we all three met later to sign the contract, I could see the clear adoration for her husband in her equally dark eyes.

As I approached the house and parked in the driveway behind Ben's truck, I thought of how much better Ben had fared in the looks department. Where both of them sported the salt-and-pepper hair now, Bobby's had thinned considerably so it was see-through as well. But it wasn't just that. Ben's face still looked young, his body still taut. Bobby appeared soft, his skin lackluster. His two years on Ben could easily go for ten or more.

And then maybe also that was the softer life of marriage compared to a single man's need to keep fit.

I studied the front of the house as I approached, with its low-hanging trees and short-trimmed landscaping. The landscaping was new; the last time I'd been there it was overgrown and shaggy. What had been white siding with brown trim was now blue trimmed and power washed.

He opened the door before I reached the porch, stepping to the side for me to come in. I hesitated for a second, unsure if the action was welcoming and cute or just trying to hurry and be done with me.

"Was I stomping?" I said, covering the two steps to the small brick porch that was so common to the older houses of our neighborhood.

"Heard you drive up," he said, pointing behind me. "Gravel works like a one-minute warning."

I met his eyes and flashed on his meaning. Instead of saying anything, I just walked past him.

"Nice hat," he said.

I ignored him, letting my gaze travel the room. It was different, seeing life in there. It wasn't set up as a bachelor's house like one might think. Dark mocha furniture flocked the dark red living room in front of me, on top of a thick braided rug that covered most of the original wood floor. Black-and-white photographs of trees were framed in what I recognized as black walnut frames. A long panoramic charcoal print of the dock at our river—before the restaurants took over—sat on his mantel, leaning against the brick like it was relaxing. To the left, an old wooden dining table sat with a single teakwood bowl of fruit in the middle.

When I'd walked through with Karen, it had been white walls and stripped bare, the old furniture long since sold or dispensed of. Ben had made it a home.

I turned to him slowly in surprise. "Wow."

A smile tugged at a corner of his lips. "You expected futons and Walmart shelves?"

"You did all this?"

"I've had the furniture for several years," he said. "But yeah, I painted everything before I moved in."

"Oh my God, it's amazing," I said, turning in a circle again. "It's so different."

"It needed to be different," he said, closing the door and heading to the kitchen. He gestured with a lean of his head for me to follow him. "It was weird at first, just being in the same walls, but I've made it mine now."

I walked slowly, watching him. I glanced up the stairway as I passed it and noticed that nothing was white anymore. Not the walls, the steps, or the ceiling. Everything was some form of earth tone. A slow song from the eighties came on, and I chuckled to myself as I followed him.

"Wow, that's an old one," I said.

He turned and walked backward, holding out one hand. "Dance?" My face must have registered humor or shock because he laughed. "I won't bite."

I might. "I don't think so," I said, laughing, but his words about being tight and controlled niggled in the back of my mind.

His eyes went neutral again. "Of course not." He gestured around him. "What do you think of the new kitchen?"

I looked around at the gleaming granite and dark, rich wood cabinets, recalling the all-white and Formica nonevent it was before.

"It's gorgeous," I said. "Why didn't you ever let me come here?"

The words fell out of my mouth without thinking, and he turned around as I spoke, looking as surprised as I felt. I blinked, wishing I could take them back.

"Why didn't you ever let me in your house?" he countered.

I scoffed, ignoring the heat rising up my neck. "You were always at my house."

"Not inside," he said. "I never met your parents, you never met mine." He shrugged and pulled two waters from the fridge. "It's how our game worked."

The old anger flared. "Game?"

He handed me one of the bottles, stopping just a foot from me. "It kept the lines neat, Em," he said softly, fizzling my anger like a match in water. Something in his voice made me ache for him. For what we once were.

"Until we blurred them," I said, my voice sounding raspy and raw to my ears.

The smoldering look in his eyes was the old Ben. The one that once knew all my secrets and loved me anyway. He blinked the moment free and broke eye contact, looking back toward the kitchen as he raked fingers through his hair.

"No one ever came here," he said, walking behind the island bar. "We didn't want anybody here." He held out a hand for the file I'd forgotten I had. "So what was the deal with the Realtor lady at your mom's?"

I cleared my throat, the temperature and subject change

knocking me off balance. I laid the file on the smooth cream-and-brown granite and turned to the page in question.

"Old history," I said.

"So am I, but you don't run off when I arrive," he said, thereby yanking my gaze back to his.

I started to point out the difference, but then wondered if there really was one. "Good point," I said, sliding the paper to him. "One of you climbed off my husband and screwed me over. The other one climbed off my roof."

His eyes narrowed. "So he didn't change," Ben said, effectively ignoring the comment regarding him. "I wondered about that."

"No," I said. "He didn't." I pulled the pen off the folder and handed it to him. "Evidently, neither did you."

"Me?"

"You know what?" I said, laying the pen down. "You and Bobby deal with this and bring it back to me when you're done."

"Where are you going?" I heard him ask from behind me as I made a beeline for the door.

"Home," I said, remembering even as I said it that I had to go back for Cassidy. "Damn it," I muttered.

"What are you so angry about?" he asked, making me turn around.

He kept walking so I did, too, backward. "This push-pull thing you do," I said. "I don't understand it, and I'm tired of it. I'm sick and tired of avoiding the one thing I really want to know."

I felt the hardness of the door press against my back, and he kept moving forward. I sucked in a breath and lifted my chin to appear defiant as he put his hands against the door on either side of my head and looked down at me from so close I could feel his breath on my lips.

"Why you made the choice you did?"

He said each word slow and deliberate, matching a rawness I hadn't seen in his eyes since he'd been back. That, coupled with the sudden need to close that half inch between us, hit me in the gut with so much emotion that for a second I didn't make sense of the words themselves. When I did, I was confused. *Choice?*

"What about what *you* chose?" I whispered, forcing myself to focus on his eyes and not his mouth.

A shrill ring broke the quiet and he clenched his jaw and reached into his pocket. His eyes never left mine, but I used the moment to put my hands against his chest and gently push him back.

"Hello," he said, his voice cracked and rough.

I turned and let myself out, grateful for that phone call. Another thirty seconds at that proximity and I would have spilled my guts, forgiven him for everything, and tested out that rug.

CHAPTER

9

I HAD TO GET MY HEAD RIGHT. I REPEATED THAT MANY TIMES in the car and thought hard about making that a voice recording to play while I slept. I was slipping, I could feel it. The draw, the chemistry, the pull of history—all of it conspired to dull the edges that needed to remain sharp and painful.

A really good twitch would have had Ben and me lip wrestling earlier. And I would have been a willing participant. No tightness, no folded arms, no second thoughts, no anything holding me back. Being that close to him again made me temporarily forget all the reasons I shouldn't be that close to him.

Holly's car was gone when I made the curve to Mom's house, so I assumed she'd had enough or made her escape when I did. Dedra's was gone, too, and that's really the only one that mattered to me. I'd made peace with Kevin's ways years earlier, knowing fully well he'd never be faithful to any one woman. I didn't have to worry about it anymore, and we were able to have an easy kind of coexistence. But it was Dedra's face that never left me. Her lack of remorse or moral code. For some reason, every time I saw her, I still saw the expression on her face in the mirror behind the bed as I walked in. I still saw the catty twist of victory in her eyes and mouth as she unblinkingly met my stare and rode my husband in my bed.

There were other women. I even knew who some of them were, but I didn't witness their indiscretions personally; and they all had the good grace to either avoid me completely or apologize profusely. Dedra, on the other hand, was an arrogant bitch that insisted on staring me down and grinning like a Cheshire cat at every possible opportunity, and I never stopped wanting to pull out every one of her bleached teeth.

I walked in through the garage, an easier feat with sneakers on, and saw Mom and Aunt Bernie through the back door of the laundry room. They were walking around the perimeter of the backyard, pointing at this and that and discussing something with interest. It hit a soft spot in my heart to watch the two of them together, and I found myself feeling glad Aunt Bernie was there.

As sometimes annoying and abrasive as she could be with her take-charge ways, my mother always seemed to get a charge out of her being around. It was like a little hidden part of her personality came out every time Aunt Bernie came into town. Something that was just them. Kind of like me and Holly, I guessed. We didn't have much in common or always see eye to eye, but there was some kind of bond there. Sort of. I was pretty sure I'd miss her if she moved away. I know my yard would.

I walked in the back door, calling Cassidy's name, but no

husky little voice answered. Then my cell buzzed, and I clicked it to read a text from her.

Hey, I got called into work . . . they suck . . . Aunt Holly drove me home.

"Well, okay then," I said to myself. "Go home or go upstairs?"

My room was calling me, and to be honest, there was something I'd wanted to do ever since that flashback I'd had, watching mini-me go out on the roof.

I headed up there, looked around at the real work that needed doing, and then walked to the window and lifted it. I hesitated a second when I did, kind of waiting to see if weird whirling things were going to suck me back like the last time, but nothing happened. So I finished raising it the rest of the way, leaned out to look around and ensure I wouldn't fall to my death, and then stuck my leg through.

It wasn't as graceful as it once was. Instead of the one fluid movement out the window that I so vividly remembered, there were several stages of scoot-and-grunt that I was grateful no one was around to witness.

Once out there, I stretched and looked toward my tree. Or what I'd always called my tree. Not so much from the ground. From down there, it was just a tree like the others, but up there, it was a canopy that wrapped itself around my little world like my own private cave. Being fall, there weren't the leaves that made it really private, but I still felt the familiar tinges of warmth and belonging that I'd always felt there. After all the years that had passed since I'd been up there, it amazed me that it still touched me that way. Especially since the last time I'd been there was when I'd waited all day for a man that never came.

I went to my favorite spot. Where the flattened gambrel roof of the garage butted up to the house, and made a perfect seat with a place to lean up against. I sat with my knees drawn up and closed my eyes. I thought my life was so complicated back then, with my frequently errant boyfriend and my family's seemingly ever-present financial struggles. The only thing that had always felt normal and constant was my friendship with Ben. All that seemed so tame and inconsequential in the light of adulthood and divorce and a so-so career and a house with a personal agenda.

The roof was where I went to sort things out, and I think that's why it called to me. I looked up into the nearly bare branches of the tree, where only a few die-hard green leaves still clung for their lives. Many a problem had been solved there, staring up into that tree. I wanted it to work its magic, somehow fixing the mess that had rolled into town in the form of Ben Landry. If he'd never taken that job with my mother, he'd have no reason to happen upon a curly-haired blonde and wonder if she was his. He could have stood next to her in the grocery store and never given it a second thought. But day after day of looking at her, talking to her, getting to know her, I just knew that somehow the puzzle pieces were going to click one day.

And not just for him. Possibly for her, as well. And then what the hell would I do? I closed my eyes again and prayed for clarity. For a solid answer.

"What are you doing out here?"

I jumped at the break in the silence, and head-jerked to the left, where Ben leaned out the window I forgot to close.

I sighed and glanced upward. "Not what I was going for," I muttered.

. . .

On the lighter side, I got to watch Ben grunt his way through the window like I did, getting one leg stuck so that he nearly crawled out. I put a hand over my mouth so he wouldn't see my amusement.

"Okay, why the hell would you want to do this all the damn time?" he finally said through his teeth as he blew out a breath and climbed the short incline to where I sat. "You always made it look like nothing."

"It was nothing. You just must be out of shape."

He glared at me before landing next to me, and as he did I felt the shimmy of déjà vu bubble up through my body. We were in the same spots we'd always had, side by side.

"So—you didn't say why you were out here?" he said, staring forward.

"No, I didn't," I agreed, since I really had no concrete reason to give him and didn't want to just say *because it felt right*. "But why are you?"

He shook his head slowly, rolling it back and forth against the wood behind us. "No idea."

I chuckled, and for that moment, there was an easy silence. The tension of before was lifted, and I wished it could stay like that. Friends again. I watched his profile for as long as I dared, remembering the shape of his face against the sky, with the air-conditioning unit as a backdrop. I'd seen that view so many times by moonlight, it was kind of odd to see it in the light of day.

I was aware of his closeness as we sat side by side and as I closed my eyes and rested back against the house, I could feel the heat at my shoulder.

"Do you remember this?" he said softly after a minute.

By the direction of his voice, I knew he'd been watching me. I forced my eyes to stay closed, insistent on not being a giant reaction to everything he said or did. Still, my heart sped up and I felt the goose bumps trickle down my back.

"Of course," I whispered back, not intending it to really be a whisper but that's all that came out. "Spent more time out here than inside."

With my eyes shut, I focused on my other senses. The way he smelled of soap and paint and something vaguely woodsy, the steady rhythm of his breathing next to me, and the mental image of his right knee propped up next to both of mine.

"Things always made sense up here," he said.

"Yeah."

I heard the wistfulness in my own voice and it made us look at each other. His expression wasn't angry that time, just—searching.

"This is where the magic happened." He looked down, kind of sad, before looking forward again. "And I'm not just talking about *that*." He jutted his head toward the ground. "Down there wasn't always a good place for me. Up here, there were no rules, no boundaries, no school crap. No parents," he said, his voice thickening on the word. "We had no secrets up here. No lies."

"We were the best of friends," I said.

He turned to me. "We were the best of everything."

His expression was so open and unlike anything he'd shown on his face since he'd been back that I had trouble making my tongue work. "I miss that."

The look that passed between us was like a magnet, making

it impossible to blink or look away. A pain of longing started low in my chest, pulling at my ribs, making my eyes burn.

"Sorry about earlier," he said finally. "I didn't mean to get so intense. Guess you bring that out in me," he added, grinning a little as he faced forward again, breaking the moment and lightening the mood.

"You don't need to be sorry."

He tilted his head in a small shrug. "Well, but I don't need to be so demanding, either. The past is the past. We can't undo it."

My skin felt like it suddenly caught fire. "No, but we can explain it."

He met my eyes and lifted an eyebrow. "Okay."

But I knew in that moment that any explaining would have to sit for a second. The ringing had descended upon me, spinning around me like a moving wall of sound, the vacuum of air sucking in tight. I shut my eyes and inhaled the biggest breath I could, knowing it was about to get hard to do that.

"Shit." I gripped his arm involuntarily. "Hang on, Ben," I said, although my voice sounded like it was somewhere else. I dimly felt his hand over mine and heard the concern in his voice as he said my name. Asking what was wrong. I felt a touch on my face but that was for someone else. That was for the Emily that was still there.

"Just—give me a second," I said weakly, then it all went black and I heard the rushing of wind and felt the bands of hell around my chest as they squeezed.

❦

I lurched forward and popped my eyes open, gulping in the muggy air of another time on the roof, one by moonlight the way it was intended to be enjoyed. I looked around in a panic, reaching for the house by habit to make sure I didn't fall off. Not that I would likely be able to in my little—I tested it with my foot—yep, in my little bubble.

"The roof," I said to myself. "Well, this could be anything."

I wasn't alone for long. The noise to my left pulled my attention to the window as it opened and a bare leg came out. It wasn't mini-me that time, but a teenaged version of myself. I laughed out loud as I watched myself climb out in panties and a strapless corset bra, a small radio in my hand that was tethered to a cord I'd plugged in under the window.

"Oh my God," I said. "Prom night? Seriously?"

I couldn't imagine what I had to learn from that night. I still remembered it pretty clearly. Kevin's indiscretions ended the night early, and I came home and stripped before hitting the roof, where the night could absorb all the crap in my life.

I watched myself in wonder, as seventeen-year-old-me turned on the radio and anchored it next to the house and pulled out the small blanket I used to keep hidden in a zip-up comforter bag under an eave. It was right by where I sat, and I could see my younger face in the bright moonlight, all taut and smooth. I wanted to tell her to wash her face every night and use moisturizer. Not that I qualified for hag potential or anything, but looking at the beginner version definitely showed the difference.

She laid out the blanket just three or so feet from me, facing the backyard, and sat down. She looked forlorn, sitting there with her hair all done up so pretty, little blondish brown curls falling down, in her underwear. And showing way too much ass, I decided, feeling a little embarrassed that I'd gone out there like that.

Right on cue, Ben appeared, scaling the tree like a monkey. My stomach contracted as I laid eyes on the beautiful boy I used to know. His crooked smile was arrogant and fresh. His body language was cocky, graceful, and sure, even climbing the shallow incline of the roof. He stood over other-me with an amused expression as she lifted one hand dramatically.

He leaned over and kissed it. "What happened to your clothes, Rapunzel?"

"Ha-ha," she said, her hand going straight to her hair, where she started pulling out bobby pins one at a time. Tiny curls cascaded down as they were freed. She tossed all the pins and clips over the side and laid back, closing her eyes. I remembered that moment—being so pissed off and just wanting to strip away everything of the evening and throw it away.

Ben stood over other-me for a second, looking all sexy in his button-down Levi's and ever-present hoodie jacket with the sleeves pushed up, dark hair that any girl would kill for hanging to his shoulders. Then he sat down beside her and gave her body a long pan that I didn't remember because she never saw it.

"So, why are you out here in your underwear?"

"Because I couldn't stand to be in that thing anymore," other-me said. It was surreal, hearing her talk, her voice closer to being mine but not quite yet.

"I thought you liked your dress," Ben said, leaning sideways on an elbow.

"I did," other-me said. "Till Kevin blew this night all to hell, like usual." I saw Ben shake his head. "He spilled beer on me in the car, ditched me for most of the prom. I hung out with three other couples till they got tired of babysitting me and went to dance."

"Where did he go?" Ben asked. I could hear the familiar irritation in his voice that was still there today.

Other-me picked up her hands and flopped them down again. "I don't know. Smoke a joint, maybe? Make out with Kathy Carmichael?"

Her voice sounded miserable, and I wanted to shut this memory off. I couldn't stand to remember that I put up with Kevin's crap back that far.

"Kathy Carmichael?" Ben said. "She'll put out for anything." Then he glanced sideways. "Sorry."

Other-me shrugged. "She was hovering, so I'm just guessing."

"Why do you stay with him, Em?" Ben said, his voice soft. "He's a dick for not seeing—I mean, damn." He gestured at other-me's body. "I saw that dress, and you're looking like this? He's a fucking moron."

She laughed. "You're good for my ego."

"I'm serious, you've—" He pointed at her boobs, which were shoved nearly out of the top. I remembered thinking there was almost no point. "You've got like Viking titties going on here, Em. What's up with that?"

"It's the corset thing," other-me said, fidgeting with it. "Shoves everything up."

"No shit," he said, staring. "In fact, here." Ben unzipped the hoodie and pulled it off, showing hard muscles I remembered weren't from working out but from toting lumber at his job. "Put this on."

"Why?" other-me said, laughing as she threaded her arms through the too-big jacket. "You see more of me in a bikini."

"I don't know," Ben said, smoothing out his Van Halen T-shirt that clung to his body like a glove. "Something about knowing it's just underwear is too much."

She slapped a hand over her face. "*Oh my God. You're so full of it.*"

"*No, I'm not.*"

"*Whatever.*" Other-me lay back down with Ben's hoodie wrapped around her. "*So why didn't you go? You could've got someone half naked and gotten laid.*"

"*Did that earlier,*" he said with a grin.

She chuckled. "*Okay.*"

"*And evidently, I just had to come here to see the half-naked part. Is that gonna be a trend?*"

She swung a hand at his chest. "*Ha-ha, you're funny.*"

"*So Kevin doesn't even know you left?*" Ben asked. Other-me shrugged, and he smiled. "*Want to go egg his car? Stab a tire?*"

"*No,*" she said, laughing.

"*Maybe I'll rig up his locker,*" he said.

"*Let it go,*" she said.

I laughed because I knew he hadn't. He'd tortured Kevin behind the scenes for weeks, leaving dog poop in his car and putting red pepper powder in his gym shorts.

"*So, how's Bobby liking his new apartment?*" she asked.

It was Ben's turn to shrug, and he lay out flat next to her. "*He's away. What's not to like?*"

"*You staying there tonight or going home?*"

"*Nah, he's got a girl there tonight, so—*"

"*Then be careful,*" she said, looking at him and reaching out her hand.

He took it and laced his fingers with hers. "*I always am.*"

I felt hot tears burn my eyes as I watched the scene I thought I'd remembered. I knew we were close, but time had faded my memory of exactly how special our bond had been. How had I not seen it then? Not that it would have mattered. He would have just gotten what he wanted earlier and moved on.

That part I'd always understood. It was the leaving town that always befuddled me.

"So have you heard yet about going full time after graduation?" she asked.

He shook his head. "My boss has been gone a lot. I'll hit him up again next week. I'm pretty sure he likes me, so hopefully he'll give me the hours."

"I wish I could just go to Egypt or somewhere, intern with an archaeologist instead of all that school," she said.

"Yeah, but all that school is the partying time," he said with a smile.

She snickered. "Yeah, that's me. Party girl. And going to the college here is not party time. It's probably live-with-my-parents time."

"Nah, you can get a cheap place on the other side of town," he said, playing with her hand. "Hey, did you even get to dance?"

"Nope."

"What a dick."

"Walk away, Ben."

A slow song came over the radio. "I'll do better than that." He got to his feet and held out a hand, and I gasped as the memory hit me.

"What are you doing?" other-me asked, looking at him with a funny grin.

"Oh, shit," I whispered from my little bubble as my eyes filled with tears. "Damn it, Ben, I forgot about this."

"Dance with me," he said, pulling her up.

"Are you crazy?" she said. "We'll fall off."

"Nah, we've done worse. Come on." He pulled her into his arms

*as she fluffed her hair out. "You look too good to waste a good song,"
he said, grinning down at her.*

"Yeah, in a hoodie?" she said.

*"Exactly," Ben said. "What other guy can say they danced on a
roof with a hot girl wearing nothing but his jacket?"*

"I have on more than that."

He shrugged. "Not when I tell it," he said, grinning down at her.

*Other-me laughed, tossing her head back. The way they looked at
each other, if I hadn't lived it myself, I'd think they were lovers. But
they weren't. Not yet. They danced a little awkwardly, standing at
an angle, but he held her tight enough to leave no question. I remembered looking into his eyes as we laughed over our crooked dance and
thinking how easy everything was with him.*

*"I owe you another one of those one day," he said when the song
was over.*

*Other-me looked happy again. He had that effect. "Really? Why
is that?"*

*"A real dance, in a real place—to that song, even," he said, point-
ing at the radio.*

"So that wasn't real?" she said, laughing.

*"Nope, figment of your imagination. So you can never dance to
that song with anybody but me. What was the name of it?"*

*She raised eyebrows at him. "You don't even know what the song
was and you want me to pledge it to you forever?"*

"Yep."

*Other-me rolled her eyes and did a little Japanese bow. "Okay, I
promise. Goes for you, too."*

"Not a problem."

"Because you just go straight to the deed, right?"

"Pretty much," he said, giving the arrogant smile. "So what's the song?"

"'I Love You.'"

"I love you, too."

Other-me blew out a breath and even I could see the impatience on her face. "That's the name, goof, it's by Climax Blues Band."

"All right," he said, gesturing toward her with a nod. "I need to get going. Keep the jacket for now."

She stretched and bent to pick up the blanket. "Yeah, I'll probably go read or something. God, we've become old fogies."

"Why?"

"Two years ago, we'd have stayed out swimming all night, now look at us."

He grinned and looped an arm around her neck for a hug. "Yeah, we're old."

"Be careful tonight, Ben." Other-me pulled away to look up at him. "Seriously, don't provoke him."

"You worry too much," he said with a wink, backing up. "Go read. Put some clothes on," he said with a chuckle as he climbed onto the tree and disappeared from view. She folded the blanket, put it back in its place, and grabbed the little radio on her way back in.

I sat there, wondering why I was still there. The scene was clearly over, and it was by far the longest flashback I'd been sent to see. Everything was quiet for a second and then Ben's head appeared at the roofline again.

"What the heck?" I said.

He walked with careful steps over to the window, and peeked in for just a second. At first, I thought he was being a perv, but then he left the window, walked right past me with a troubled look on his face, and pulled the blanket back out.

146

He wrapped it around himself and sat down right next to me in his usual spot, not a foot away. I didn't dare breathe, although I knew he couldn't hear me. There I was, studying his profile again, wishing I could ask him the questions I couldn't ask his older self.

But more than that, I was floored to realize he stayed there, sleeping on our roof. And it made me wonder how many other nights he'd done that. Found the only safe place he could. He closed his eyes hard, as if he were forcing them, and my heart broke.

"Ben—"

It was all I had the chance to get out before the breath was knocked clean out of me. I was pulled back fast, blackness swirling around me, pushing on my chest, shoving me forward.

❧

"Emily!"

Ben's voice was loud in my ears as the air filled my lungs in a gulp. I coughed and felt my body tremble uncontrollably. And when I opened my eyes I was looking straight into Ben's. He was kneeling in front of me, my face in his hands, and when I saw the fear and worry in his eyes, my weakened defenses broke.

"Emily, talk to me."

"Ben," I said, with no actual sound.

He heard me though, and massive relief flooded his face. He closed his eyes and rested his forehead against mine, taking deep breaths.

"Holy shit, Em, you scared the life out of me."

"I'm sorry," I said, feeling tears run down my cheeks, hot as fire. I couldn't stop. Looking at him now, thinking of all the time that had passed, and yet there we were again. On the roof.

"What the hell is going on?" he said, his mouth so close to

147

mine I could feel the words. He pulled back a little then, study-ing me, wiping my tears away with his fingers. "Are you sick? Are you—are you having strokes or something?"

I shook my head. "No, I'm fine." But the flood wouldn't be stopped, and the physical closeness was like a drug I couldn't leave behind. As he put more space between us, I pulled him back, wrapping my arms around his neck and letting the sadness wash over me. Something in the furthermost recesses of my mind told me to shut it down, but I couldn't. I couldn't let go.

CHAPTER

10

Ben inhaled sharp and deep, and I prayed he didn't think I was mauling him, but then he wound his arms around me and pulled me in tight. It felt right, being wrapped up in him there. It felt like the old days, when I could sink into him and everything was okay. Until seeing that in action again, I'd forgotten just how incredible that was. And knowing there was no logical way to have that again just made my heart hurt more.

"Talk to me," he whispered after several moments.

"It's not that simple."

He pulled me back gently, and then caught my hands in his before I could get completely away. "Look around you," he said, nodding to either side. "Where we are. This is the one place it *is* simple."

I looked down at his hands holding mine, and thought back to when that was a normal occurrence, not something making my skin tingle. We'd once had no secrets, but I had a big one now. One I couldn't tell him, not even up in the place where the magic happened. My eyes filled again, and I blew out a breath, frustrated with the amount of water I could evidently spew forth.

Before I could say anything, he pulled me a little closer, and it was my turn to suck in a breath as I saw the dark intensity in his eyes.

"Emily, I just watched you stop breathing for a full minute, and I don't think I've ever been so fucking terrified in my life. Don't blow me off again." He shook his head slightly. "Not up here."

As I blinked the tears free, I tried to hold my head up to look confident and assured. I needed to let him in on at least what he'd witnessed. He was right—sort of. The roof was where everything was safe.

"Ben, you're not gonna believe me."

One side of his mouth curved upward, but it didn't reach his eyes. He was still worried. "Give it a shot."

I gave him a wary look, not sure if I could stand the rejection again if he thought I was nuts and left. I let go of his hands and wiped my face, swiping under my eyes and cursing the fact that I was not a pretty crier. He thought I was dying or having convulsions or something, though, so I guess he wasn't too uptight about swollen eyes.

"I keep getting sent back in time."

His eyebrows shot up. "Say what?"

I nodded and looked away. "Yeah. See? I told you it—"

"Emily," he said, stopping me. "Don't get defensive. Just talk to me."

I looked in his eyes and didn't see the urge to bail. Not yet.

So I licked my lips and took a deep breath. "Remember prom night?"

He blinked in surprise, and then got a faraway look as he dug up the memory. "Sort of."

"Up here." I pointed to where we were. "Right there, actually. In my underwear—"

"Gave you my jacket," he said, his expression looking a little foggy, but like things were beginning to dawn.

I nodded. "Yes, you did."

"What about it? What's that got to do with—"

"You pretended to leave, but came back after I went in, got the blanket out of the bag, and slept right here," I said, pointing down. "Wrapped up in the blanket."

Clarity and backpedaling borne of survival mode took over his features. "You—I didn't know you knew about that."

"I didn't," I said. "And there may have been other times you did that, but I just saw it. Just now. I just relived that night."

Confusion showed all over him. "What—how?"

I shook my head. "I don't know. Something to do with this house?"

"This house?"

I held up my hands. "It only happens here. And the things I go back to are only in whatever room I'm in."

Ben closed his eyes. "Hang on. Back up." When he opened them, there was no ridicule or sarcasm. "You're serious."

"I couldn't possibly make this up. I'm not that creative."

He looked at me for a long moment, and then sat back next to me, leaned up against the house.

"Okay. Start from scratch."

. . .

I told him all of it. About the first time when he'd arrived, seeing my parents buying the house, seeing Holly as a toddler and my dad just starting the hardware business. About seeing myself as a child and the first time he'd come over. About finding out my mother used to clean houses to help pay the bills, and how they kept bailing out my uncle. And about prom night.

"It's like it's going in order," he said. "Progressing through your life."

"Not just mine," I said. "My mom's, too."

"But you're not there—like interacting?"

"No, I'm watching," I said. "I can't move, and no one can hear me."

"And it's just for a minute?"

"I guess," I said. "You've told me before it was ten seconds, this time was like a minute. But for me, it's real time. This time had to be like thirty minutes. I mean, think about it. You were there. We talked, we danced—"

"We danced," he said. I looked at him, and he had an odd distant look on his face. Almost a smile. "I remember that."

"And you spent the night up here," I said softly. "How often did you do that?"

The almost-smile vanished. "More times than I care to count."

"Why didn't you tell me?"

"Because you knew enough already," he said. "I took care of myself. Found a place that he couldn't reach."

"But—"

"You would have brought me inside, Em," he said, meeting

my gaze with a hard edge. "Your parents would have eventually found out, they would have called mine, tried to be all helpful, and then my dad would know where to come looking. It wouldn't have been safe anymore."

I nodded. "Sorry you had to deal with all that."

"You don't need to be sorry," he said, a smile in his eyes as he echoed my words. "You were the good stuff back then."

A laugh escaped my throat. "Back then?"

"Yeah." He reached over and rested his hand on mine, giving it a little squeeze.

I tried not to focus on the warmth of his fingers or how I could feel his pulse beating against the back of my hand. I tried to push down the burn in my stomach and not give in to the thoughts of how much I'd missed him.

"So what am I now?" I dared to ask.

He blew out a breath. "Complicated."

I chuckled. "So you believe me?" I asked.

He shrugged. "Of course."

I looked at him warily. "That simple, huh?"

"Well, like you said, you aren't creative enough to make something like that up."

I elbowed him and he laughed.

"Something's trying to tell you a story. Or show you something, Em," he said. "All you can do is pay attention."

A couple of sparrows chased each other, landed in the tree, then onto the roof. They stopped, mid-chatter, to stare at us like we were aliens.

"Well, now you know I'm not stroking out," I said. I wanted to go with that flow. Keep it light. Enjoy feeling like friends again. But another part of me was telling me to ask the tough questions while we were "where the magic happened," even though I knew that probably meant the magic would be over.

"So—if I was the good stuff then, Ben, why did you leave me?"

The silence that followed was deep and thick, as I waited for an answer and then wished I'd never gone there. I stared at his hand on mine, and I swear I felt the temperature go frosty.

"Because you had other plans," he said finally, but his voice had changed.

I head-jerked toward him. "I had what?"

"You belonged with Kevin, not me. That was a pipe dream. Look at the house you live in. The daughter you have together."

My mouth worked, but words weren't lining up correctly. "A pipe—"

"I couldn't give you that," he said. "I wouldn't take the chance on turning out like my dad. I'd rather never have kids than be that kind of father, so I got fixed as soon as I could afford it."

I stared at him, the words about never having children burning my chest. But it wasn't the sweet, caring Ben of a few moments before. It was the angry version again. The one I had so much trouble understanding. He pushed to his feet, still holding my hand, and pulled me up.

"You're like Jekyll and Hyde, you know that?" I said.

"And you're hell-bent on fixing the past instead of just enjoying now." He gestured around us. "This was nice. We actually—connected again. But that's not good enough for you."

He headed to the window and I followed him reluctantly. He made it back through faster than he'd made it out, and he turned, holding out his hands to help me back through. My guess was that chivalry was the only thing pushing that action. He grabbed me around the waist to haul me down from the window seat, which put me square in his arms when my feet touched the floor. He didn't let go right away, just looked hard into my eyes.

"You're being called to visit old times. Okay. But there are certain times I don't want to revisit," he said, his voice quiet. "If you end up there, I don't want to know about it. I don't want to dig it up and talk about it."

"Why? Ben, you want to talk about *magic*—"

"Because it serves no purpose, Em." He let me go and held his hands out. "It just stirs up old shit. It's like talking about my dad. What's the point? It doesn't change anything. My mom? She was a victim, too, in a different way." Ben took a deep breath and rubbed his face and then his hair, making it stick up in little spikes. "Me and you? I have no desire to go backward and reopen old wounds. I'd rather focus on now."

I was about to ask what old wounds he had to draw on regarding me when he lifted my chin and kissed my lips. Even through my shock, I felt the energy ripple between us, and his breathing quicken.

"Starting with there."

He turned and walked out, leaving me to stand there like a goon, just as Bernie and my mother walked in. My mom turned to glance behind her after she looked at me—probably because I looked like I'd been shot and dragged through the mud with all my crying.

"You okay?" she asked.

"He really just did that," I mumbled.

"Just did what?" Aunt Bernie asked as she came in and looked around. "Girl, you still have a lot to do in here."

"Yeah," I said, annoyed that they had horned in on my moment. I shook my head free of the fog that accompanied Ben's lips, and then got annoyed again that there *was* even fog. Or a moment. "Um—yeah," I repeated, looking around. "Still a lot to do."

I grabbed a box from the closet and left the room, leaving them behind me. I'd just start loading up my car with crap and then I wouldn't have to come back every day. Although that was a joke since I knew I would.

I got increasingly irate at his audacity as I lugged an unfortunately heavy box down the stairs. I put it down to open the door, and then cursed my remote for not opening my trunk.

"Need some help?" Ben called from the garage.

I pinned the box against the car with my body and ignored him as I opened it with the key.

"Hey," he said, walking up, a folded sheet of plastic under his arm.

"I've got it," I said.

"Oh, I see that," he said, laughter in his voice.

I got the box in the trunk and whirled around. "Where do you get off just kissing me like that?"

His eyes widened in humorous surprise. "Was it hideous?"

He knew it wasn't. He knew it had curled my toes. "You don't want to face anything heavy, answer any tough questions, just skip off into the future—"

"I'm pretty sure I never mentioned skipping."

"Like I'm supposed to trust you now," I continued, ignoring him. "And then you lay that kiss on me."

He laughed, which just lit me up more. "I didn't tackle you, Em."

"How would you feel if I just walked up and—did this." Before I knew it, I had his face in my hands and my mouth was on his. What was intended to be aggressive immediately turned soft. Searching.

Shaking, I let go and stepped back, not knowing what the hell I was doing. His eyes were heavy and his breathing was fast.

"How would you—what would you do?" I asked weakly, though I managed to keep my head up as I turned to walk away.

I felt his hand on my arm as he spun me back around and backed me against the car. His hands came up to my face and his mouth and body landed against mine at the same time. All the air left me as I expected something fiery and got soft and deliciously slow instead. When he dove deeper, I defied all my own defenses and pulled him in, winding my arms around him. Just when I began to lose myself in his kiss, he stopped and backed away slowly.

His fingers trailed down my cheeks as he met my eyes with an expression so full of heat it could have self-ignited.

"Probably something like that," he breathed, sounding a little ragged.

"Okay then," I croaked. "Glad we're clear."

"Your move?"

I held up a finger, pretty impressed that I could. "I'm good," I said, sliding sideways around him.

I headed straight back into the house and up the stairs, not missing a beat. "Oh my God, oh my God, oh my God."

I was on fire. I went to the bathroom and splashed cold water on my face, then groaned at the sight of myself. I glowed, I was so red. And I still had paint globs sticking out of my hat and puffy eyes from crying.

"What the hell am I doing?" I said, running the icy water over my wrists to cool off. "This isn't a game. You aren't fifteen."

"Why are you talking to yourself?" my mother said from behind me, making me jump.

I blew out a breath and grabbed a nearby towel. I pressed my face into it and wished for that one second that I could stay in there.

"Because I'm losing my mind," I said into the towel.

"Well, that's unfortunate," she said.

"Isn't it?"

I put the towel back on the rack, since I wasn't at my house, where I'd throw it somewhere in the vicinity of the sink, and I gave her the best smile I could come up with.

"What's going on?" she asked, her wise eyes seeing more than I wanted her to.

I shook my head. "Nothing I can get into right now, okay? I'm gonna load up some boxes and I'll be back later for dinner."

She nodded, a look of concern definitely playing on her face, but she knew me. She knew that I'd talk when I was ready.

"Okay. Wash your hair."

I laughed and rubbed at my eyes, which no longer had an ounce of makeup. "I'll be presentable, I promise."

I chanced a glance from the corner of my eye when I passed the garage with the next box, and he was leaning against the workbench with his head down. It gave me a little rush of— something—just knowing I wasn't the only one fighting myself.

I nearly ran the next two trips up to my room and back, grabbing everything that would possibly fit in my trunk, not even caring what it was. I nearly had to sit on it for it to latch closed, but as soon as it did I was gone. I drove off without even looking back. I needed space from him. From the chemistry that had sparked the second he'd arrived and had been simmering ever since. And that particular day, with the paint and the roof and the flashback and then that whole mouth-to-mouth fiasco—I felt like I needed to shower in ice.

I remembered his kisses, for the most part. It had been many, many years, and a long stretch of Kevin in between, but I did remember that he had skills in that area. Skills that had turned me into a puddle of gush and given me Cassidy.

Nothing in my memory bank had prepared me for the fire he'd just lit up in me from head to toe. In that thirty second stretch at my car, I'd thrown out my worries, my dignity, and all the reasons I needed to stay away from him. In fact I would have probably done him right there in the driveway, forgetting about the neighbors and my mother and aunt as well.

"I am such a slut," I said to myself as I made it to my house, walked in the door, and knocked three open magazines out of the way so I could flop onto my couch and wallow in the chaos that seemed to blanket me.

OTHER THAN DINNER THAT NIGHT, WHICH WAS BEN-FREE DUE to his plans with his brother, I managed to stay away from my mother's house for four whole days. Four days. I met with clients, made new spreadsheets, created a house tour schedule where I bounced from showing to showing like a chicken on crack. I made sure I was busy, and I made sure I was rarely even home, spending one of those days at the office I detested just so no one could drop by looking for me.

Not that I thought anyone would really drop by looking for me. Or try to find me. Or call. He—or whoever—wouldn't have my number, but it was listed in the real estate section of every newspaper and then there was always my mother. She'd handed over my address like it was a recipe for cheesecake. Why would my phone number be any more of a hassle? He would just have to ask.

Or I could stop obsessing about a man I had no business thinking about or wanting to think about. Ben Landry was everything I needed to avoid. A gorgeous man with the ability to drain my brain of logic with one touch. And Cassidy's father. That was reason enough. I couldn't "move forward" with him, when eventually he or Cass—or even Kevin—would put the pieces together.

Plus, he could talk all the noise he wanted to about leaving the past in the past and all that, but how could I ever trust him not to bail on me again without knowing why he did it the first time?

No. It was infinitely better for me to stay away while he was there, and keeping a distance from that house had an appeal as well. I enjoyed having entire days spent in one time period.

I was stir-frying some chicken and vegetables, feeling very liberated and domestic even though it all came from a bag, when my doorbell rang on the fifth day. I looked at my reflection in the microwave door, knowing that Cass was at work, Holly and Greg were on a date, and Mom was busy with Aunt Bernie. Was that hope I was feeling, or dread? Or both.

I turned the fire off and headed to the door with a positive attitude, refusing to even look out the window to see who it was. It would be whoever it was supposed to be.

And when I swung the door open, it was Kevin. My arms dropped to my sides along with my spirits.

"Funny. You didn't figure into any of the possibilities," I said, smiling at him and his perfectly ironed shirt and bleached teeth.

"What?"

I shook my head. "Nothing. What's up?"

He shrugged and tilted his head. "Just wanted to talk to you for a second."

"Is my phone not working?"

"It tends not to, when you see it's me," he said, smiling back.

I laughed. "Okay, come in. I'm making some dinner; have you eaten?"

"Nah, but Sherry's making an organic vegetarian etouffee, so I'd better wait."

I stopped and gave him a look. "Are you sure? I have chicken."

He appeared to waver for a second, then shook his head. "It's okay. But go ahead, keep doing what you're doing."

He headed to the collage of Cassidy while I went back to the stirring. I felt a pang of guilt that I hadn't felt in years, as he smiled at some of the photos. With him raising her, and Ben not in the picture, it got to where I thought of Kevin as her father. It was easy to believe the lie when there was nothing around to dispute it. Now, she was grown and living her own life. And lately, I constantly felt about two hairs away from everything being yanked out from under all of us.

"This is when she loved me," he said with a sad little laugh.

I swallowed the lump rising there. "She loves you, Kev; she's just trying to make her own way. You have a hard time letting people do that."

"I guess."

"So, what's up?" I asked after a pause. "I don't know if Cass has done anything with that paperwork, if that's what you're wondering."

He shook his head minimally, still looking at the pictures,

and the little warning bells went off in my head. Kevin was nothing if not opinionated and in-your-face. For him to come to my house and then not come look me in the eye—told me it wasn't going to be his normal rant.

I decided to abandon my dinner for the moment and pour myself a glass of wine. I poured two on instinct and offered him one as I sat at the table.

"You aren't going to eat?" he asked, glancing back at the stove as he sat down.

"It can wait; what's going on?"

He met my eyes and chuckled. "Is something going on with you and Landry?"

My whole body relaxed. "Jesus, Kevin, is that what you came over to ask me?"

"No, I'm just wondering."

"Well, quit," I said, getting back up to revisit dinner.

"Sherry wants to get married," he blurted out.

I looked back at him, at the genuine worry and anxiety in his face, and sat back down.

"O-kay. I'm guessing you don't?"

He toyed with his glass. "I should. I mean, yeah, I guess I do. I just—"

"You've been together long enough to know."

"I know," he said, pushing back his chair and rubbing at his eyes. For the first time, I noticed the perfection was waning. There were the little lines around his eyes, and some gray in his eyebrows. "And in that respect, I do." He blew out a breath. "She's perfect for me. We have a great relationship."

"You have a great relationship?" I leaned across the table

toward him. "You sound like you're describing a dog. Or a car. Or an insurance agent. Do you love her?"

He met my eyes. "I loved you."

That backed me up a good foot. I sat up and blinked at him. "Wh—What—"

"I loved you with all I had, Emily. Since junior high, I was in love with you. And look what I did with that. I still had to screw it up. I couldn't be happy with what I had, I still needed what I *didn't* have."

I didn't want to go down that road. I scooped my hair up and tried to look patient, but reminders of what the whole town knew my husband was doing behind my back was not my idea of memory lane.

"So you're saying you might do it again?"

He scoffed and looked away. "I've already done it again. And again. That's my point."

I dropped my hair and stared at him. "Seriously?"

"I love her, Em. She's amazing." He got up and pushed his chair in, lining it up with the others. "But clearly, that's not enough to keep me faithful. Should I let her marry into that?"

I wanted to shake him. "No!" I got up and left my chair out on purpose. "Kevin, grow the hell up. You're not special. Everybody has temptations—hell, I could have had three different flings while we were married, but I never gave it a second thought. I made the choice. You have that ability, too. Get help if you need to, or let her go." I walked up to him and put my finger on his chest. "But if you love Sherry like you say you do, be a man. Don't fuck her over."

He narrowed his eyes. "Who could you have had flings with?"

I turned around and headed back to my cooling dinner. "Really? That's all you heard?"

He followed me. "I'm sorry."

I looked at him, annoyed. "For what?"

"Cheating on you. Messing things up."

His voice was soft. Sincere. Probably for the first time in all the apologies he'd made.

"I know," I said, and then looked back down at my chicken that wasn't looking so good. "Things happen as they're supposed to, Kevin. Maybe Sherry's the one for you."

"Maybe." He started to leave, then turned around. "Thanks for talking to me." He shrugged. "I didn't have anybody else."

I gave him a small smile. "Anytime."

"So is Landry the one for you?"

I closed my eyes. "Bye, Kevin."

He chuckled and left. But I knew he'd registered the fact that I hadn't said no.

CHAPTER

11

Two more days of giving my mother's house a wide berth, and I didn't know if I was happy with myself or depressed. Mom called to check on me but said nothing about Ben. Holly called to talk about Mom's party, which she and Cass had decided would just be a girls' night out somewhere.

Ben hadn't made one single effort.

This thought kept poking away at me as I tried to enjoy a quiet evening at home with a good book and my fleecy pajamas. The same paragraphs passed in front of my eyes over and over, but I wasn't seeing the content. I kept checking my phone, and Facebook, and e-mail, and then I'd end up playing a puzzle game I downloaded an app for, and then get disgusted and go back to the same tired paragraphs.

Isn't that what I'd wanted? To stay away from him? To keep my life all zipped up in its neat little pouch, without the distraction and danger of him messing it up? Maybe. But I had to face the additional fact that while that may have been what I wanted, I'd expected him to give it a little more of a fight.

That last kiss of his had certainly felt like more than just a passing interest. Almost a week afterward, I could still remember every second of it, the way he smelled and the way he felt and the look in his eyes that had gone with it. But maybe afterward, he'd second-guessed it. Maybe he wished he hadn't gone there and had decided to back off as well. He'd certainly done it before.

Irritated, disgusted, and put out with myself for feeling so pathetic, I decided I deserved a treat. Ice cream. And not just any old wannabe ice cream in a bucket, either. I wanted the real deal with scoops and mix-ins and a waffle cone. There was the dilemma of putting on real clothes, versus going to a drive-through, but I was always paranoid of getting in a wreck and being left to stand on the side of the road in my silkies.

So I split the difference and threw on black sweatpants with a purple T-shirt, found a pair of sneakers to slide into, pulled my hair into a ponytail, and off I went in search of two scoops of Dutch chocolate with chopped pecans.

The place I had in mind—Crème de la Cream—was only a mile and a half away, and I could already taste the perfection. When I pulled into the lot, there was only one car there, and I rejoiced at my good fortune, not having to show my bare face and mismatched attire to a crowd.

The aroma of freshly cooked waffle cones in various flavors hit me as soon as I opened the door, and my mouth reacted. I opened it to spill out my favorite combination when the bathroom door opened and who should rush out with a flourish but Dedra Powers.

"Emily," she breathed, all happy and fresh and made-up and

clearly on her way home from a date or something nice. Unless she was one to park on the couch in Prada heels and a Gucci bag, Dedra had had a better night than I did. Her smile curved, cat-like. "Have a craving, too?"

I made a point to close my mouth, and then smiled. "Yes." I turned to place my order before my head started spinning all the way around. Then the chime went off signaling another customer coming in, and we both turned to see Ben walk in.

"Really?" I said under my breath. Or I thought it was. Seemed to bounce around that room, so maybe it wasn't.

He hesitated in the doorway when he saw me, like he wasn't sure if he should turn back and run the other way. While I understood that feeling all too well, it hit me a little too close to home. After a few seconds passed, he walked up slowly, looking a little distant but never breaking eye contact with me.

"Emily."

I would have given all the ice cream in the world to have Dedra's clothes at that moment. In my size. Looking at him in his worn, soft jeans and blue sweatshirt with the sleeves shoved up, all I could think of was the hideous purple shirt I had on and the fact that I sported no makeup. What a way for him to see me after six days.

"Hey, Ben."

"Oh, Ben—Landry?" Dedra piped in, leaning between us so we had to look at her. "Are you Ben Landry?"

Ben blinked and looked at her. "Yes, ma'am."

She fidgeted and smiled the way I'd seen women do around him since we were old enough to fidget. "Wonderful," she said, holding out a hand. "I'm Dedra. Dedra Powers? Mrs. Lattimer told me about the work you're doing at her house."

Eyebrows moved up slightly, and I knew he fought not to glance toward me. "Dedra Powers. I do believe I've heard your name."

"Well, not in vain, I hope," she said on a giggle, and I shook my head. She looked my way. "My goodness, your mom has a lot of questions," she said. "You'd think she'd absorb some of your knowledge."

I smiled as I remembered my mother's words about calling Dedra night and day. "Well, I guess she wants to get her money's worth."

Dedra smiled back, although her eyes showed something else. She turned her charm back to Ben. "I told Mrs. Lattimer that I'd love to get someone with your talent under contract as a handyman."

I saw his eyes light up with amusement, and he nodded. "Well, we'll have to talk then." He pointed ahead. "Right now, I just want something sweet."

"Oh, I love their frozen yogurt," she said. "They have the best nonfat peaches and cream yogurt. I get it sprinkled with crushed almonds just to be bad," she said, leaning into me conspiratorially.

I stared at her. Down at her. Because she was one of those tiny petite people that wear size zeros and model Barbie clothes. Then I turned my back on both of them and smiled at the clerk behind the counter.

"I'll take two scoops of Double Dutch Chocolate, mixed with chopped pecans—and almonds," I said.

"In a bowl or cone?" the clerk asked.

"In a cinnamon and sugar waffle cone," I responded, stepping to one side. "Your turn."

The smile Ben was fighting to keep off his face was worth all six days of self-banishment. And it hit me like a ton of cinder blocks to know just how much I'd missed it.

Dedra ordered her nonfat pointless drivel in a plastic cup, and then Ben pointed at mine as the clerk handed it to me.

"I'll have that, too," he said, then walked around Dedra like she was a traffic cone. "Busy this week?"

I felt my heart speed up as he stepped closer, and I took a slow breath to even things out. I refused to show a reaction, knowing he'd expect one.

"Crazy. Had a lot of appointments on hold from the previous weeks, it was time to get people taken care of."

He nodded as if trying to tell if I was lying. "Well, I have those papers signed for you; they're in my toolbox at your mom's house."

"Oh, good."

"Yeah." He nodded over my head toward where Dedra was chatting with the ice cream girl about the nutritional content. "Interesting choice to hang out with. Did I interrupt a big night on the town?"

I laughed in spite of myself and gave up waiting to eat my cone as it began dripping down my hand. I licked my fingers with all the grace of a hippopotamus. "Yes, don't I just look ready to hit the town?"

"Well, Ben," Dedra said from behind me just as he was about to say something. She clicked her little heels right around me and laid a beautifully manicured hand on his arm. "I'd love to talk to you about your work. Here's my card," she said, deftly pulling one from the side pocket of her bag. "Please call me."

I knew that please-call-me tone. It was the universal please-fuck-me tone known to women everywhere.

"I sure will," he said, smiling down at her in such a way that probably melted her yogurt. He met my eyes as she left. "What?"

I chuckled. "You just can't help yourself, can you?"

One corner of his mouth twitched up. "Oh, come on. You jealous?"

Any playfulness I'd felt was doused by the bucket of cold water that comment brought. "No," I said coldly. "And don't ever play that game with me over her."

I headed for the door and he double-stepped it to get in front of me. "Em. Emily. I'm sorry, I wasn't thinking, that wasn't cool for me to say that." He leaned over to make me look at him. "Seriously. I'm sorry."

"Okay," I said, acting like I didn't care. I held up my cone. "Gotta go."

He pointed to the little outside patio tables and chairs off to the side. "Or you could sit with me a minute and eat our ice cream together."

Crap.

"Or—I could do that," I said.

Thinking that didn't sound very upbeat, I smiled, but he didn't look wounded or anything so I let it be. I claimed a chair and worked methodically at my cone, trying to think of brilliant conversation.

"Not too cold tonight, that's good," I said. Not what I had in mind.

He nodded, licking around the sides of his cone, and I was momentarily paralyzed by the memory of his tongue in my mouth before I pinched myself to grow up.

"Did Cassidy bring those books to you?" he asked.

All other thoughts blew away like the wind. "Cassidy? What books?"

"She found like three boxes of books in a hall closet, and your mom said they were yours. She stuffed them in her car and was going to bring them over."

Hearing him tell me what Cassidy was doing had a surreal feel to it. Like I needed to hit rewind and do it right.

"Oh. Um, no, she hasn't made it by, yet. When was this?"

"I don't know, a few days ago. She's been helping your mom out quite a bit." He pointed randomly. "She's funny."

"Funny," I repeated.

"Yeah, the way she sees things," he said, a small smile tugging at his lips. "She can get into some babble fests, but somehow she always brings it around to make perfect sense. She's got a good head on her shoulders."

I couldn't even taste the chocolate anymore. "Because?"

He looked at me funny. "Because she knows what she wants."

I laughed. "Really? How on earth did you get all that?"

"She talks," he said matter-of-factly. "All the time," he added with a laugh. "By the way, your mom's party is day after tomorrow in case no one has told you yet. I've heard the plans more than once."

"Yes, I knew that," I said.

"She may not know what she wants education-wise, but she's smart about life. She sees the world—really sees it. Not just what she's told to see."

I nodded, feeling clammy all of a sudden. He'd just described himself at that age, and he was too smart to not figure that out soon.

"Yep, she's a one-of-a-kind all right," I said, and I tossed the little remainder of my cone in a nearby garbage. I pushed out my chair. "Well, I'm going to head back home."

"Okay." He sat back in his chair, looking like he was staying awhile. "It was good to see you."

"You, too."

I stood to go, but the problem was that I couldn't seem to actually follow through. He had that look going on. That pin-me-to-the-wall, root-me-to-the-floor look, where he mastered the phenomenon of not blinking. I gripped the cold metal chair instead and thought about kissing him. Why the hell not. That's where my head kept veering off to anyway, the way he sat all slung back with his clothes clinging to him just right.

"Are you not talking to me again?" he said, his face showing no emotion.

I blinked myself back to reality. "What?"

"I'm just curious, so I know when to leave you alone," he said, rising to his feet in one slow movement. "When you start answering questions like a robot, that seems to be the time."

I sighed. "There isn't a grand plan for what I'm doing, Ben," I said, hoping I sounded world-weary and sophisticated. "And I'm standing here talking to somebody; I thought it was you."

He laughed, but not a happy kind of laugh. "I'm guessing you're avoiding the house so it doesn't suck you backward. You're avoiding me so I don't"—he leaned toward me—"suck you forward. Life's just easier that way, isn't it?"

"You know, you're one to talk about avoidance."

My roots had been released, and I turned on my heel and headed for my car. Quickly, before he could catch up and glue me to my car with his tongue again.

"Meaning what, exactly?"

"You know damn good and well what it means."

"So you keep telling me." I kept walking. "See you tomorrow," he called out.

"We'll see."

That was weak and we both knew it. I might have been strutting away like I had Dedra's haughty little pumps on, but in reality I had Emily Lattimer Lockwood's sneakers on, the ones with holes in the toes.

MOM'S HOUSE LOOKED FANTASTIC. LIKE WHY-WOULD-YOU-EVER-want-to-leave kind of fantastic. The den all done up in the earth tones, with no crappy paneling, made it look almost like a new house. Well, a new house with the old carpeting, but that would have its day as well. It looked empty without Mom's chair and the big old couch that was supposed to be there, and I wondered where she and Bernie were hanging out. I guessed the kitchen.

The cabinets had been given just a simple piece of trim around each door, giving them a whole new look. The windows all had snazzy new trim and fresh paint. The downstairs bathroom had new brushed nickel faucets and some new shelves that weren't there before.

Ben had been busy.

"You like?"

His voice directly behind me as I admired the new shower-head massager startled me so badly I had to grab the wall to keep from taking the shower door out. His rumbling laugh sounded warm as I turned around, and the smile in his eyes that went with it made me falter.

"Told you I'd see you today," he said, pulling some of the smile back.

"It's night."

A fact I thought I'd planned out well. Facing the house, avoiding him. So much for that.

"Yes, it is," he said, crossing his arms. "It's been a crazy day. You?"

"Something like that."

"And now you're here."

"Well, I thought I'd stop avoiding uncomfortable situations," I said. "Face it all head-on. You should give it a try."

On that note, I tried to step around him, which in the tiny bathroom required me to put my hands on his arms to move past. I looked away from his face as I did, but I heard him take in a slow, deep breath as our bodies touched, which was quite remarkable considering how loud my heart was beating in my ears.

"Mom?"

That one I heard, as I exited the bathroom with Ben on my heels, and Cassidy gave me the funky eyebrow.

"Having a cozy moment?" she said, a wicked grin on her face.

"Want a Christmas present?" I responded, widening my eyes to signify moving on.

She laughed. "Hey, Ben."

"Mr. Landry," I said, laying a hand on her shoulder.

"We passed up *Mr. Landry* a ways back," Ben said in my ear as he passed, sending a trickle of goose bumps down that side of my body.

"Yeah, once you've squeezed large furniture through small doors together, you hit the first name basis," she said. It was almost flirty. And I was almost sick.

"So what brings you here this late?" I asked, changing the subject. "Mom's not here, she and Aunt Bernie went shopping."

"Oh, that—can't be good."

"No, I'm sure it won't be," I said. "But then stranger things have happened lately, so who knows."

Ben turned and gave me a subtle look when I said that, then headed back down the hallway to Mom's room. I guessed her room was getting the makeover next.

"Aunt Bernie'll have her in green eye shadow, Mom. Blue fingernails!"

I laughed. "Not in the same outfit. So what are your plans?" I asked as I played with her curls. She leaned her head over as she'd done since she was three, an instant easy woman for anyone to play with her hair.

"Well, first I'm stealing some time with Tandy," she said with baby talk words for the dog, who wagged her tail from her bed. Tandy didn't bother with barking at the door anymore; it had become too much of a revolving door for her to keep up with. "I'm waiting for Josh to meet me here and we're gonna go up in the attic and dig through some boxes."

"Wow, doodlebug, you really know how to live it up."

She giggled. "I know, right? But hey, he offered."

I shrugged. "Can't turn that down."

"What are you gonna do?"

"Get the rest of the boxes out of my room, and box up the stuff still on the shelves and the dresser." Another thought pinged. "Oh, you had books for me, Ben said?"

"Yeah, they're still in my trunk; want me to go move them over?"

I threw her the keys and headed upstairs, glad that Ben was working downstairs. Glad that Cassidy was working two floors above him and had no reason for endless chitchat. I felt a sense of sadness when I entered my old room that I hadn't felt before. Like everything was about to be left behind. I'd heard people talk that way when selling their houses, like the walls were alive and soaking up their memories, and they were leaving them behind. I always thought that was an off-the-wall sentimental notion, but I was feeling something like that right then. I suddenly didn't want to pack up the books that had tided me through many a grounding, when all I could do was curl up on my window seat and read. I didn't want to take down the Madame Alexander dolls my dad had bought for me when I was little, or the hand-blown glass clowns that stood side by side on my dresser.

My gaze fell on the window, and it seemed easier somehow to go there. Not outside—I wasn't going outside again—but just to sit on that seat and look out at the night. I sat and pulled my knees up to me, thinking of what group of items I would hit first, but the second I laid eyes on the roof, it started.

"Oh, you've gotta be kidding me," I said, gripping the windowsill.

The wind rushed in my head, the blackness seemed to pull me out that window no matter how I tried to fight it—I even tried to stand up to break it before it started, but I couldn't feel my legs. I didn't want to go this time. I wasn't curious, I didn't want the show I knew was coming. As the tightness squeezed the breath out of me, I realized with crystal clarity what Ben meant when he said he didn't want to hear about it. Because I knew where I had to be going, and suddenly more than anything in the world I did not want to relive it.

When the air rushed back into my lungs and I jolted forward like someone slammed on the brakes, I wasn't really on the window seat anymore, but out on the roof where I'd been the last time.

"No fair," I said. "Breaking your own rules!" I didn't know who or what I was saying it to, but I threw it out there anyway.

And as I expected, the voices coming from the tree were getting closer. I could hear the laughter and giddiness as two people emerged over the roofline. Ben wasn't alone that time. I was with him. Climbing up that tree in a party dress that clung to me as I dripped river water. Ben pulled himself up on the roof, his black button-down shirt sticking to his wet skin like it was painted on, and then he hauled me up with him.

Laughing and trying to be quiet, they half walked–half crawled across the roofline to retrieve the secret blanket. I watched them, hugging my arms across my body, already feeling the burn behind my eyes. I couldn't think of her as younger-me anymore. She was me. It was too vivid a memory to think of it as watching; it was going to be relived.

It was my twenty-first birthday.

"Oh my God, I can't believe I just did that," she said, flopping on her back on the blanket, only a foot from me.

Only a foot from me. It was going to happen within sneezing distance of me and I could not leave. The thought was bizarre. Even weirder was the crazy thought that crept into my head about time and if something was happening now, did it happen then, too? Did I sit here and watch myself the first time? Oh my lord, what if I'd had an audience then, too.

"I can't believe you did that, either," Ben said, shaking his hair so that water slung across her. It was shorter than in earlier years, but not as short as now. He sat beside her, then landed sideways, propping his head up with his elbow. He had filled out since the last time, his shoulders were broader. He was a man.

"Hey!" she said, whopping him across the middle with the back of her hand. "You were right there with me."

"Yeah, but I'm a hooligan," he said, dropping his head in laughter. "I can't believe that old man actually called us that."

"I'm just glad he didn't call the police."

"Yeah, you're all of age now," Ben said, poking her. "You'd go to jail for indecent exposure."

She fidgeted and adjusted her dress, which looked out of whack. "I'm all crooked now," she said, giggling. "I couldn't get everything back on right, being all wet."

"Well, feel free to take it off," he said. "I mean, you've already done it once."

She put her hands over her face. "Oh, man, you're never gonna let me live that down, are you?"

"Never," he whispered, close to her. "And don't act all holy, chickadee, I know you looked, too."

"Well, you took so damn long, I couldn't help it."

Ben laughed. "Yeah, yeah, try that again. I didn't take that long, I had to hurry and get in the water."

"Why?"

He grinned. "You don't want to know."

She looked genuinely confused and propped up sideways on her elbow to face him. "What?"

He laughed. "Nothing." He looked at her in silence for a few seconds. "Happy birthday, Em. I hope it's been a good one."

"Best ever."

"Even with dickhead out of the picture?"

"Because he's out of the picture." She scooped wet hair back. "It's been two weeks, Ben. I told you I'm not going back to that cheating prick and I mean it."

He gave her a look. "You have said that before."

"It's done this time," she said. "I've wasted enough of my life with him. All the other girls in town can have him. If they haven't already."

He laughed. "I'm sorry, I know it's not really funny."

"Next subject," she said. "Thank you for making me go party tonight when I just wanted to sit around and mope about losing my apartment. It was just what I needed."

"What I'm here for. I still say you could have moved in with me and Bobby and saved yourself the parental drama."

"Kevin would have flipped out—not that that really matters. But moving in with him was bad enough. If I did it again with another guy, my parents would disown me. And seeing you all that up and personal with women you'd bring home—I don't know, that would have been weird."

His eyebrows knitted together. "Why?"

She shrugged and then smiled. "I don't know. Maybe because I never have to share you. When we're together you're always mine."

He put a finger to his lips. "Shhh. Don't tell anyone, but I'm always yours anyway."

She shoved at him. "Ha-ha. But you didn't think I could keep up with you tonight, did you?"

Ben held up a hand. "I stand corrected. You can drink like a sailor. And still not drown in a river."

"And then climb a tree," she added.

He pointed at her. "In a party dress."

"Which you looked up; that's why you wanted me to go first."

He chuckled. "Sweetheart, I wanted you to go first so I could catch you if you fell. I just saw all your goods, back there at the river, remember? Looking up your dress would have been kind of like eating the chocolate and then drooling over the wrapper."

She laughed, and he moved a wet lock of hair out of her eyes. Somehow, I remembered that simple gesture for years to come. Out of all the moves that night, for some reason that one stuck with me.

"Eating the chocolate, huh?"

"Yeah, there's a metaphor for you."

"I'll never look at a chocolate bar the same way again." She sighed and sounded happy. I knew she was. "Oh, man, I had so much fun tonight. And speaking of every woman in town—do you know how many people hate me tonight?"

Ben frowned. "Why?"

"For being with you," she said, laughing. "I'd forgotten how bitchy girls can be. Every woman at every club we hit wanted to gouge my eyes out and step over me to get to you."

"I could say the same thing about the men."

"No."

"No?"

She shook her head. "Women are evil. I had three of them tell me in three different bathrooms about what a good lover you are."

Ben nearly choked. "What?"

"I'm serious! 'His kisses make your clothes melt off' or some such thing."

He looked sincerely shocked. "No shit? What if we'd been on an actual date?"

She put a hand to her chest in mock indignation. "We weren't on a date? You mean I got naked for you and it wasn't a date?"

Ben laughed. "You got naked all on your own."

"And you didn't even need to kiss me. Damn, you're good."

"I can't believe somebody said that."

She waved a hand. "That's nothing new, Ben. I heard about your 'talents' all through high school. Girls always wanted to know if we'd messed around."

"And you said—?"

"No. Should I have lied?"

"I kissed you in the eighth grade at—"

"Carla Martin's party. Yeah, truth or dare doesn't count."

They locked fingers and twisted the union back and forth, and my heart sped up as I knew it was coming. It was like watching a freaking soap opera that I'd already seen.

"So why is it you've never made a move on me?" she asked.

His eyebrows shot up. "Is that a request?"

She shoved at him with their joined hands. "Quit being a pig, I'm serious. I mean I know you don't think of me like that, but—"

Ben laughed out loud. "Don't think of you like that? Emily, I'm a guy. I think of every woman like that. Back there at the river?" He pointed off the roof. "I had to stay in the water because I had a raging wood."

She slapped a hand over her eyes. "Oh my God."

He pulled her arm down and made a face to make her laugh. "Yes, I think of you like that. But I—I have to be different with you."

"Different?"

"Other women, I act on it. I get laid. I move on." He shook his head and smiled but the smile was changed, sadder. I saw it now, but I didn't know if I saw it then. "You matter, Em. I'd be toast."

She chuckled. "You'd be toast? You're saying I might melt your clothes?"

He fake-grimaced. "It's never happened, but you could be the one to do it."

She leaned in closer to him, flirty. "Sounds like a challenge."

He smiled down at her and seemed to weigh out his words. "Careful there. That fire's unpredictable."

"Meaning?"

He leaned in to match her. "Meaning that with you—I don't know if I could stop."

CHAPTER

I remembered the heat that had gone to my belly and lower when he'd said those words. The feeling that invisible barriers had been broken.

"Why with me?" she asked softly.

His smile faltered, and he appeared to be fighting something. He brought it back though, and took a deep breath as he gave her a questioning look.

"Is this true confessions night?"

She tilted her head. "I think so."

He stared into her eyes for a long moment, and then looked down at the shingles between them before meeting her gaze again and holding it. "Because you're all I've ever wanted." I heard her deep intake of breath, and I remembered the feeling behind it. "And I can't believe I just said that out loud," he continued, shaking his head with a little laugh and breaking eye contact.

She took his hand and interlaced her fingers with his, making him look at her again. "Want to know my confession?" she asked finally after a forever silence.

She let go of his hand and gently took the front of his shirt in her hand, pulling him to her until her lips were on his. She kissed him softly until he responded with kisses of his own, his hand traveling her face.

"Em," he said against her lips. "What are you doing?"

"Confessing."

His mouth broke into a smile. "I like your method." His hand moved behind her head as he pulled her in for more. After a moment, he stopped with difficulty, both of them breathing a little faster.

He rested his forehead against hers. "There was a reason not to do this."

"Mm-hmm, because you wouldn't be able to stop," she said.

He ran a finger along her cheek. "No, because you're the real deal," he whispered. I could have recited that line in my head, I still remembered it that well. "It wouldn't just be sex with you. You'd take my heart."

The tears fell freely down my face. I wanted to go back. I wanted to put fingers in my ears and go "la-la-la" and not see or hear any of this again.

She touched his face and his lips and then wound her fingers into his hair. I couldn't see her eyes but I knew they were misty. I knew she was trying to say the words.

"And that's a bad thing?"

"Em, if we cross this line, I can't watch you be with other men," he said. "I can't watch you go back to Kevin again."

"I don't want anyone else," she whispered against his cheek, and I saw him close his eyes as one tear squeezed out. He quickly rubbed *it away before she could see, and my heart ached to know that. "And you already have my heart."*

I watched his eyelids flutter and his hands tremble a little as he pulled her face to his again, and kissed her slow, soft, and from what I remembered, agonizingly thorough. He pulled her body close, wrapping her up in his arms as he cradled her head and dove deep.

I wanted to leave. I didn't want to sit that close to myself and Ben as we made love. I leaned my head back and closed my eyes, listening to their words, their breathing, their laughter over awkward angles and hard surfaces, the sounds of their kisses and soft moans when places were touched just right. Their confessions of love and how Ben wanted to see her face as he made love to her. Their build as they moved together to come at the same time, crying out, and then actually crying. I opened my eyes to find that I was, too.

"Oh my God, Ben," she said, her voice shaking with tears as she wrapped herself more tightly around him.

"You're crying," he said.

"You're shaking," she responded.

He laughed and kissed her forehead as tears trickled from his eyes, too. "It's because it's you, Em. That was—I swear to you, I've never made love before. I've never—"

"Me, either," she said, little sobs jerking her breaths. "I've never felt anything like that before."

"Emily—"

"I love you, Ben."

He dropped his head and held her tight. "I love you, too, baby."

The words echoed in my ears, and it made me sit up. Was it coming? The ringing? "Please, God, let it be over," I said. "There's nothing new here." Tears streamed down my face as I struggled to my feet and yelled at the sky. "There's nothing new here! Enough, already!"

The jerk backward made me grope for the wall of the house as my vision went black and all the air was knocked from my lungs. I shut my eyes tight, hearing only the rush of the wind go past me until a giant intake of breath brought me back to the present.

⁓

"Shit!" I exclaimed, blinking my room back into focus as I found myself back on the window seat. I got up quickly, pushing away from the seat, and then reaching for my bed as my head spun, unable to catch up. "Shit, shit, shit."

"Mom?" Cassidy's voice said from somewhere near the door. I held my pounding head in my hands and kept my eyes closed. "Mom, you okay?"

"Mm-hmm," I said as I sank onto the bed and tried to swipe at my eyes with shaking hands.

"No you're not," she said, rushing to kneel in front of me. "What's wrong? What happened?"

I just watched the rerun of your conception.

"Nothing, baby, I just—" I looked up and saw Ben leaning against the doorjamb, a crowbar still in his hand from—whatever he was doing with a crowbar. Like he'd come running for something. My stomach contracted at the sight of him, standing there looking concerned, when my last image of him was making love to me—her—me. "I just tripped and landed hard on my knee, that's all," I said, focusing on Cassidy again. "You know how wimpy I am about my knees."

"But my God, you don't usually sob over it, Mom; are you sure you're okay?" She was looking at me intently. "Ben and I both heard you from where we were; we about collided in the hallway."

I shook my head, taking slow breaths to get myself back under control. "I'm fine, Cass, it's okay. Go back to what you were doing."

She looked at me with skepticism. "I don't know, Mom. Nana said you've been acting funny."

"Funny?" I said. "What kind of funny?"

"I don't know—odd?" She raised her eyebrows to enforce the point. "Kinda like now?"

I put my hands over my face for a couple of seconds to get my gears realigned, and then I ran fingers under my eyes again and smiled. "Hopefully, I will never tell your children that you are acting odd. I'm fine, I just lost it for a second—when I fell. Please quit hovering."

I stood up and pulled her with me, wrapping her up in a mighty hug at the end.

"Okay," she said, not sounding totally sold, but headed that way.

"Okay," I echoed.

I met Ben's steady gaze over her shoulder. The look in his eyes said he knew where I had gone, just as I'd known before I got there. He didn't want to talk about that one, and that just burned me up even more. Time had dulled the edges, but reliving that night cemented the hurt and betrayal all over again. How could he have declared such hardcore feelings as he did, and then walk away. Run away. Out of town, out of state, wherever the hell he went. How could he have left such an amazing love behind? Because *I had other plans*? Bullshit. I felt raw.

I stroked Cassidy's hair and tried to shoot those feelings at him like daggers, but he didn't look guilty. Or defensive. He just turned away and walked back down the hall without a word.

Her phone buzzed, and as she dug it from her pocket, I saw the image of her dad. Which was followed by a sigh of disgust as she realized she couldn't ignore him with me watching.

"Hello?"

I went to the window and closed the blinds before anything else decided to yank me around. Without any more thought, I started grabbing the Madame Alexander dolls and laying them on the bed. Then as Cassidy's voice got increasingly edgy, I grabbed the desk chair and stood on it to pile book after dusty book into my arms. Four sneezes later, I stepped down carefully and dumped all the books on the floor. Cassidy was pacing by that point, her expression taking on its trademark glaze-over that always infuriated me to no end. When it involved me. With Kevin, I figured it was his problem.

It was about school, as usual. Her lack of it and his opinions on that matter. While I somewhat agreed with him, at least in the beginning when she'd dropped out after one semester, the horse was beyond dead. Two and a half years of beating that carcass had done nothing to change her mind about college, and had only created a canyon between them that his constant harping kept widening.

She finally lied about her phone going dead and cut the call short, pressing the plastic against her forehead afterward with her eyes closed.

"He makes me so crazy," she said to the room. "I want to go run for days without stopping after I talk to him, just to blow the jitters off me. How the hell did I come from him?"

I gave her a small smile and rubbed her arm, mentally shaking off that question. "You know, you used to be inseparable. Always talking, always working on projects together."

"And then I grew my own brain instead of branching off his, and he can't stand that he isn't calling every shot."

I sighed. "I know, doodlebug. He just wants you to have everything in life you can have and not have to struggle."

She twisted away from me, irritation making her itchy. "I'm happy with my life, Mom. I like what I do. It may not be out of a book or a diploma, but it's me." She dropped cross-legged onto the floor and picked up books randomly, turning them to see their covers one at a time. "I like not having everything mapped out line by line, dot by dot. I live my life. I don't schedule it to death."

"You also miss things that way, baby."

She held out her hands, a book in each one. "What am I missing? I don't sit home and lay around watching TV. I go out every day and make a point to talk to someone new, do something new, take a new route to work, walk on the wrong side of the street— whatever. I may not follow the rules but I see my life in color. Not in bullet points on a calendar."

Her cell phone buzzed again, and she glanced at it.

"Text from Josh, he's almost here," she said, the sulk firmly implanted in her voice. I helped her up and hugged her before she walked away.

As hard as it was from the parent perspective, I envied her. She was making her life more challenging, no doubt, but—to be so comfortable with living day to day. To be so comfortable in her own skin and with who she was. I would have loved to know what that felt like.

I FOUND SOME BOXES DOWNSTAIRS AND LOADED UP WHAT I'D disrupted, feeling a little guilty about disturbing such a long- and deep-rooted location. I stayed far away from the window and any other revelations it felt it needed to show me. Every time I saw us making love in my mind, heard Ben's voice telling me he loved me, remembered the emotion and the tears, I had to grip my middle to keep it together. The raw, mean, jagged hole had reopened there and threatened to pull me in every few minutes.

I didn't want to see him again. I didn't care anymore what his reasons could have been. I'd been dancing around the subject because time had taken some of the details away, and I wasn't sure it was worth asking. Twenty years later, was it really relevant? I mean, outside the Cassidy factor that he wasn't even aware of.

After going down the home movie trail, I realized that nothing could fully justify his leaving. Not after the monumental connection we had that night. No love before or since had ever been that strong, at least for me.

No, it was best to just let it be. Let him finish whatever work he had left to do, and then he'd be back at his own house with no reason to see me again.

I was searching for my keys in the kitchen so that I could make a quiet exit when I heard the commotion at the front door. Or on the front porch, I realized as I rounded the corner and saw the door wide open and Cassidy and Kevin arguing.

"Damn it, Kevin," I muttered.

I headed for the door and felt Ben walk out of the hallway behind me. And just the fact that I didn't even see him and could feel his presence—get goose bumps on my back because of it—completely pissed me off. By the time I got to the door, a whole four feet later, I was primed to join the fight.

"Seriously?" Cassidy was saying to Kevin. "God, Dad, let it go!"

She was bowed up and waving her arms in the middle of the

porch, the tiny light above her making her golden head appear to glow. Josh stood to one side, leaning against one of the wooden posts, looking as if he wished the concrete would open up and suck him through it. Kevin stood on the bottom step, hands in his jacket pockets, looking worn out.

"Cass, you won't listen to me when I call you, *if* you even answer the phone."

"I told you my phone was going dead."

He held his hands out. "And so I came to you."

"Why?" she said, turning in a circle and catching sight of me. "Mom, please tell Dad what I told you."

"No, *you* tell your dad what you told me," I said, leaning against the doorjamb. "Y'all talk to each other for once, not through me. But does it have to be in the front yard? Can you do it inside?"

"I have," she said, raising her arms again. "Over and over. He didn't understand it any of the ten times I've repeated it."

I pointed at Kevin. "Him, Cass, not me. Talk to him."

"Oh my God, whatever," she said, storming down the steps and past him, Josh on her heels. She turned around and walked backward, the dark absorbing her. "I'm telling you both—see, my words are flowing your way—I'm not going back to college. I'm not going to business school. I'm not going to sit down and write a life plan on career paths or opening a restaurant, or a bookstore, or a toilet factory. I am fine. Leave me alone." On that, she got into her car, Josh scrambled to climb on his bike, and they were off like a speedy parade.

Kevin watched her, looking defeated as he usually did regarding her. They were so close once. When she was little and didn't have her own brain yet.

"Well, that went well," he said to the retreating taillights.

"Kevin, what did you expect?" I said, walking out and away from the heat at my back. "You know how she gets when she feels cornered."

"And why am I always the bad guy?" he said. "Why does she always feel like I'm cornering her? Why can't we just talk?"

"Because you don't just talk, Kev, you lecture. You tell her what she's supposed to do, instead of asking her what she's going to do."

Kevin frowned. "She's twenty-one. She doesn't know what she's going to do."

I remembered being twenty-one and clueless. And pregnant. Unable to balance a checkbook. That wasn't Cassidy. "Yes, she does. In fact, she knows herself better than we did at her age."

"We were having *her* at her age," he said, and it was everything I could do not to turn back and see if Ben was still there. "Our options went away. She's *throwing* hers away."

"We have to trust her," I said. "She's smarter than you're giving her credit for."

"I know," he said, looking at the sidewalk, then behind me. "Can I help you? Are you ever not here?"

I turned around to see Ben coming out the front door, keys in his hand, clearly leaving for the night. He hesitated a step to give Kevin a look, then moved it to me as if to tell me I was a moron for ever loving such a dipshit.

"Good night, Em," he said, handing me an envelope. I remembered the papers.

"Oh—thank you. Forgot about that."

Ben didn't respond, just walked to his truck. Kevin's face showed disgust and the urge to say something, but I cut him off.

"Good night, Kevin." I went in the house to turn out the light and lock the door and found him still standing there when I shut it behind me. "What?"

"If we wouldn't have gotten pregnant—"

I groaned. "Oh, come on, it's late."

"Just—I'm serious," he said. "If all that wouldn't have happened, would you still have come back to me? Would you still have married me?"

I blew out a breath and decided not to play the game anymore. "No," I said, and the word seemed to bounce around. "I would have gotten my archaeology degree and moved to Africa or Egypt or—somewhere."

Kevin blinked, looking stunned. "Huh." He turned and walked toward his car, very slowly.

I felt a little bad. "What would you have done, Kevin?"

He stopped but didn't turn around. "I don't know. Gone to college somewhere, then come back and married you. But I guess you would have been in Africa."

"And you would have gone and gotten laid."

He chuckled and resumed the journey to his car. "Yeah, probably so."

I WASN'T GOING TO RIDE IN BIG BLUE. AUNT BERNIE, HOLLY, Cassidy, myself, and my mother were dressed to go out, looking good, feeling good, and I wasn't about to ruin that by piling in a giant trailer.

Aunt Bernie was the one who'd brought it up, pointing out that we all had smallish cars and five people would be crowded. Holly eyed the monstrosity warily.

"I think we'll be just fine," I said. "It's just across town, we won't be in the car long."

"Seriously?" Cassidy said, looking like she was ready to burn up Manhattan instead of Main Street. She had on a tight little red dress that fell off one shoulder and was made to bring men to their knees. "Come on, Mom, it'll be a hoot!"

I stared her up and down. "Dressed like that, you want to drive around in a Smurf-mobile?"

"Hey!" Aunt Bernie said, hands on royal blue hips. Royal blue everything. It was evidently the color of the day. "You know, we can just leave your little butt here on the curb," she said loudly.

I held up my hands. "Sorry. I just pictured a little nicer evening." I gestured at Mom in her black pantsuit and pearls she wore to any nice event, and Holly in her little green dress that was eerily similar to my requisite little black dress, but made her hair look gorgeous. "I was told to dress nice for Mom's birthday."

"And we are," Cassidy piped in, linking arms with Aunt Bernie. I wanted to know what day she sold out to the other side, because I'd missed it. "And I think that makes it even more fun to ride around and make it a party bus."

My mom laughed and turned around before she could get targeted.

"A party bus?" Holly said. "Have you ever been on a party bus?"

"As a matter of fact I have," she said, crossing her arms. "And I think with the right *attitude*," she said, throwing a glare my way, "we can make this whatever we want it to be. For Nana."

"Oh, lord," Holly mumbled, smoothing her dress and looking around as if people who knew her might be hiding in the trees.

"Mom, what do you want to do?" I asked.

She just grinned. "Anything that will get us going. I'm hungry."

"Well, there you go," Aunt Bernie said. "Let's get to The Grille."

"The Grille?" Holly said quickly. "I thought we were going to Phillipe's?"

"Oh, hell no," Cassidy said, laughing. "We'd never get reservations there, why'd you think that?"

"Be—cause of how you said to dress, I guess—" Holly said, trailing her words miserably as reality settled on her.

"Come on," Cassidy urged. "Where's your sense of fun? We dress to the nines and make a splash, looking like movie stars going to eat burgers and nachos. Party it up with some beer and champagne on the bus, just like it was a limo."

"Well, except that I'm driving it," Aunt Bernie said.

"I can get Josh to come drive it, if you want," Cassidy offered.

"Oh, good God, no," Aunt Bernie said, patting her on the back. "Nobody drives Big Blue but me. He'd hit everything on the way."

"And where will you park it?" Holly asked.

"I always find a way," Aunt Bernie said, looking proud.

I looked at Holly, knowing it was inevitable. I was riding Big Blue.

"Okay," I said, looping an arm around Cassidy's crazy head. "Let's do this."

"Yay!" she squealed like a little girl.

We piled in one by one, and Aunt Bernie looked like a kid with a new puppy, showing us everything, pointing at the stereo and the TV and the microscopic kitchen. But I was a little distracted by the pink and purple shag carpet.

"Wow," I said, sitting on an equally carpeted bench seat.

"Holy crap," Mom said.

"Isn't it pretty?" Aunt Bernie said. "I just had it redone."

I saw Holly's eyebrows raise and I felt mine go, too. "This is new?"

"Yeah, it was brown before, didn't you see it?" she said, and then waved a hand at my blank stare. "No matter. I got a great discount on the shag; it was a steal."

"I'll bet," Mom said, cutting her eyes at me on her way past. "I'm surprised they had so much of this color in stock."

"Can you live in here?" I mumbled through my teeth so Aunt Bernie wouldn't hear. She was messing with things up front by then anyway.

"I'll need sunglasses," Mom mumbled back.

"I think it's hysterical," Cassidy said, spreading her arms out. "What a fun place to live."

I looked at her. "You know I just told your dad how level-headed you were, don't ruin it."

"Don't worry, Mom," she said with a wink. "I'd have blue carpet."

"Joy."

We settled in, felt the world tremble as Big Blue rumbled to life, and held on to whatever was next to us as Aunt Bernie lurched us away from the curb and away from sanity.

"Oh, Jesus," Holly said, working her way up to a chair.

"So, do you know where The Grille is?" I called out.

"Not going there, yet," Aunt Bernie called back. "Cass wants to make a pit stop first."

"Pit stop?" Holly repeated, looking like we were going to throw her out. Or maybe she was hoping.

"Gonna get some beverages for the bus," Cassidy said with a grin.

In looking at her, I realized I was officially old. I remembered being crazy and spontaneous and living for the fun, so I knew where she was. But she was trying to drag a couple of old farts and two more older farts along for the ride. Well, Holly was born old, so she was probably terrified. I think the rest of us at least had a memory of living it up.

"Why didn't you do that ahead of time?" I asked.

"More fun this way," she said, looking out the window.

"Not for her to park this beast, it's not," Mom said.

"Oh, it's fine," Aunt Bernie said. "I'm used to squeezing in all kinds of places. Hold on, ladies, I'm turning in."

She made a turn that included going over a curb and a parking divider, bouncing the whole lot of us a foot out of our seats before she came to a squeaky stop in front of a small convenience store.

Cassidy jumped up as the rest of us still held on to anything stable. "Okay, come on."

"You go ahead," Holly said, smiling.

"Let the clerk think you're a movie star," I said.

She fluttered her eyes in a half roll and blew out frustration with all us old women as she yanked the door open and took her sparkly self in the store.

"That Cassidy is a firecracker, I'll tell you," Aunt Bernie said, falling into her cackling laugh.

I scooped my hair back and let it fall. "Yeah—she's something, all right."

"Poor guy in there probably thought he was being invaded," Holly said, peeking through a window.

"How you doing back there, birthday girl?" Aunt Bernie yelled, looking through the rearview mirror instead of turning around.

Mom gave a thumbs-up and a cheesy smile. "I'm good."

I laughed, and even Holly snickered.

"Got it!" Cassidy sung as she stepped back up into Big Blue. "Wine coolers for Aunt Bernie and Nana, champagne for Aunt Holly, and light beer for me and Mom."

"Sounds like a plan," I said, reaching for one.

"Drink up, ladies," Cassidy said. "Let's get a little fun juice in us before we go eat."

"Holy shit, doodlebug, you're gonna get your nana drunk, girl," Mom said. "I haven't eaten all day."

"Oh, here, I got some snacks, too."

She pulled a bag of pretzels out of the bag. I had the feeling it was going to be a long night of twenty-one-year-old energy. God help us all.

CHAPTER
13

THE BEER HELPED. THE WINE COOLERS THAT I ASSISTED AUNT Bernie in drinking helped, too. Holly even stooped from drinking champagne to wine coolers and was kicked back with her bare feet up on a table, looking more relaxed than I'd seen her—ever. I almost hated that her husband was missing it, but then again he might not have recognized her.

We kind of stopped worrying where Aunt Bernie was driving to, because it just seemed to not stop, and it was easier if we didn't look. Mom sat cross-legged on the bed, surrounded in wall-to-wall pink and purple, and grinning like a fool. She really needed more than pretzels. Cassidy looked the most normal, but then she was young and most likely just getting started.

I imagine that we looked like some sort of mutant aging girl band, filing out of the giant powder blue Winnebago that Aunt Bernie took up half The Grille parking lot to fit in.

"We should make a bathroom run first," I said, feeling pretty sure that my makeup at that point was probably as blurry as my brain.

"Good idea," Holly said, following me.

Cassidy stayed behind with Mom and Aunt Bernie, who either didn't care or firmly believed they still looked spiffy. Cassidy still did. I sighed as I envied her that. Holly and I were old enough to know we were faded and young enough to be vain about it.

We weaved a little as we hit the bathroom, and I laughed as I saw Holly's smile.

"You're so smiley," I said. "Look at you."

She stared at herself in the mirror like she was studying a painting. "I am. Huh."

"You look good like that," I said, cleaning up my eyeliner that had bled down a bit. "Should do it more often."

"I would need wine coolers for that," she said, chuckling. "And they're too fattening."

I gave her a look that I realized took my eyes a smidge too long to do. "I think you have the room."

I fixed everything else while I was there. Hair, powder, blush, lip gloss for a bit of sparkle. Holly repainted her lips like it was for a grade. And then we walked out like Charlie's Angels, minus the blonde and the guns and the bell-bottoms.

Cassidy already had a tall table snagged, and Mom and Aunt Bernie were settled in with a basket of chips and some salsa.

"Didn't know your drink orders," Cass said. "We got beer."

"Beer's good," Holly said, making me raise my eyebrows at her. "What?" she said, looking defensive. "I'm not anti-beer."

"Since when?" Mom chimed in.

"I just—prefer other things," she said. "But I can drink a beer."

"Whoo-hoo!" I hollered—maybe a bit too loud. "Holly has converted. She's one of us."

"Oh, whatever," she said, but the glow and smile on her face were evident.

Probably just hearing those words sobered her up enough to make that smile authentic. I'd never thought about it before, but the buzz clarified some simple things. Like the fact that Holly had rarely fit in with anyone. She always kept herself so perfect that no one could qualify.

We ate, we drank, we ate some more, the beers slowed down. Aunt Bernie sweet-talked the elderly manager about leaving her home on wheels in the parking lot overnight so she didn't have to drive and we could all just walk the few feet to crash. I was surprised that he went for it, but I think she threw in some of my mother's catering ability for free. And there was the strong possibility that he liked the bright blue fingernails and eye shadow, as he kept looking at them with fascination.

There was an eighties theme going on at the jukebox or sound system or whatever the heck they had there. Cassidy dragged me and my mother out for a three-generation dance combo.

"I have pictures," Holly whispered in my ear when we got back to the table, giggling like fools.

"Your ass should have been out there," I whispered back.

"I'm not that drunk," she said, laughing.

My mom was having a great time, I noticed, and I winked at Cassidy when she caught my eye. She'd done good, planning this for her. And it was perfect—the crazy combo of dressing up and partying down. We'd just had to relax to realize it. My baby actually knew what she was doing, and I made a mental note to stop making her prove it.

Then the air changed. I was laughing hysterically about something, grazing on cake the manager had brought to my mom with great fanfare, when I saw Ben stroll up to the table.

The cake went solid in my stomach like concrete, and Holly nudged me.

"Yeah, I know," I said.

"Happy birthday," he said, going straight to my mother and giving her a big hug.

"Aw, thank you, Ben," she said, instantly glowing. My lord, he could light up anything female.

He thumbed behind him. "I saw the—party machine—out there, figured there couldn't be two of them."

Cassidy beamed and wiggled a little in her seat. "Told you—party bus!"

He laughed, looking at her, and patted her shoulder as he stood just to her left. "You did good, Cass."

My chest started to feel heavy with anxiety over that scene, so I gripped my not-so-cold-anymore mug for grounding.

"So, how's the party, ladies?" he said, looking around at each one of us, landing on me last. I felt it all the way to my toes.

"Fantastic," Aunt Bernie said, her voice beginning to sound normal. I wondered about that. Was it normal or had I just heard it for too long? "You should join us."

"Oh," I choked and then coughed on it as Cassidy gave me a funny look. "I'm sure Ben doesn't want to hang with a bunch of drunk women."

Even as I said it, I caught the amusement in his eyes as I realized that's exactly what most men want. Granted, one was too young and two were too old, so it probably lessened the likelihood.

He chuckled at my discomfort and held up one hand as he rested the other one on Cassidy's shoulder. "That's all right, I'm just picking up some dinner and going back home. Y'all have fun."

"Look at you two," Aunt Bernie said, leaning toward Mom for a better angle. "You could come from the same gene pool with those eyes."

Everything ignited from my chest up to my scalp. The worst observation that could possibly be made was coming out in front of everyone. Ben. Cassidy. The whole freaking world. Holly grabbed my leg under the table and I felt her nails dig in. I welcomed it. It reminded me that I hadn't stopped breathing yet.

Cassidy giggled and leaned into him, batting her eyes and making me want to erupt from my chair.

She twisted to look up at him. "Are you my long-lost, crazy Uncle Ben?" she said, laughing and including the table with it.

He shook his head as if we were all nuts, and laughed. "I doubt it. Y'all behave."

He walked to the bar and placed his order as the bass from some random song vibrated through my bones. I felt like I'd been made. I couldn't even look at Cassidy, it was as if my gaze was glued to the napkin holder in front of me. It was chrome and shiny with smears and scratches in the surface, and I could see my reflection. It fit, I thought. The smears and scratches.

"Honey, you okay?" I heard my mother say next to me.

"Uh-huh," I said, on autopilot. I stabbed at a piece of cake with my fork, noticing the tremble, and shoved it in my mouth for movement.

"That man is so good-looking," Aunt Bernie said, shaking her head slowly. "Whew. How he's still single is beyond me."

"Oh, he's hot," Cassidy said, laughing at the look her comment brought from me, which I guess was the magic that spurred life back into my nerves. "What?"

"Please—don't say that," I said, trying to act casual without giving even more of my fraudulent self away.

"Why?" she said, snatching cake off Mom's plate. "He's a hot older guy, I can notice that." She licked her fingers and winked at me. "As far as that goes, I wouldn't be against an older guy if they looked like Ben."

I could feel the nachos roll around in my stomach and turn to something like battery acid. I had to keep it cool. I had to keep it cool.

"Well," I began, on some crazy kind of screeching note. I cleared my throat. "Twice your age is a little more than *older* so let's take it down a decade, shall we?"

Cassidy laughed. I laughed. Holly and Mom and Aunt Bernie laughed. And I fantasized about pouring ice cubes down my dress.

"Oh, I don't think there is any question who our little Ben has an interest in, anyway," Aunt Bernie said, sitting back in her chair like the cat who chowed on the canary.

"Little Ben?" I said, feeling a tiny bit of relief seep into my veins now that he'd left the table. "Really?"

"Yeah, no kidding," Cassidy said.

"What?" I said, looking back and forth at them.

Cass scoffed. "Mom, it's obvious you and Ben have sparks."

"Sparks?" I said on a laugh, fanning myself with a paper menu.

"Please, they have lightning bolts," Mom said, and I focused a please-shut-up smile at her. "You do!" she continued. "You should see the two of you in the same room together."

"I think y'all had something way back when," Cassidy said, her voice all mysterious and her face taking on an expression like something was about to get juicy.

Holly ordered another round of beers, probably to change the subject, but it didn't work. Regardless, I was immensely grateful.

"No, no," I said, trying to make light. "Ben and I were just—best friends."

"Mm-hmm," Cassidy said, widening her eyes. "Josh is my best friend, too."

I opened my mouth to once again play the whole thing down, when I heard the beginning simple piano notes. And my skin lit on fire.

I CLOSED MY EYES AS THE CHORDS SUNK INTO MY SKIN.

"No, no, no," I said, "he didn't."

I felt Holly twist around to look. "He didn't," she agreed, leaning into me. "He's at the bar looking as beat up as you do—but he's coming. This song mean something?"

"Oh—probably—" *You picked me up from off the floor . . .*

I felt his hand on my shoulder at the same time his mouth was next to my opposite ear. "I think I owe you a dance."

Just the vibration against my ear was enough to render my knees useless. "It's—you don't have to—"

"Please don't shoot me down in front of everyone," he whispered again.

I let out a little nervous laugh that allowed me to take a few breaths and slid from my stool without making eye contact with any of my table mates. Least of all, Cassidy. I don't think I could have made it to the dance floor if I'd looked at her.

I was doing good just to walk with my hand in his, as he led me out there. I stared at it all the way till he picked a spot in the very center and turned to pull me to him, at which point I made it to his face. And that was my downfall.

The lights were knocked down to nearly nothing, and his face was inches from mine as he decided on the make-this-count route and zeroed out the space between us. I was so close that I could feel his breathing get faster, and his eyes even in the dark let down every wall. In that instant, there was no unexplained anger, no arrogance, no distance. No words spoken, even. I thought we'd try to ease the awkwardness with dumb conversation, but suddenly there was nothing necessary to say. At that moment, we were who we used to be. As he pressed my hand against his chest and moved his other hand up to the base of my neck, we moved together as one and there was no bad history or tension or sadness.

The music, the words talking about meeting your soul mate, that person that becomes your best friend, your lover, the one you want and need and love—it sank into me like lead. I felt the weight of it as his eyes wouldn't blink. As he held me tighter and his face got closer, until finally both arms were around me, one up in my hair, and I buried my face in his neck and hugged him to me as tightly as I could. It was the music and the dark, I decided. It was like being outside at night, where we knew how to be. We knew that world. The need I felt for him was overwhelming, and I was aware of the trembling that I assumed was from me but we were so intertwined it was hard to tell. I knew the song was coming to an end, and somewhere in the back recesses of my mind I knew reality was about to descend and other people that I couldn't recall names of at that moment were about to reenter my life. But right then, I would have given just about anything for that song to go on long loop and play over and over again.

If ever a man had it all, it would have to be me. Because ooooh . . . I love you . . .

It was over. Another song started to play, and it was another slow song, but it was as if we both knew we only had the one. Or was it just me? Had I imagined his response, his reactions? Had it been just a dance for him? I kept my eyes closed as I loosened my hold, and I felt his hands move slowly from my back up to cradle my face. That's when I realized he was shaking, too. It wasn't just me. *It wasn't just me.* His lips were warm and soft on my forehead for one lingering second, and then I opened my eyes and looked up into his—and my chest felt like a bear sat on it.

His face looked so torn between sad and happy, frustrated and content. In the dark, I could still see the emotion in his eyes that looked like I felt.

"Thank you for the dance," he said, his voice hoarse.

I couldn't say anything. He backed away and then turned to head to the bar, where a steaming bag of something awaited him. I felt a familiar ache as I watched him pick it up and walk away, nodding to the women at my table on his way out. I felt numb, like he'd taken everything I had with him. Again.

That's what it was, I realized. It was the same empty, sick, horrible feeling I had after we'd made love all night and then he'd left me. Something I never wanted to feel again. My God, I was twenty-one all over again.

"Are you okay?" asked a girl dancing next to me.

"I'm good," I said, nodding. "Shit," I muttered, scooping back my hair and forcing my feet to move. "Get it together, Emily." I swiped under my eyes as I left the dance floor, where fifty other people were locked together oblivious of me. Unfortunately, my table was not. They were all staring at me as if I'd rolled out of a spaceship.

I grabbed my purse with an annoyingly shaky hand. "I'm gonna—go to the ladies' room," I said without meeting anyone's eyes. "Back in a minute."

"Mom?" Cassidy said, her voice thick with concern.

"Yeah, baby," I said, flashing her a quick smile. "I'm okay, just need to freshen up a little."

"Em," Holly said, her voice low.

I met her eyes for just a second and squeezed her arm as I walked around her. "It's okay."

I held my head up as I made it across the room, passed the bathroom, and went straight out the back door to the patio no one was interested in because of the muggy cold. The chill hit me like a wall, making me suck in the air. I needed it. I needed to freeze everything up. To ice down everything that boiled inside, and numb the hurt that was clamping down on my heart.

Being wrapped up in him again was too much. Too good. Too much reminder of what he left me with and why I couldn't trust him not to do it again. I rounded a corner of the wall and leaned my back against it, breathing in the cold air fast to stop the burn from coming back up.

But it wasn't to be stopped. Everything stung on its way out. My skin felt hot, my eyes burned, my stomach threatened to upheave the nachos. My chest felt as if it would cave in from the lack of oxygen, as my sobs took over and beat the crap out of me. I slid down the rough brick wall till I was half sitting, half squatting on the ground.

Why the hell did he have to come back? If he didn't want me then, fine. So why was he back now, acting as if he did? Holding me like that. Looking at me like that. Stirring up old shit.

"Emily!"

I jumped half out of my skin at the sound of my mother's voice, and I scrambled unsuccessfully to get to my feet.

"Jesus, just—stay where you are, I'll come to you," she said, slowly getting to the ground. "Just takes me a minute."

"I—just needed some air, Mom, I'm—"

"Oh, yeah, I can see you're the picture of wonderful," she said. "Everyone has meltdowns behind buildings when things are going well."

"I know," I croaked. "I must look like a lunatic."

"Luckily I speak the language." My mom took one of my hands. "You're in love with that man."

New tears. New burn. "Well, that made me feel better, thanks." The hiccupping sobs returned. It was all kinds of fabulous that other people could see what I was killing myself to keep hidden. Of course, the latest floorshow probably hadn't left much to the imagination. We danced like people in love.

"Damn him," I hissed.

"Because he's Cassidy's father?"

I gasped so hard and deeply it hurt my throat. I wanted to deny it. I wanted to yell and be indignant and say how crazy and out of line that question was. But it was my mom, and no theatrics I could produce would fool her. She'd seen it all. So I let the rest of the burn come, the trembling, snot-filled, body-wracking sobs. I cried till I had nothing left.

"When did you know?" I asked finally.

"Tonight."

"Just now?"

She shook her head. "At the table, when Bernie mentioned the resemblance, your face went ten shades of gray. I remember Ben Landry back then. Further back, even. He's the one that used to meet you up on the roof at night when you were kids."

My jaw dropped. "You knew that?"

"I also knew about his daddy, honey. So I figured you being his friend was a good thing. And if our roof got him away from that son of a bitch, then so be it." She shrugged. "I poked my head out now and then, saw y'all eating chips and listening to music. Didn't think I had anything to worry about?" she said at the end with eyebrows raised.

I pictured some of the later nights spent drinking beer and smoking joints, sneaking up and down that tree to swim at the river, prom night in my underwear, and *the* night in question. I was really glad she didn't poke her head out those times.

I shook my head. "It happened after Kevin and I broke up that last time. We realized we had something—had always had something." I lifted my shoulders and let them drop. "Then he disappeared. I got pregnant, was depressed, Kevin was persistent—"

"Oh—oh, lordy, Emily," she said, squeezing my hand. "I remember you being so mopey and despondent. I thought it was over Kevin. Then when you turned up pregnant and he stood up for you—I thought you got what you wanted. Why didn't you tell me?"

I closed my eyes. "Mom, I wasn't sure. It could have been Kevin's, too. We'd only been broke up a couple of weeks. I think I knew in my heart, but I didn't *really* know till she was born."

Her eyes narrowed. "And where did Ben go?"

"I don't know. Never saw him again until he showed up at your front door the other day."

She grimaced. "Oh, honey," she said, letting a little chuckle loose. "I'm so sorry. Dear lord, no wonder you acted so crazy." Her eyes widened. "Does he know about Cass?"

"No."

She sat back and crossed her arms, wheels turning. "Oh, God, Kevin wears me the hell out, but he does love that girl."

My eyes teared up again. "I know. Which is why I keep avoiding everything. Old history with Ben, new history with Ben, anything that puts him and Cassidy together. Mom, I don't know what to do anymore. He left me. He didn't know there was a baby, but he left me and I made a life for us."

"I know, baby."

"I can't rip her life up just because he came back."

"No, but you don't have to rip yours up, either," she said, patting my hand. "You deserve a second chance."

"Nana?"

"Oh, shit," I said, pushing to my feet and hauling Mom up with me. I wiped at my face and scrubbed my hair out with my fingers.

Cassidy came around the corner with Holly and Bernie. "What the hell are you doing? And, Mom, what is—oh my God, what is the matter? You look horrible!"

"Wow, baby girl, thanks," I said, attempting a laugh.

"Why are y'all outside in the dark?" she asked, her forehead creased in concern. "We started thinking y'all got mugged in the bathroom, then there was no one in the bathroom, and the bartender said he saw somebody go out back."

"I tried to tell them it was no big deal," Holly offered.

Mom glanced at Holly and then back to me, I guess figuring out that Holly was in on the crazies. "Well, it wasn't," she said. "Cass, your mom and I were just having a little mother-daughter time, and she's on her period so she got a little—"

"Really?" I said.

"Oh, honeybugs, I understand that hormonal stuff all too well," Aunt Bernie said. "I used to cry the paint off the walls."

"Okay, let's go in," I said, not wanting any more of Aunt Bernie's menstrual stories.

"You're upset about Ben, aren't you?" Cass said, grabbing my hand. "Mom, come on, I mean it was pretty clear he loves you."

My throat closed up. "Let's go in," I croaked.

"You might want to go find that bathroom, now," Mom said, wiping at my face.

"Yeah," I said.

As we went in and they headed to the table, I hugged her around the neck before I veered off to the ladies' room.

"I'm sorry, Mom," I whispered.

I felt her chuckle. "Nothing to be sorry about, baby girl." She backed up and looked me in the eye, and I could see the girl, the young woman she was in my flashbacks. "It's okay, honey," she said quietly. "We've got this."

CHAPTER

14

I was in a pickle, as my dad used to say. Holly would call it a conundrum. My mom would say I was in a bucket of shit. I leaned toward her version.

I was falling in love with him again. Just saying that in my head was enough to make me nuts. I couldn't love him. I couldn't put Cassidy in that place of too much contact, and I couldn't put myself in the spot of trusting him again. The last time I let myself love him, he told me he'd be back and didn't show till my mother hired him to work on her house. He said I'd had other plans. No. I didn't leave my house for two days, waiting for him. I had no other plans. He was my plan.

I sat in my car, looking at Mom's house, wanting to just go back home. I'd stayed home the day after the girls' night, gone in to the office the day after that to attend my required meeting, and there it was, another day, and I couldn't get out of my car.

Ben's truck was there. Mom's car was there. Big Blue, of

course, was there. I didn't want to see him, not then and not ever. I knew, at that point, that it could never be normal with us. If we shared oxygen somewhere, we were destined to draw together like magnets.

And I was quite done with the spanking my mother's house was giving me. I felt twitchy just thinking of the walk in. I didn't want it anymore. I thought the early stuff was cool, but I really didn't see why it needed to show me what I'd already lived. I thought of asking Holly or Cass to get the remaining things from my room, but how would I justify that? And there were the general things still in the hallway closets and the attic. And the kitchen. And the garage.

I made a mental note to never move.

"Grow up, chickenshit," I said, swinging my car door open. "Let's go deal with this."

And deal with it, I did. Opened the front door, making the knocker bounce once, and stood face-to-face with Ben.

"Hey," I said, taking one step back. Then forward again. I refused to show weakness.

"Hey," he said back, and then gestured at the door with another paintbrush. "I'm painting in here today. Guess I should lock the door."

"Oh—yeah, that'd probably be good." I thumped my own forehead on my way up the stairs. "Really, Emily?"

I didn't even stop to see where Mom was or if she needed any help. I wanted to get my stuff done and go. I had crap in my own house that needed cleaning out and none of it needed to tell me anything.

I hesitated outside my old room, my hands on the facing. I did not want to cartwheel backward into space. Pretty much, there

wasn't anything I dreaded more at that minute, and so just the
thought of stepping foot in there and hurtling back to watch
myself wait for him in misery gave me a headache.

I put a toe in and followed gingerly behind it. "Crap, crap,
crap," I muttered, looking around. Still some boxes in the closet,
and I needed to strip the bed and check the dresser and night-
stand drawers. And probably get that furniture out of there, as
well. Which would require help. Another day. Ugh.

I went straight to the closet and began pulling the few boxes
out, stacking them in the hallway. The way I looked at it, if I
could get everything into the hall, then that was less opportunity
for time travel. Nothing worthwhile that I could remember had
ever happened in the hallway.

I had made some headway, and was bent over in the bottom
drawer of my dresser, when I felt him. I stood and turned around.

"Enjoying the view?"

He made a crooked little smirk. "Actually, yeah."

"This isn't the entryway," I said, trying to look cute.

"Damn good thing you're around then," he countered.

I bit my lip as I smiled, intent on holding back the effect he
had on me. He had that no-blinking-sorta-cocky-almost-smile
thing going, and I felt my skin tingle.

"Yeah, I'm good for something," I said, and halfheartedly
pulled open a drawer full of someone's extra clothing. My mom
must have used it for storage. I met his eyes again. "What's up?"

He walked through the room to the window, the window I
refused to go near, and pulled a blind slat up to look outside.
"You got to me the other night," he said softly.

And not expecting that, my knees went dead. I gripped the
dresser so I didn't crumble like a stack of cards.

"That song," he continued, turning to face me, letting the slat go. "The song, the dark—"

"Yeah—I know what you mean," I said, shifting my feet like an eleven-year-old boy. "It's like that's our element or something."

"And it makes me crazy." He looked at the window. "One second, we're one way, and the next second we're at each other's throats." He turned back to me. "I don't even trust my own instincts with you anymore."

I laughed. "Which are?"

"Most of the time? To kiss you for days."

I swallowed hard. "And the rest?"

"To run the other way."

I raised my eyebrows. "Well, you're good at that. I say go with your strengths."

There, I thought. Be cocky right back. Give him something that will piss him off and make him go away. He didn't go away. He blew out a breath and shook his head, instead. He paced the room and stared at me.

"You're a piece of work, Em."

"I'm a piece of work?" I walked slowly up to him, so close he had to back up a step. "That's rich coming from you."

"Me?" he said. "You're all over the damn place."

"Because I don't trust you," I said—not really intending to say it out loud until the words fell out of my mouth. "And I don't trust myself around you."

"Ditto," he said, his voice thick, his eyes hard.

I narrowed mine to study him, closing the inches between us. "What the hell, Ben? We dance like lovers. You can't catch a breath when I get close to you."

He touched my face. "And you tremble when I touch you," he

said through his teeth, winding both hands into my hair and causing me to forget my words. "And then bolt."

"Because you act so angry," I said, feeling the pull of his mouth just centimeters away. "And then you look at me—"

"Like you look at me," he finished. "And that's why I have every right to be angry."

"For what?" I said. "For saying things you didn't mean? For leaving town? Leaving your family? Leaving *me*?" I said, feeling the hot tears surface. "What the hell do you have to be angry about?"

Even at the close proximity where I could feel his breath on my lips, I could see the confusion in his eyes. "Leaving you. I'm so sick of hearing that." He let go of me and backed away, making all my nerve endings reach out. I needed to feel him close again. I followed him, but he stepped back again, putting two fingertips against my chest as he tilted his head a little. "You left me."

That stopped me. "What?"

"You heard me," he said, his voice barely audible.

I shook my head, a scoff coming out of my mouth. "I left you," I repeated. "How do you figure that, Ben? I was here." I pointed a finger at the floor. "Right here, in this room. You were gone. Basic math."

"You were here," he said, his eyes darkening as he stepped toward me again. His face showed something other than anger, however. Even in just seconds, I recognized pain. Hurt. Betrayal. The way his eyes used to look after his father would go at him. "But you weren't alone. *Basic math.*"

I blinked, running back through the memories as best I could, trying to match up what he was talking about. "What—I don't underst—"

"I loved you," he said, the words formed slow and emphatic. "I put everything I had out there on that roof. I gave you— everything."

I felt tears spill down my cheeks. "So did I," I whispered.

"And then you chose Kevin."

"What?" I backed up that time. "I did—what?"

"After every low-life thing he did to you, you still—"

"No," I said, holding up a hand. "What the hell are you—"

My words, my thoughts, my breath—were interrupted by the ringing, the pull, the darkness tugging at me. "Oh, shit, not now," I said, groping for his arm.

"Of course it's now," I heard him say, like it was from far away. I could sense the sarcasm even as I was leaving.

"Don't leave," I said weakly as my chest constricted. "Please don't—"

But it was too late. I was gone.

❧

I was standing there in the middle of the room, watching me stand there in the middle of the room. My face was so happy—the one on other-me. She glowed. She was in love. I wanted to yell at her to let it go. That it was all a pipe dream. That's what he'd called it. A pipe dream.

I knew what day it was. I knew from her funky natural-dried, river-water hair and the crumpled up party dress in the corner. From the sun in the window and the lighting, it was early morning. Ben had just left. Forever. Or it may as well have been.

She went to the still-open window, I knew to relive it for a moment. I remembered sitting there and closing my eyes and remembering every single decadent detail. I couldn't wait to do it again. To look in those eyes and feel it all again. I remembered feeling on top of the world, like I couldn't believe how lucky we were to finally admit what had lurked under the surface all those years. To finally put it out there. He'd promised he'd be back later in the day. And I knew she'd sit there, happy in her moment, assuming that was true, until she found out it wasn't.

There was a soft knock on the door.

"Emily?"

She turned around, blinking to pull out of her basking reverie. "Yeah, Mom?"

The door opened, and a not-quite-gray-yet version of my mother walked in. Her hair was still strawberry blonde, but fading to something a little less vibrant. The slim and trim figure of her youth was starting to go a little soft.

I looked down at myself, realizing she was my age. I hadn't gone there just yet, thank goodness. At least not noticeably. I wouldn't be sporting a bikini ever again, but in clothes I still did okay.

"Hey," she said, perching on the bed. "You just gonna live out of boxes, huh?"

She pointed to the boxes stacked precariously against the closet, two on the floor left gaping open. I remembered that feeling, of not wanting to make it permanent. Losing my apartment to Kevin and dropping out of community college to work full time had been bad enough.

"Quite possibly. It's temporary. But I'm grateful," she added quickly.

Mom nodded with a chuckle. "How was the big birthday night?"

A slow smile spread on other-me's face, but she subdued it before it could get too crazy. "Maybe the best birthday ever."

"Really?" Mom said. "Better than the Silly String birthday."

"I'd have to say it bumped it down a notch."

"I'm glad," Mom said, getting up to pat her arm. She touched her matted hair and then pointed to the dress in the corner. "Do I want to know?"

Other-me laughed. "Probably not."

I heard the door knocker downstairs, and Mom headed for the bedroom door. "There's sausage and pancakes if you're hungry."

"Okay, I'll be down."

Other-me grabbed the damp dress off the floor and headed downstairs. I was alone in the room, but I knew it wouldn't be long before the person at the door would be up there filling up space with hot air. I closed my eyes and waited, praying that this flashback wasn't going to include the next day and a half of misery.

I didn't have to wait long, but not in the way I expected. A sound at the window caught my attention, and when I opened my eyes I drew a quick breath.

Ben was there.

"Em?" he called softly. A mischievous smile played at his lips as he poked his head in. "You in here?"

"Oh my God," I said. "What the hell—"

He looped a leg through the window, laughing. "This is crazy," he said to himself. "I need to start using the door."

He was halfway in when voices drifted up the stairs, getting progressively louder. He stopped as we both realized they weren't nice voices.

"Oh, no," I said, tears filling my eyes as little puzzle pieces started to fall into place. "No, no, no, Ben, you didn't—"

The sound of other-me's angry words stopped for a moment, and then continued toward us, and Ben ducked back out of the window just as she barged in. Followed by Kevin.

"Emily, come on," he was saying. "You always forgive me."

Kevin looked so young, so baby-faced. I would have been more in awe of that, more shocked by seeing how much he'd aged, if I weren't horribly drawn to that window. From my angle, I could just see his face, but she couldn't. I wanted to yell and jump up and down and tell her he was out there.

"Exactly," she said, whirling on him. "Key word there is always. As in over and over and fucking over. I'm done."

"Don't say that, baby."

She held up a hand and looked away. "Don't call me baby."

"Em, please," he said, leaning into her line of vision. "Just—just listen, okay?"

She glared at him. "You have thirty seconds."

He sat on the bed, looking miserable. "I don't know why I do the things I do," he said, sounding so much like the Kevin that had come to my house the other night. "I don't want to. I love you, Em, and I keep messing it up." He looked up at her with tear-filled eyes, looking remorseful and beautiful. "It's always been you and me, Emily. I'm nothing without you. Please." He stood up and reached for her but she pushed his hands away.

"Don't," she said.

But he was persistent, and he took her hands. "Please," he repeated. "I'm begging you. I swear to you that I'll change. I will love you forever." Sadly, I knew he meant every word. But he'd never, ever, be able to live up to his intentions.

"Kevin—"

"Baby, please," he whispered, taking her face in his hands and leaning his forehead to hers. "I'm sorry."

"No," I choked out, watching Ben's face in the window. I head-jerked from the couple in front of me to where he sat just out of their *sight. As Kevin kissed her, the tears fell down my cheeks, hot and scalding. "No, Emily!" I yelled. "Pull back! Ben's right there!"*

Ben's face went cold. I recognized it. It was the one he had every time we got near this subject. The same glazed-over shell of pain that he'd get every time his father beat the shit out of him.

That damn kiss went on too long. I yelled at them to hurry and get back to the fighting, but I knew better. I knew I wasn't changing history. And as I pleaded with other-me to no avail, I watched Ben leave.

You weren't alone. You chose Kevin.

"No!" I wailed, falling to my knees. It was my fault, all along. He didn't stay long enough to see—

"Stop that!" she said—finally, but too late. She pushed him back and wiped her face. "You don't get to do that anymore."

Kevin was crying. "Please don't say that, Em. I know you still love me."

"I did," she said. "But you killed that. A little bit each time, till now there's nothing left." She hugged her arms around herself and walked to the window—to the window! Fifteen seconds too late, she walked to the fucking window. "Please leave, Kevin. We're done."

"I don't believe that."

"You never do," she said, her voice a monotone. "Now, I don't care."

"Emily—"

"Bye."

After several moments of head-hanging and tear-wiping, he trudged out. Other-me sat on the window seat with a huge sigh, her face in her hands. When she lifted it, she let the smile return and gazed out the window, remembering again.

"He's—not coming back, you stupid girl," I spat. "You let that idiot in for too damn long, and Ben—" My stomach burned as I said

his name. I couldn't believe it had all come down to that one moronic moment. Twenty years of separation because he reacted too fast and I didn't react fast enough. "Oh my God."

He mercifully answered, because the blackness and the ringing and the noise and the tightness descended on me all at once, sucking me back with an attitude.

❦

I was alone.

I blinked around at the room that had been my haven as a child, had been my gateway to freedom, and now was the portal to a memory I could never fix. Tears streamed down my face, sobs stuck in my throat as I struggled for normal breathing. I sank to the floor as my knees gave way.

"Okay, that's it," I said, hiccupping. "I've had enough." I grabbed the comforter off the bed nearby and yanked, sending pillows flailing in all directions. I pulled it to me and leaned my head on the floor, pulling the soft cloth around me. "I can't do this anymore, God. Please be done."

I thought of my life and what I'd done with it after Ben left. Marrying Kevin, having Cassidy, working as a receptionist till I could afford night classes for real estate. Driving to dance recitals and softball games and divorcing Kevin. Nothing special. Certainly no African adventures or Egyptian archaeological digs. But a life that gave me Cassidy.

If Ben would have stayed, the only thing that would have changed was the man. My heart hurt at the thought of that. I could have lived my life with that man. Been a family that I didn't have to lie about. How different would we have been? How different would Cassidy have been? How stupid were we?

I got to my feet and wiped my face, then snuck down the hall to the bathroom, not sure where Ben was. I did quick repair and then went looking. He wasn't in the entryway, and his paint supplies were propped on a workhorse over some plastic sheeting. I peeked out the door, careful not to disturb the knocker in case it alerted Mom.

His truck was gone. That was okay, I knew where he lived.

CHAPTER

15

Ben's house being only a few blocks away didn't leave me much practice time. There is an argument to be made that I didn't have to leave right away, either, but once I knew he was gone I couldn't get in my car fast enough.

As I pulled into his driveway, I winced at the crunching gravel under the tires, knowing I'd just knocked down my thinking time by half. I had no idea what to say. *I didn't choose Kevin, you stupid moron,* probably wasn't the best way to start.

I walked slowly, knowing he already knew I was there. I wasn't even sure why, other than the need to set the record straight. He needed to know. Or maybe I just needed to say it. Still, he didn't swing the door open ahead of time, he didn't stand there waiting for me. Maybe he was going to make me sweat it. Or maybe he didn't care anymore.

I shouldn't have cared, either. The one thing I was doing with absolute certainty—hunting him down to rehash history—was the one thing I knew better than to do. And yet, there I was on his doorstep. Not knocking, just standing. Wishing for a bench or somewhere to sit and sort out my words. I swiped fingers under my eyes and glanced back toward my car, giving myself one last chance to bail, but then the door finally opened.

I swung around, greeted by a very closed-off face and crossed arms.

"Hey."

"What do you want, Em?" he said, his voice low and weary. "We've already done this."

I shook my head. "Not this, we haven't."

He sighed like I'd just signed him up for the draft and rubbed his eyes. "What now? Where did you go?"

"The morning after."

"Fantastic."

"Ben," I said, stepping forward. "You were there."

"I'm aware of that."

I held my hands up. "Well, I wasn't. But this time I saw you."

He turned around to walk back in. "What difference does it make?" He motioned with his hand. "Come in if you need to ramble, otherwise, I'm watching a movie."

"A—movie?" I asked, taking tentative steps forward to follow him.

"I decided I'm taking the day off," he said, landing on his couch. The television screen was paused in an unfortunate facial pose for some man about to lose an eye.

I allowed myself a slow, steadying breath in and out while he fiddled with the remote. I looked from the screen to the picture on the mantel. The charcoal one I knew instinctively he'd done himself, of the river and the dock. A memory he pulled right out of his head and put on paper forever. He hit play and let the guy have his eye gouged out before turning back to where I stood standing behind the couch. Resignedly, he paused it again.

"What?"

I studied his face, the way his jaw worked when he was irritated. Something I managed to see a lot of.

"You left too early."

His eyebrows knitted over his nose. "I told you, I decided to take the day off. I told your mom."

I shook my head before he ever finished. "Not today. *That* day."

If a look could be a groan, he had it. "Emily, I already told you I wasn't going there with you."

I walked around to stand in front of where he was sprawled across his couch, legs and arms spread over pillows. I knelt so that we were more eye level.

"You left too damn early," I repeated.

"I saw enough."

"You bailed without having any faith in me."

His eyes flashed. "Okay, damn it, you insist on the play-by-play?" He swung his legs down so that I had to scoot back. "I came back to surprise you. To be spontaneous. To tell you I suddenly couldn't stand to be away from you."

I breathed faster, trying to keep anything from showing.

"But you weren't alone," he said.

"No, I wasn't," I agreed. "I was fighting with Kevin."

"Not for long," he said, his voice monotone. "I may not remember a conversation from last month but I remember that day vividly."

"And if you'd stayed fifteen seconds longer," I said, hearing the shake come into my voice, "we would have been talking about it *together* over the last two decades."

There was a pause, and his cocky anger fizzled slightly in his eyes as he tried to make sense of what I said. "What are you talking about?"

"I told him no, Ben."

"And accidentally married him anyway?" he said, the sarcasm coming back.

I closed my eyes and listened to the air coming in and out. "No," I whispered. "That was two months later." When I opened my eyes, hot tears spilled over. "I never knew you were there, Ben. I never knew you left. But I saw it today. You left the window right before I told him we were over and to leave, that I didn't love him anymore." I blinked more tears as they came. "And then I sat on that damn window seat all day, waiting for you, because you said you were coming. I slept on the roof that night. Waited again the next day, till I finally went to Bobby's and found out you were gone."

I saw the different stages roll past in his face. Denial, question, realization.

"I didn't choose him, Ben. I chose you," I whispered, not able to see him clearly anymore. "I—thought you—"

"You thought I changed my mind," he said, like he was thinking out loud. He sat back in the cushions and put his palms against his forehead. "Jesus."

I rose slowly to my feet and wiped at my face, thinking I had to look like an alien after all the crying. "I just felt you should know."

His gaze followed me up. "So you ended up with him, why, then?"

I licked my lips and hoped he'd assume the Kevin angle. "I ended up pregnant," I said quickly, averting my eyes. "He insisted on making it legal and I was too scared and clueless to do otherwise."

"Well, then it turned out as it should have," he said, bringing my attention back to him.

"What?"

"You had a kid together, Em," he said, still sunk back against the dark chocolate leather. "What we had wasn't important." He flipped a hand sideways. "We both moved on."

Acid pushed an ugly laugh up my throat. "Wasn't important? We moved on?" I gestured behind me. "Is that why you drew a picture of our dock to keep in your house? You could add one of the roof and have our whole history."

He moved his line of vision past me to the picture, and his flippant air went somewhere else.

I walked away, not feeling my steps, not feeling my feet, not feeling the air around me. I walked out the door and left it open, not stopping until I was inside my car. I never looked behind me once I got the car moving down the street. I never checked to see if he watched me leave.

I STARED SIDEWAYS AT CASSIDY'S GIANT COLLAGE FOR AN HOUR from my spot on my pillow on my couch. At the pictures of her and Kevin at different events, at various ages. I closed my eyes. He would have never had that opportunity to be her father if Ben would have stayed, but Ben never had the chance at all.

My eyes felt so puffy and worn out, I just wanted to sleep. I wanted it to take me deep down where the fingers of sleep grab you. I'd changed into pajamas the moment I walked in the door, deciding I needed a break from everything. From Ben, from that house, from my job—although to be honest, I'd kind of already been doing that. From my family, from my life. I thought about watching TV, but I ended up lying there with the remote in my hand, never turning it on. I wanted to pass out and not dream, just sleep, so I clamped my eyes shut tight and tried to force it, but the ringing of my doorbell made me give up.

"Ugh!" I moaned out load, wondering why other people were home in the middle of the day like me. Didn't other people have real jobs with real hours? I lay there for a minute, under the premise of maybe-they-would-go-away, but then the bell rang again.

Rolling out from under my favorite quilt, I went from knees to feet and trudged to the door, feeling twice my age and never giving any thought to who it might be. Honestly, with my luck lately, I figured it would be Kevin again.

I unlocked the latch and opened it without looking out the window, and then stood there wishing for sexier pajamas when it was Ben.

"Hey," I said.

I felt every nuance of the word as I forced my tongue around it. Because he wasn't just standing there. He was standing there with one arm leaning on the house, looking like he might fall over if he didn't. His expression was hard and intense and raw, but worn out, as if he'd fought himself to come over. His eyes panned my red flannel pj's, and I held my chin up anyway.

"Were you asleep?"

Was I asleep. "I decided to take a day off, too," I said.

He nodded slightly but fixed his eyes on mine and didn't say anything. I gripped the door handle in my left hand and squeezed to help the anxiety.

Finally, his eyes closed, as if he were struggling with something. When he opened them, the look pierced right through me. "Em, I don't want to waste any more years," he said, the words barely making sound.

All the air went out of me, and tears instantly filled my eyes. Again. Damn it. *Shut the door*, my brain said. *Close it, and walk away. Don't listen. Don't say a word.*

I didn't. I didn't say anything, I just walked into his arms and wrapped mine around him, inside his old blue jean jacket. It was warm and familiar, oddly enough, and as I buried my face in his chest, I felt him take a long, deep breath. He pulled me tight against him, lowering his face to my hair and whispering my name.

I felt the kisses in my hair, soft and moving toward my face as his hand wound into my hair and held my head. All the reasons not to be there were waving in the back of my mind, but it felt so right, so normal to be in his arms like that. We fit into each other perfectly, and suddenly I couldn't let go. I wanted to stay wrapped up in him forever.

I hadn't opened my eyes. I was a little afraid to—afraid of what I'd see. Scared of seeing my own anxiety reflected in his eyes. Of seeing the raw everything that we were, exposed again. But as he trailed his lips down my forehead to my nose, and pulled back to look at me, I had to look.

And the tears in his eyes did me in. I broke.

"Ben," I whispered, brushing his lips with mine.

Both of his hands cradled my head as he kissed me back. Teasing my lips once, twice, three times. On the fourth, I pulled him against me and he made a rumbling sound deep in his chest as he deepened his kiss and claimed my mouth.

I felt that kiss in the soles of my feet.

His kisses make your clothes melt off. Oh, I had the feeling they were about to. It was so slow and delicious, like he was tasting everything, memorizing my mouth. I didn't know about my clothes, but the rest of me melted into him. When we finally came up for air, breathing like we'd just run a marathon, his hands shook. He traced my cheek, my lips, but his eyes never left mine.

"Probably—should come inside," I managed, vaguely aware that we were on my porch.

He picked me up off my bare feet and walked into the house, with my arms around his neck and my fingers in his hair. He kicked the door closed and let me down slowly, letting me slide down his body. That was it.

I was on fire for him. I pulled his face down with me and kissed him with all the passion I had burning inside me. Everything that had lain dormant for the past twenty years came raging to the surface. Ben responded the same, diving deep and aggressive. When he pulled his mouth away, he trailed down my jawline, down the side of my neck, moving my hair aside to taste the skin toward the bottom. I moaned at the sensations his tongue sent sparking through my body, and I twisted my fingers in his hair.

"Mmmm, Ben—"

He unbuttoned one button at a time, following each opening with his mouth until he was kissing between my breasts. Then I was off my feet and wrapped around him, his hands holding my ass. I could feel him hard against me, and I locked my legs around him tighter. I was out of my mind with desire for the man who'd made me crazy with love the first time.

He made a growling noise deep in his throat and turned and pinned me against the wall, pushing hard between my legs and making me gasp and wrap my legs tighter. "Where's your bedroom, Em?" he said, his voice ragged.

I pointed, and he walked there, carrying me until he laid me on the bed and came with me, pressing his body against mine as his mouth ravaged mine and his hands went on the move.

Mine did, too. Gone were the jacket, the flannel shirt, the T-shirt. I made easy discard of them, wanting skin against skin as he freed my top, peeled off my pj pants in one movement, and came back up slowly, kissing his way up my thighs.

"Oh, God, Ben," I moaned, arching my back as he lingered torturously before working his way back up past my belly to my breasts, which he then made love to with his mouth till I was nearly begging.

He traveled back up to my face and kissed me, soft and then hard, soft and then hard, over and over till I rolled him over and worked a rhythm against him. He moaned my name and grabbed my ass as he moved with me, his eyes heavy and full of heat. It was erotic and primal and nearly put me over the edge, but I wanted the full show. I kissed down his chest, to his stomach, unzipping his jeans as I moved lower. He grabbed my head and made a sound of ecstasy as I licked my way down till he was free of restraint and in my mouth. He was huge and ready, but I teased him with more, dragging a nipple along the length of him as I crawled back up slowly and rubbed him against me until we were both shaking with need.

"Em—"

"I want you so bad," I breathed, sliding down over him and catching my breath as all my muscles went taut. "Oh my Go—"

He made a long moan and dug his fingers into my hips, moving me how he needed me to move. I was done for. It had been far too long since a man made me feel like that, and all I could do was hold on to him and hope I didn't pass out from lack of oxygen. I was going over the edge as he shoved up deeper. I was going—

"Ohhh!" I couldn't breathe. I couldn't think. He pumped harder and all I could do was cry out in some crazy voice, as I heard him build up a roar of what sounded like pain if I hadn't been watching his face.

My name never sounded so good as it did being forced through his clenched teeth in the throes of orgasm. Again. And again.

I fell onto his chest as we both heaved in air and waited for the blood to return to our heads. And just when I thought I couldn't be surprised anymore, he grabbed me tight and flipped us over so that he was on top, smiling down at me.

"Wow," I breathed.

"Impressed?"

"Kinda. Especially since you're not even breathing hard anymore," I said, huffing.

He chuckled and moved the hair out of my face. "Well, I guess I recover quickly."

"I'm a little out of practice, sorry."

"Oh," he said, shaking his head. "If that's out of practice, you're doing just fine."

I smiled and closed my eyes, still in my basking place. "That was—"

"Amazing," he finished for me, as he kissed my nose, my cheeks, and found his way to my lips again. "Hot, sexy—"

"Mmm, oh, yeah," I agreed.

"Better than the roof?"

I chuckled. "I don't know; that had its own special touch."

"I don't think my bones could handle that now," he said.

I moved my hands along his shoulders, up to his face. "I think your bones do just fine."

His fingers were in my hair, playing with the strands, and his eyes were playful. "Well, now that the crazy monkey sex is out of the way, we'll see how well they hold up."

"Oh?"

"Oh, yes, ma'am," he said, dropping a kiss on my lips. "See, I'm taking a little break, here."

"Uh-huh."

Another kiss. "And then I'm going to make love to you very slowly."

"Mmm, sounds good."

Another kiss. "And then I'm gonna take a little longer break."

I giggled. "Mm-hmm."

"And then that one's on you."

"Really?"

"Yep, your choice."

I kissed along his jawline. "And if it's on the swing in my backyard?"

He looked down between us. "I think I just got hard again." We both laughed, and his eyes were warm. "I don't care how we do it, I just want to see your face."

Something in that simple sentence froze me, brought me back to reality, and he must have sensed it because he leaned back to look at me. I know he saw it in my eyes, the fear behind the desire.

"What?"

I shook my head. "Nothing."

"No, there was something. The whole room changed temperature." He caressed my cheek with his thumb. "Talk to me. What did I say?"

I looked in his eyes. "The—seeing my face thing. It's stupid, I know, but it brought me back. You said that then—"

Realization dawned. "Emily, let me tell you something." He moved off me and lay to my side, on one elbow. "I made a mistake back then. One that cost us." He closed his eyes for a second like he physically felt the pain. "When I leave here today, I *will* be back. And the time after that. And the time after that."

A sinking feeling joined the celebrating one in my gut. Cassidy.

"For whatever reason, we've been given a second chance," he said, pulling me up close to him. "I'm not blowing it."

We can't have a second chance, my brain screamed. But everything else was making a much louder noise. My heart pounded in my ears. "I love you." I froze as I said it, surprised that it fell out of my mouth like that.

His eyes misted a little, and that got me even more. "I've always loved you, Em."

BEN DIDN'T LEAVE THAT DAY AT ALL. OR THAT NIGHT. EVERY-thing was an opportunity. Making something to eat created a new perspective on my kitchen counter. Watching TV on the couch gave it new love. Showering—well, let's just say we took a few. We never did make it to my swing, but I figured there was time for that.

I watched him sleep, as I woke up and couldn't get enough of seeing him lying next to me. I wanted to take a picture to keep with me, to prove I didn't imagine the phenomenal day and night we'd just experienced. To hold on to this image of the man who could still give me goose bumps just lying in my bed. I wanted to believe in what he kept saying about fate and second chances, but he didn't know what I knew. I just couldn't trust that it had staying power. Not with the giant wrecking ball looming over our heads.

What would happen if the truth were found out? Or *when*. Because life was never that simple and it shouldn't be. The truth would come out, sooner or later, if Ben and I remained together. And there really wasn't an *if* there, either. I was madly in love, again. I was everything I'd tried so hard not to be.

It was that damn house's fault. Because that was logical.

What would happen to Cassidy if she found out that the man she'd always called Dad—wasn't? They had their differences, but still, she loved him. Kevin adored her—it would crush him. And Ben—what would he say? How would he feel? I knew that answer and I pushed it away.

Ben stirred in his sleep, and I used the opportunity to curl up against his warmth. His body responded without ever waking up, a rumble of contentment in his chest as he pulled me to him, our bodies fitting each other perfectly.

THE NEXT TWO DAYS WERE A BLUR OF WORK AND SEX. I HAD showing after showing after closing after contract signing, which was a good thing after all the downtime. Every other waking moment—and the non-waking ones, too—were spent naked. Ben was insatiable, and I have to admit that my sex drive had skyrocketed. I remembered hearing about the mighty Ben Landry's sexual prowess when we were young, how he spoiled women for any other men. I was definitely spoiled.

But it was more than that. I knew the sex would calm down with time. I had my best friend back. The one I could talk to without reservation and listen to his voice forever. That was the good stuff.

I pulled up to Mom's house late one afternoon, just as the sun was disappearing behind the trees and the sky looked sleepy. I'd spent an entire day dragging one particularly picky couple all over the county to find the perfect window lighting. Of course, the lighting changed throughout the day, so what they nixed in the morning was the one they loved in the afternoon. I joked that they could just sleep in every day, but I don't know that they were normal enough to find that funny.

I parked behind Ben's truck, feeling the giddy tingle in my stomach at the thought of him in there. Holly drove up just as I got out.

"Where've you been?" she asked, lugging some foldable boxes out of her backseat.

"Working." I held up the bag of fast-food remains I'd chowed in the car. "And eating."

"That stuff is so bad for you," she said.

"So is starving," I said defensively. "It was necessary. It was a long day."

She got a wicked grin on her face, kind of foreign for Holly. "Mm-hmm, I bet."

I looked at her funny as I took some of the load off her and we walked up to the porch. "What?"

"I saw Ben's truck at your house last night," she said, all sing-song-y.

Everything went hot from my shoulders up. I wasn't quite ready to share it yet, but clearly it was going to be shared anyway. And just as I was about to make it sound all talky-talky and non-committal, Ben opened the front door.

"Saw you coming," he said, holding it open wide for us to maneuver her boxes in.

The look that passed between us did not go unnoticed by Holly. And I couldn't deny it, either. There was nothing noncommittal about what I wanted to do with him right there in the entryway. And it wasn't even just a sexual thing. I saw the whole package from our whole lives when I looked in his eyes, and it had little to do with the way my skin tingled thinking about the night before.

He closed the door and went back to his work, but my smile couldn't be pulled back.

"Oh my goodness," she said, leaning the boxes against a wall. "You got laid."

"Shhh," I said, my head on a swivel, although a giggle came up like I was fourteen.

Holly laughed, too, and shoved at me. "Mom's outside with Aunt Bernie, picking up sticks."

"Why?"

Holly did a weary shrug. "You know Mom and her leaf and stick fetish." She lowered her voice. "So what changed this around?"

I put my hands over my face. "I don't know. Being weak, I guess."

"That dance the other night at The Grille—"

"Yeah, that—probably didn't help."

Holly laughed again. "So, what now? Are y'all, like, dating?"

I opened my mouth to answer and then realized I had no idea what to call it. "I think we kinda skipped that step."

Her eyes got wide. "It's that serious."

"It's—that serious."

We looked at each other, both realizing the implication of that, which took the levity down considerably.

"Does he know about Cassidy?" she asked, to which I shook my head. She bit her lip and nodded. "Okay then."

"I know," I said. "I don't sleep anymore, thinking about that. Mom knows, by the way."

"Oh, shit."

I held up a hand. "No, it was okay. When I had my little nervous breakdown that night—she guessed."

Tandy pushed through the doggie door flap and did her huff-and-puff routine at us before settling into her bed with a glare.

"You have no idea how sucky your life is about to get," I said to her.

"So what did she say?" Holly asked, bringing my attention back to her.

"Not much, really," I said. "She didn't get upset."

Holly snickered. "Well, at this point, Ben's got more brownie points than Kevin."

"True." I shook my head, chuckling in spite of myself. "That's horrible."

"Well," she said, taking in the empty living room and the just-enough-to-get-by kitchen. "Off to clean my room, well, as much as I can around Aunt Bernie's stuff."

And off the subject, per classic Holly.

I didn't know what I was there to do, actually. Maybe watch Ben work? No, that would be juvenile. My room was done, and I had no desire to go back to verify that. Not that there was anything else to beat me up with in there, but I wasn't taking the chance.

Truth was, I had gotten so accustomed to going to my mother's house almost every day that it seemed like the natural thing to do. If Aunt Bernie hadn't been there occupying her attention, she'd probably be eating it up.

I wasn't going to stalk Ben, so I headed up the stairs with the intention of seeing what needed doing in the attic. I passed my door without hesitation, and before I could get to the pull down, I noticed my dad's office door open slightly.

I went in and flicked the switch, flooding the lonely old room with light. The telescope had been put back in its place from where we'd moved it, and I flicked the switch back off to go peer out of it. It took some adjusting to find the right angles again, but the familiar places were there. Waving, as though they'd been waiting all along. The Big Dipper. Orion's Belt. I made a mental note to ask Mom once again if I could bring the telescope to my house rather than put it in a cold, dark storage building where no one would enjoy it. I didn't see her attaching it to Big Blue.

I turned on the lamp behind my dad's desk and saw that the other stuff was already gone. It struck me hard in the gut to see it that way. All the weird décor, the wooden duck, the tins, the calculator—all the stuff on his desk was gone. I felt a burn in my stomach as I pulled out the drawers and saw they were empty. The thumbtacks, even. I looked up at the poster, though, that was still on the wall and ran my hand over the dusty surface. I wondered when my mother had done this, and if she'd needed me. Or maybe it had been something she needed to do alone. Regardless, it was like a physical loss, not being able to come in there and feel his things. I'd always thought it was kind of silly, but now I realized how comforting it had been.

I sat in his chair, listening to the familiar squeak of the springs and the clicking noise as I swiveled a little to look at the poster. No sooner had I done that, when the tingling and tightness around my body began.

"Lovely," I muttered, gripping the chair arms and closing my eyes. The sound of wind rushing by filled my ears and everything went topsy-turvy for a second until I jerked forward and sucked in a giant breath of air.

CHAPTER

16

Still sitting in my dad's chair, I took the usual few seconds to catch my breath and look around. I had an immediate rush of warmth as I got to see all his things back in their places. Knowing they'd be gone again when I returned, I panned the room slowly, memorizing the way it was supposed to be, wishing I could film it for posterity. There were extra things, too. Some large boxes lined up on the far wall, probably attic overflow. Possibly Uncle Tommy's stuff, or some of Mom's craft stuff.

The quiet didn't last, which I didn't expect it would. I figured there was something to be learned by my little trip, and that hadn't happened sitting alone yet. Dad's voice came down the hallway, accompanied by one that grabbed my heart.

"Well, let's go see," my dad's voice said, entering the room. He looked exactly as he did when I'd last seen him, with gray taking over most of his short hair and a slight paunch to his belly.

Holding his hand was Cassidy. Her hair was pulled back in a ponytail that bounced golden curls like springs. By the stretchy leggings and sparkly yellow butterflies on her shirt, I put her at around seven or eight years old. My hand automatically went to my chest as I took in the little girl Cass had once been. Skinny and prissy, free of makeup and beauty products, just eager dark eyes waiting to drink in the stars and constellations.

"Is it dark enough?" she asked, her little voice melting my heart.

"Oh, I think so," he said. "Question is, are you eight enough?" I smiled as I remembered him doing that. "Because only true-blue eight-year-olds can see Orion's Belt."

"I've seen it," she said, with all the grown-up-ness she could pull off. "You showed me the three stars when we were in the backyard like a year ago."

He winked at her as he peered into the scope and moved it to line it up just right. "But not the whole shebang," he said. "Not like you can see it through here."

He moved to the side so she could look, and she did it like he told her to, not touching it, keeping her hands down by her side.

"Whoa," she breathed. "Look at everything else around them. How come you can only see the three when we look up at the sky? There's like kagillions!"

"Because space goes on and on forever," he said, leaning an arm against the window. "We see the closest and the biggest. The stuff the sun shines on."

"I want to go see it all one day."

Dad laughed. "You want to go to space?"

"Yeah," she said in awe, still taking it all in through the little eyepiece. "I could do that. I could be an astronaut."

Dad shrugged. "You can be whatever you put your mind to, whatever you're willing to work for. Because if something's hard to get, it's—"

"Gonna be the good stuff," she finished with him, smiling up with two missing teeth.

"That's right, doodlebug," he said, tweaking her nose. He sat down on the window seat and gazed at her.

"I want to go everywhere," she said, climbing onto his lap and looking up at the poster with the red circles. "Space and Japan and Greece and Hawaii."

He widened his eyes in mock surprise. "All that?"

"That's just one summer," she said, her head cocking with attitude, as he laughed. "I'm gonna see all of Europe, and South America, and Australia the summer after that. And Alaska."

"Wow," he said. "I want your job."

"Oh, I'm gonna have a great boss, too. She's gonna let me take off on my trips whenever I want, and pay me lots of money."

"Good for you!"

"Yep."

"Cassidy?" came my voice from downstairs. "Come on, baby, we have to get home. Tomorrow's school."

"Ugh," she said. "Today should go on forever. Birthdays should be longer than regular days."

So it was her eighth birthday. That thought jiggled something in my memory, but I couldn't pick it out.

"Yesterday was your birthday, it probably was longer. Today was just like icing. Like a freebie. That's the good part of when birthdays fall on a weekend."

"I guess."

"And you need lots of school if you're gonna be an astronaut and

snag that rich job of yours," Dad said, tickling her ribs. *"So give me a hug."* She jumped up and attacked his neck with a giant bear hug. *"Ooh, yeah, that's a good one. Love you, doodlebug."*

"Love you too, Paw-Paw."

She ran downstairs, and Dad continued to sit in the dark, leaning against the wall that jutted out from the window. He looked off at nothing, and I wanted so badly to talk to him. To tell him all the things I never got to say. Because you always think you have later to say them.

The light filled the room, and my dad blinked as Uncle Tommy walked in. *"You sitting in the dark?"*

"Hey, bud, thought you were already gone," Dad said.

"Nah, I had to hit that birthday cake again," Tommy said with a chuckle. *"Nice to see everyone tonight; thanks for the invite."*

I had to think a minute, but then I remembered a party that Uncle Tommy came to right after his second divorce. He was evidently lonely and Mom and Dad decided he needed some family interaction. My kid's eighth birthday was, I guess, the closest thing on the agenda.

"Glad you could come by," Dad said, getting to his feet, looking tired in the bright light. He hugged his brother in that backslapping way that men do and moved as if to leave the room, but Tommy stayed put.

"Um, wanted to talk to you, if you have a second," he said.

My alarms started going off. Dad's probably were, as well, but he didn't show it. He just looked worn out.

"Okay."

Tommy sat on the desk, so his back was to me, but I could see Dad's face.

"Well, you know things have been hard since the hardware store went under," Tommy began, and I saw Dad's eyes lose a little shine.

"Yeah, I have a little bit of an idea."

Tommy held up a hand. "I know, I know. You've had to struggle, too. The store just—"

"Don't even go there," Dad said, his voice quiet. "That was seven years ago. And the store didn't do anything. You did."

Tommy sighed, a deep, miserable sound that even made me feel sorry for him. "I know," he said again.

"And you need money," Dad said. It wasn't a question.

"Just till the end of the month, when I get paid," he said. "And only if you can spare it."

"And if I can't?"

There was a pause, and all three of us knew that Tommy would do something stupid to get it, which is why they kept trickling it to him. "Then I'll figure something out," he said. "I'd pay you back, though."

"No, you won't," Dad said, walking around behind his desk. Tommy turned to face him. Dad leaned on the desk, right next to me. I could have touched him if my bubble of freakydom would let me. His hands splayed above the drawer that held his never-used thumbtacks. "Do you know that I've been trying to save for years to take my wife, my family—now just my wife again—on a trip?"

"What?" Tommy said, looking thrown by the change.

"All she ever wanted to do was travel," he said, still looking down at his hands. "I promised to take her, but it never happened. We had kids, and I promised to take them. Never happened." He stood up and looked at the poster. "Kids are grown and have kids of their own now; it's just me and Frannie again. I'd love to make good on just one of those promises."

"So what's stopping you?" Tommy said, making my dad turn to him with a look that should have withered him.

"You."

Tommy looked taken aback and gave a little chuckle. *"What do I have to do with it?"*

Dad turned back to the poster, lifted up the free corner at the bottom with no tack, and reached behind it sideways, to his elbow. When he pulled out a metal box, I cried out.

"Oh my God." The freaking box. It was behind the damn poster?

He set it on the desk rather hard, making the pencil cup jump. He opened it, and there was a small stack of cash, with notes scribbled on bits of paper. I strained to see them, but I couldn't make them out from my angle. He grabbed a section of the cash, counted out five hundred dollars, and shoved it at Tommy.

"Take it and go," Dad said.

"That's it?" Tommy asked, fingering the bills like they'd betrayed him.

"Are you kidding me?" Dad said, rounding the corner of the desk. *"Four months ago, I gave you a thousand. Six months before that, fifteen hundred. Last year, another four thousand throughout the year. And every other damn year before that,"* he finished, his voice rising. *"Why am I never able to do anything with my money? Why have I never taken my family anywhere? Why did my livelihood go down the damn toilet? Why am I having to live check to check at a shit job and watching Frannie work her ass off to help make ends meet at this point in our lives?"* Dad advanced on Tommy, and I held my breath. I'd never seen him angry like that. *"Because you are a leech and a user and all I ever do is throw good money at you."*

Tommy picked up the bills slowly, not saying anything, as Dad closed the box and put it back in its place.

"Thank you," he finally said after a full minute, then he walked out the door, never looking up.

Dad leaned against the wall after he put the box back, and then looked at the poster again. He lifted the corner and pulled the box out, glancing at the door suspiciously.

"What are you doing, Dad?" I asked, not really intending to ask it.

He carried the box to the far side of the room, looked at the door again, and opened a flap of one of the large cardboard containers. He dug around in it, pulling things up I couldn't see, and shoved his box down into the middle somewhere, putting the other things back on top and closing the flap back.

I laughed out loud. "I don't blame you," I said. "I wouldn't have trusted him, either."

Dad rubbed at his face, raked his fingers back through his hair, and walked downstairs. I looked down at the pencil cup, the big antique calculator, and the desk calendar. And my skin lit on fire.

It was turned to May 7, 1998.

ॐ

"Oh, no," I breathed, as I looked back up to where my dad had left. "No, Daddy, wait!"

But he couldn't hear me. And I couldn't change anything. Tears filled my eyes anyway as I wished for a do-over so that I could have looked at him closer. If I'd realized this was the night he died, I would have paid attention.

I rested my face in my hands and recalled the hysterical phone call from my mother at three in the morning, when she'd found him in his recliner with the TV still going. Bonanza was on. I heard the music through the phone. I let the tears come, thinking how tired I was of crying. "I love you, Daddy," I whispered.

The suction began, and I didn't move, didn't brace myself, I just waited. The noise of air and high-pitched ringing filled my ears, the air was squeezed from my lungs, and I hurtled through whatever it was that kept throwing me back and forth until I pitched forward like someone kicked me.

୨୦

I sucked in a giant gulp of air and gripped the desk as the vertigo slowed down.

"Shit," I muttered, blinking in the dark. "Okay, that—oh my God." I got up and walked on shaky legs to the door, and shut it behind me.

"Whoa, Emily honey, are you okay?"

My mother would pick that precise time to come out of her bedroom.

I turned and nodded, swiping at my eyes. "Just having a nostalgic moment, I guess." I opted against, *Well, I just saw Dad a few hours before he died, and by the way he gave Uncle Tommy five hundred dollars.*

She put an arm around me, and we walked to Holly/Aunt Bernie's room, where Holly was smiling through Aunt Bernie's rant on downsizing, while giving the unmade bed-with-clothes-on-it an evil eye.

"You saw Big Blue," Aunt Bernie was saying. "She has all I need. None of that crap that used to hang on me like a noose was necessary."

"Well," Holly said. "Right now, I like my crap. Think I'll let it strangle me for a little while longer."

"Suit yourself," Aunt Bernie said, kicking her shoes off and looking for her slippers, which were in two different places. I knew it had to make Holly nuts to see her old room so messy. "Sure wish I would have started sooner."

She excused herself to go start baking something, and no one was about to get in the way of that, so Mom and I sat cross-legged on the messy bed and watched Holly wrap tiny ballet dancer figurines.

"House is looking good, Mom," Holly said.

Mom smirked. "Well, some of it's just putting lipstick on a pig, but if it'll help sell it."

"Sure you still want to?" Holly pressed.

Mom widened her eyes. "Yes, I'm sure. So—I hear things are happier with you and Ben?" Mom asked, nudging me.

I gave Holly a look, and she stuck her head in the box. "Really?" I said. "Can't imagine how you heard something like that."

"Well, it's a good thing," she said. "No reason to hide it."

"Oh, lots of reasons to hide it—not that we're hiding it," I corrected. "We're not really doing anything—purposely. There's not a plan or a thought process behind—"

"Lordy, you've got it bad," Mom said, interrupting me with a shake of the head.

"No kidding," Holly said, taking a figurine out of the newspaper to wrap it again, better. "She's at the babbling phase."

"Excuse me?"

"You are, honey. You do that," my mother said. "When you get all giddy over a man, you do that."

I stared at her, amused. "Right, because there have been oodles of them."

"I can't believe you just said *oodles*," Holly said.

"I can't believe y'all think I babble."

"I can't believe you never told me the truth about him," Mom said.

I sunk back against the comforter and miscellaneous clothes that smelled like old perfume. "I was so devastated that he left, Mom. And then everything kind of settled in, and I was afraid of blowing it all up. I had this beautiful baby, and Kevin just—" I sat back up. "You know, for a while I think he actually went on the straight and narrow. She changed him, made him want to be a better man."

"And then you started believing your own hype," she said, her eyes wise. Even Holly stopped her wrapping and just listened.

"Yeah," I said softly. "I told myself it was what it was."

"And now?" she said.

I met her eyes. "What do you mean, now?"

"Do you keep up the lie, or come clean?" she said.

"Are you serious?" Holly asked, piping in. "Do you realize what the fallout would be?"

"Oh my God, I don't even want to think about Kevin ever finding out Cass isn't his," I said, covering my face. "And it being Ben would be the nail in the coffin."

"Shhh," Holly said suddenly, darting her eyes toward the door.

My stomach contracted to the size of a pea as Cassidy took two very slow steps into the room. "Hey, doodlebug," I said, wondering if my voice really sounded that high. "Didn't hear you come in."

But the look on her face turned on the faucet of doom that started at my fingertips and seeped steadily through my skin to my core.

"What did you say?" she said, her voice taking on a monotone quality.

I couldn't feel my lips. I pulled them between my teeth but the nerve endings left me. "What do you me—"

"What did you just say, Mom?" she said. Her eyes weren't twenty-one anymore, they were old and wise and teared up and accusatory. "About Dad and Ben."

Holly looked as frozen as I felt. A lone crystal ballerina dangled from her fingers, and her eyes looked red. I held back my hair with jerky fingers and closed my eyes to the zing-zinging going on in my head. "Come—sit down for a second."

"I'm good," she said stiffly.

Mom grabbed my hand for support and reached out for her with the other one. "Sit down, sweetheart. Let your mom talk."

But Cassidy held her hands up out of Mom's reach. "I don't want to sit. I want to know what the hell y'all were talking about."

"It wasn't meant for you to hear," I said.

"I'll bet," she snapped.

"Cassidy," I began as I stood, my stomach feeling like an acid pit. "Just listen to me for a second."

"No, you know what?" she said, backing up. "Save it. I don't even want to know what kind of fucked-up justification you have for that."

"Watch your mouth in this house, young lady," Mom said.

Cassidy didn't hear her. Her blood was boiling too loudly. She glared at me without blinking, and the tears in her eyes fell of their own accord. "And he's here in this house—oh my God." She shook her head with disgust at me. "You're just as bad— God, all this time and you're just as bad as Dad." A bitter scoff came out of her mouth from deep in her core and a fresh wave of tears came with it. "Excuse me, *Kevin*."

She turned on her heel and stormed down the hall and down the stairs.

"Cassidy Lynn, you stop right now," I called out as I tried to keep up.

She whirled around at the front door, her eyes blinded with tears. "Get away from me, Mom. Leave me the hell alone."

She slammed the door in my face and was in her car and smoking the little bug's tires before I could get down the porch steps. Her taillights disappeared around the corner on two wheels.

I left the front door gaping open behind me, and I heard the thunder of Holly's steps on the stairway, followed by Mom's slower ones keeping up the best she could. I turned to look at them, begging with my eyes for somebody to fix what I'd just snapped in two. Aunt Bernie leaned her head over the bar to see what was going on, and Ben poked his head out from the hall.

"Everything okay?" he asked.

Back and forth from Holly to Mom, I looked. I couldn't look at him. Nothing was ever going to be okay again. I could feel it.

CHAPTER

17

I LEFT TO TRACK HER DOWN. I DIDN'T KNOW EXACTLY WHERE I was going, but I couldn't sit and wait on her. I knew how anger played out with Cassidy. She would stew and analyze and isolate from the issue for a couple of weeks, until she had everything crossed and dotted in her mind and knew what questions to ask. She never liked spontaneous fights or arguments, because she couldn't control where they went, so running off to be alone and think it out was her signature move. Normally, I'd let her be.

This wasn't one of those times. This was a jacked-up, life-altering moment for her that was all my doing and up to me to set it straight.

You're just as bad as Dad.

And to top it all off, she thought I cheated on Kevin. Fabulous. As I drove around the neighborhood in the dusky dark, in the general direction I'd seen her last, I ran through the list of where she'd go. Or where I'd go if it were me. I called her and left four different messages. Texted her while driving and dared someone to stop me for that. I'd hire them on the spot to go on a search.

She wouldn't answer. She also wasn't at Kevin's, thank God. She wasn't at her apartment. Holly's car was back at her house again but sat there unaccompanied. I did a drive-by at Josh's apartment complex and didn't see her car, then circled back to my house in case she decided to trash it or something. No Cassidy. On a whim, I went by both her jobs, starting with the one in town, then heading down to the docks to Dock Hollidays. I even got out and asked there, and they hadn't seen her.

Perplexed and a little worried, I went back by Josh's, sat in the car for a minute to figure out what to say, and walked up to the second-floor apartment I was lucky to remember hearing the address for.

Josh looked frazzled when he opened the door.

"Ms. Lockwood, hey," he said, pausing for a minute before jumping to one side to hold the door open. "Come in."

"I'm just looking for Cass, Josh, have you seen her? She's not answering her phone."

He blew out a breath and stood there awkwardly, as if my not coming in messed up his plan. "I know. And yeah," he said, rubbing his face. "She was here for a second—and I mean really a second," he said, holding a hand up. "She was all freaked out and crying, and I tried to find out what was wrong—do you know what was wrong?" he asked me, looking truly upset.

I liked him a little more for that. But I could hear my heartbeat in my ears, and his nervous energy just added to my anxiety. "And then she left?" I asked, ignoring the question.

He looked deflated. "Yeah. I tried to get her to come sit down and talk to me. I don't think I did anything to make her so crazy, but she just kept saying her whole life was a lie and she couldn't trust anybody."

I closed my eyes and clutched my stomach. "You didn't do anything, Josh, this was about me."

"Well," he began, and I noticed his eyes were red like he'd maybe been crying, too. "Then what's she talking about? I mean, she yelled all that and—" He stopped and looked down at his closed fist as he opened it, like a little boy with a prize marble. Except it wasn't a marble. Lying in his palm was a beautiful little diamond ring. "She gave this back to me, saying marriage is a joke, and left." His voice cracked at the end, and I stood there staring at the bling in his hand.

"Oh my God," I said, although no real sound went with the words.

I picked up the ring and looked at it with a broken heart and weepy eyes. It was a simple solitaire, not big, but very well designed so that the diamond looked bigger than it was. It had probably taken him a year to save enough to buy it, and it was exactly what Cassidy would love, simple and not flashy. From the man who loved her. And she'd given it back.

"Josh, it's beautiful," I whispered, setting it back in his hand. "I didn't even know."

"We were—we were gonna come announce it this weekend," he said, landing heavily on the couch and just staring at the ring. "She wanted a few days for it to just be us."

I nodded and knelt in front of him. "It's not you, babe, okay? She's mad at me."

He looked miserable. "What would you have to do with—"

"You'll find out soon enough," I said and patted his knee.

"Just have faith right now, that y'all will be okay." I closed his fingers over the ring. "Hold on to that."

"Okay," he mouthed.

"Do you have any idea where she went from here?"

He shook his head. "She just left."

It was all I could do to hang on to my patience. "I know. I mean, can you think of anywhere she might go? Someplace you've gone together? Talked about going? Something nostalgic?"

He looked around his little living room with its many electronic video and audio gadgets, as if it might give him a clue, and then shook his head. "We have some favorite restaurants, but mostly we hang here or at her place."

"Okay, can you call me if you hear from her?" I asked him, digging in my bag for a stray card.

"Absolutely."

I didn't know where else to go. I called Mom to see if she'd come back, but no. I went by Kevin's again, and all was lit up and cozy there, but no little white Volkswagen bug. So I went home. I hated it, and I felt all itchy about it, so much so that I didn't even put my keys down. I landed on the couch, but that just brought my gaze to the big Cassidy collage, and I sprung right back up and walked up to it.

I felt the burn behind my eyes as I let my gaze roll from one family photo to the next, the wholesome look of it settling in the pit of my stomach like something rotten.

The doorbell ringing startled me and I ran to the door, hoping for Cassidy. But when I swung the door open, it was Ben.

"Oh, hey," I said, hearing the disappointment in my voice. "I mean—" I held up a hand. "I didn't mean it like that."

"Hey, it's okay," he said, looking at me with concern and taking hold of the hand I was flailing. "Em, what's up?"

He came in, and I walked back to the collage, letting him follow me. "We—had a big fight, Cass and I."

"Well, yeah," he said with a chuckle. "That made national news, I'm sure." He stood behind me and hugged me to him. I closed my eyes and pretended for a second that things could really be that good. That they could really match the joy I felt in his arms again. That a secret I'd kept buried for twenty-one years would just fade off into the sunset and not destroy everything in its path.

"She's not answering her phone," I said.

"Is that normal?"

"After today it probably is."

"Then let her cool off."

My chin quivered. I couldn't have this conversation like this. "This one's different, Ben. This one—it's major."

He squeezed me tighter. "Then come on, let's go look for her some more. She doesn't need to be driving around if she's that upset."

I smiled a tiny smile that hurt my heart at the same time. It killed me that he didn't even know the irony of worrying about her.

Cassidy knew. I looked in her face in each and every picture, where she smiled brilliantly under crazy blonde curls and deep intense dark eyes, and wondered how the hell I ever thought it would stay buried. And how on earth I ever kidded myself into believing that I could have a relationship with Ben without the truth.

"Ben," I said, not recognizing the sound of my voice.

"Hmm," he said, his mouth against my hair. We were rocking slightly and I imagined that his eyes were closed as he just enjoyed the moment.

"I have to tell you something."

My phone buzzed from my bag on the couch, and I pulled free of his arms to dig it out. Disappointment filled me when it wasn't Cass's number and face populating my screen, but an unknown number. I nearly let it go to voice mail, but then something made me answer.

"Hello?"

"Mrs. Lockwood?"

I usually fought the *Mrs.* reference, but there was something in the man's tone that made the little hairs on the back of my neck stand up.

"Yes?"

"Ma'am, my name is Officer Harris, I'm with the state troopers. Are you Cassidy Lockwood's mother?"

My fingers and toes went icy, as if the blood was working its way backward. Like they say happens if you're in freezing water. When your extremities shut down to focus the blood supply to your core.

To protect your heart.

"Yes?" I said again. Ben turned at the sound of my voice, which I assume was odd by the look on his face.

"Ma'am, your daughter was in a serious accident tonight—"

The room closed in and went dark. There were no rushing sounds, no tightening of the airways, no ringing in the ears, no going back in time. Just ordinary horror-filled darkness, as someone filled my head with pictures. Everything went numb as Ben reached me and held me tight against him, taking the phone from my hand and listening to the rest. I stared at the keys in my hand, but I couldn't feel anything but my heart beating against my ribs. Everything else was shutting down. Protecting it.

EVERYTHING WENT IN SLOW MOTION. I DIDN'T REMEMBER THE drive to the hospital, just that we were suddenly there. I didn't remember calling Kevin or my mother, but they arrived there at the same time we did, screeching into the parking lot.

I moved like a robot, pushing doors open ahead of me, as my mother's voice droned on behind me about Holly's dead phone and how she couldn't reach Greg. Once we made it in and to the desk, Kevin all of a sudden had a voice.

"Cassidy Lockwood," he said, spreading both hands wide on the counter. "She was just brought in."

"The single-car accident," a nurse sitting down said to the one we were facing. She pointed at a chart.

"No, the *girl*," Kevin said to the one sitting, his voice rising. "Tell me about my daughter."

I could feel Ben's warmth behind me, his hands on my shoulders. Part of me felt like his touch was the only thing keeping me plugged in. My baby was in critical condition, having wrapped her little white windup car around a big brown tree out on a lonely stretch of winding highway. The grace of God had put an actual state trooper driving by at the moment it happened, because there were no other cars out there. She would have bled to death on a tree before anyone would have found her off the side of the road in the dark.

"Sir, I'll get the doctor for you," the woman said, jumping out of her seat like it had shocked her.

Kevin was breathing hard, and Sherry was wrapped around him, but he looked at me and pulled me out of Ben's grip, hugging me to him. I felt his body shake, and I lost my composure. Somebody had to be the rock, my mind screamed. Someone had to take control.

"God took care of her, Kevin," I said, wiping tears from my face and pulling back but holding on to him. "He put somebody there. She'll be okay."

"What the hell was she doing driving out there at night?" he said, his face contorted with grief. "That road has no lights, it's pitch-black. What the hell—"

Sherry wiped at her eyes and squeezed my hand, then took the opportunity to reclaim her hold on Kevin. Which I was grateful for, as I backed back into Ben. His solid presence and grip on my arms were what I needed. He turned me around then.

"Come here," he whispered, and I melted into him. He wrapped his arms around me and made me feel so safe. So loved.

"Ben," I cried into his chest as I clutched him to me, begging God for a miracle to save my baby girl. Whatever it took.

IT WAS ALMOST AN HOUR BEFORE THE DOCTOR CAME, AND I thought Kevin was going to start pulling doors off the hinges to find her. Kevin was not an aggressive man, but this had his chemistry all out of whack.

When she came, she introduced herself as Dr. Somebody of Something, and told us that Cassidy had to be stabilized before she could leave her.

"Can we see her?" I asked.

"No, she's being prepped for emergency surgery," she said, "And that's som—"

"Holy shit, emergency surgery?" Kevin said. "How bad is she?"

"Okay, relax," the doctor said, the words bouncing off my ears like echoes, over and over. "We're going to take care of her." She put a hand on each of our arms to calm us, but all it did was make me feel trapped. I pulled away.

"Relax?" I said, my voice not sounding like me. "Would you relax? Tell us what's going on."

The doctor's expression stayed neutral and empathetic. "Your daughter has some rib fractures and some pretty bad abdominal wounds. Her right leg is broken just below the knee, and I will tell you that the bone went through the skin."

"Oh my God," I choked.

She touched my arm again. "But it was a clean break and can be set. The problem is more the rib injuries," she continued, and I tried to focus on her words as my brain kept forming the image of my baby girl mangled in that fucking toy car. "There is evidence of internal bleeding, and she lost quite a bit of blood, which is putting her in a high risk right now. She needs surgery— on her leg, yes, but that's secondary. I want to go in and find the bleeding."

"Yes," Kevin said, the first calm word he'd said since we arrived. His face was gray when I looked at him, his eyes sunk in. "Do whatever you need to."

I nodded in agreement, my words stuck in my throat. I felt Ben behind me and let that warmth soak in.

"Okay," the doctor said. "That being said, we're low on her blood type, so I'll need both of you to—"

"Let's do it," Kevin said, already rolling up his sleeve. Bells went off in the back of my head, but I was too in shock to register them. "Hook me up, I'll give her all I have."

"Are you O positive?" the doctor asked.

"No, I'm A," Kevin said, still rolling.

"Then we can't use you," she said, already gesturing to me. I saw Kevin's face fall, and then the doctor's voice sounded like she was talking from a well as she put her hand on my shoulder and asked me to come with her. But all I could do was shake my head.

"Emily, go," Kevin said, his voice cracking. "What's the matter?"

"I'm A positive, too," I said, on a whisper, feeling the bile rise up in my throat. Feeling the panic I prayed I'd never feel, but not giving a shit at that moment about something that petty.

It was my prayer. *Whatever it took.*

I turned out of Dr. Somebody's grasp before she could put words to the question in her mind, and looked up into Ben's face, the whole movement feeling like slow motion. He looked into my eyes, the question already there, but he read it in an instant. He was a smart man. His eyes registered everything right there in front of me. Confusion, disbelief, and then realization and shock, before filling with tears.

"Hate me later, Ben," I whispered, the tears streaming down my face. "Please—"

He tore his eyes from me and yanked his jacket off, letting it drop to the floor. "I'm O positive," he said quietly, swiping a hand across his face as the tears blinked free. "Let's go."

The doctor only hesitated briefly, giving me a quick glance before leading Ben off down the hall. I watched his back as he strode like a man wanting to rip something apart. Probably me.

It was done. The secret was out. And my baby was lying in a hospital bed and needing surgery because of it. The man I loved was just mentally kicked in the nuts, and the man who raised her—

"Emily."

Kevin's voice cracked on my name, and I turned around slowly, not feeling my legs anymore. I felt my mother's hands on my arms, and I thought for a minute they would have to hold me up.

He was shaking, crying, and Sherry was holding his arm. I had the most random thought that in all the years I'd known him, I'd never seen him look so bad. He looked old. Like I had literally added twenty years to him.

"What the living hell—just happened?" he said, his words clipped and ragged.

His eyes weren't there yet. He hadn't quite let himself believe what he'd just seen. Ben Landry was going to give blood to his daughter. I could see the thoughts playing out. He wasn't allowing it to be true.

"Let's go sit down," Sherry said, gesturing to some chairs nearby. "Before both of you fall down."

I nodded, and headed that way, but Kevin yanked his arm free of her.

"No," he said, swinging me around and pulling me out of Mom's grip. "You tell me," he said through his teeth. Tears and disbelief poured from his eyes. He was begging me to make it not so. The anger slipped for a second, and it was just pure grief. "Please, Emily—"

I felt my illegal hamburger coming up, inch by inch, with every sob. "I'm sorry," I managed to push out. "I'm so sorry, Kevin."

His face slowly went blank, his eyes dead. The tears kept coming but it was like there was nothing driving them. "No," he finally whispered. "You didn't—" He shut his eyes and shook his head as if that would knock the thought away. "I'm her father," he said, his voice hard and thick on each word.

I closed my eyes, unable to stand the torture on his face any longer. "I wanted you to be," I whispered. "I didn't know unti—"

He grabbed the front of my shirt and pushed me backward, making me gasp and fling my eyes open wide. Sherry cried out, and my mom yelled out expletives.

"You self-righteous bitch," Kevin spat in my face, pain so etched into his features I didn't think anything would ever make it better. "How dare you beat me up all these years!"

Everyone came running to pull at him, but I didn't fight him. I deserved it.

"Raking me over the coals for what I did," he yelled in my face. The yelling wasn't the bad part, it was the agony in his voice that ripped at my heart. "When you were fucking Landry back then."

I shook my head. I could hear Sherry talking, pleading with him, reasoning with him. I could hear my mother fussing and feel people pulling at us, but it was all like white noise.

"No, I wasn't," I sobbed. "It was after you and I broke up, just one time." I had to stop and catch a breath. "Before he left town." I grabbed at his hands. "Kevin, please, Cassidy needs us right now."

"Us?" he said, acid lacing his words. "That's rich, Em. Us." He let go of me with a fling and a push, shoving at everyone else that was groping at him as well. He started to sling another insult at me, but something inside him finally broke, and he crumpled right there in Sherry's arms in the middle of the lobby.

I couldn't breathe. I had destroyed so many people with my deception. Not intentionally, but the result was the same. I backed up slowly till I met with wall, and I slid down the smooth white surface till the floor welcomed me. There was a small couch on either side of me, but I curled my legs up against me and stayed where I was.

Mom was crying and came to sit on the couch, holding Ben's jacket. "Honey, come up here," she said, but I shook my head.

"I'm good," I said. I didn't hear the words come out but they seemed to as she patted my hands.

"She's gonna be okay," she said. "They're gonna fix everything. She'll be okay."

"Nothing's gonna be okay," I said, holding my head. "Ever again."

"It may not be the same," Mom said, trying to reach Holly again for the fiftieth time. "But it will be okay, honey. You'll see. Things have a way."

I watched Kevin and Sherry go to the chairs at the opposite wall and sit down. She was talking softly to him and rubbing his back. He was right, she was great, and he was smart to love her. He was a moron for cheating on her.

And I had destroyed him. And possibly Ben, too. But none of that mattered as much as the girl in the bed. I came close to destroying her and losing her, and that thought once again brought the anguish to the surface.

I heard a ruckus and looked up to see Josh skidding to a stop at the nurses' station.

"Cassidy Lockwood?" he said, his voice panicked. "Is she here?"

"Oh, shit, I forgot—" I began, but my mother got up and went to him, putting an arm around him and walking down the hall a little way. They stopped after several feet and he stared down at her, his reddened face making his blond hair glow. I could tell he was crying even from that far away, and she hugged him till he let go on his own. She linked an arm in his and led him back down to us and put him in a chair on our side. He didn't say anything, just sat bent over with his elbows on his knees, sniffling every few minutes. I wondered if Cassidy's ring was still with him.

A nurse came to talk to us. The police came to talk to us. An intern came to talk to us. Ben didn't return. I didn't really expect him to, but I found myself envious of Kevin having Sherry there. And then I knew how far I'd fallen, to be envious of Kevin for anything.

I reached for his jacket from Mom and pulled it to me, smelling his scent, closing my eyes to pretend he was there with me. Which pretty much knocked me down the rest of the way.

I didn't care. I kept watch on the nurses' station, looking for any kind of activity on the spot I knew her chart was kept. I watched Josh put mileage on the rug, wearing out the same spot many others before him had worn. And I tried not to make eye contact with Kevin, who was doing all the same things on his side.

I was still sitting in the same spot, my arms around the jacket and my forehead resting against it when Mom nudged me. I jumped, thinking it was the doctor, but then she laid a hand on my shoulder and I looked up to see Ben enter our little alcove.

His dark eyes were raw and swollen, the lids heavy. He didn't even look my way, but he locked eyes with Kevin. I couldn't read either of their expressions to know if it was hatred or anger—or indifference. Kevin just looked blank. Robotic. Ben walked to the back chairs and sat down alone, elbows on knees, head on fists. Kevin's gaze followed him and then landed on me, and it wasn't blank. It celebrated the fact that I'd destroyed that, too.

It was close to midnight when the doctor I found out was named Dr. Branson finally came out, looking tired. I scrambled to my feet, hoping I didn't fall on my face from everything going stiff and numb. Kevin focused on her and refused to look at me.

"Cassidy came through just fine," she said, pulling off her scrub cap. "She does have three fractured ribs on her left side, and bruising to her colon."

I grabbed my mother's hand and breathed a sigh of relief. "And the bleeding?"

"Was from a nick to her spleen," she said.

"Oh, God," Kevin said, rubbing at his face.

"No, we got to it in plenty of time, closed it up, cleaned everything out; she will be fine," Dr. Branson said, holding up a hand. "There were open gashes to her abdomen so there are staples, but she was incredibly lucky in so many ways. Just going to be in a lot of pain for a while. We did go ahead and set her leg while we had her under, since the rest of the surgery went so well."

"Okay," I said. "What—um—" I couldn't think clearly. "How long will she be asleep?"

"Till morning, at least," she said. "And I will warn you, since

269

you haven't seen her yet, she did sustain some cuts and bruises to her head and face, but they're minor and will heal. She's got a mild concussion, but nothing to worry about since she'll be here for a bit anyway." She smiled at me. "I can't tell you enough how miraculous this was. A wreck like that—somebody had their hand over all the important parts."

We thanked her, she left, and we stood there. Mom walked off to update Aunt Bernie and try to reach Holly. My entire body seemed to let go at once, as I stood there alone, and I started shaking uncontrollably. I couldn't stop. I made it to the couch and hugged myself as tight as I could, trying to will it to quit, but then the tears and the nausea came back, and no amount of mind control would stop it.

I finally got up to make a run for the bathroom. I was halfway there, when I felt light-headed and my knees gave way. I felt the earth coming up at me, but I never landed. Arms that I'd know in my sleep caught me. He adjusted me against his chest, and through the haze and the head-to-toe buzz, I felt his words in my hair.

"I've got you, just breathe," he said. "Steady breaths."

"I'm—I'm good," I heard myself say.

"Yeah, just come on," he said, walking me somewhere.

Ben walked me into the ladies' room, apologized to two women in there, and brought me to the sink to run cold water over my wrists, which wouldn't be still. I looked around for the nearest stall, refusing to puke in front of him, and half crawled to the toilet. I retched violently, as my body felt like it was beating me up for everything I'd ever done. I sobbed harder as my stomach convulsed over and over. Dimly, I was aware of him kneeling behind me and holding my hair, and as mortifying as that was I loved him for it. Especially since I knew he hated me right then.

The trembling receded, the buzzing got lower, and I blinked in the light until my vision was semi-normal. I was exhausted. It was worse than any hangover I'd ever had.

"I'm—sorry," I said on jerky breaths. "I don't know why this—happened."

"Shock," he said. "The comedown can do that."

He handed me a cold, wet paper towel, and I held it against my face. What I really wanted was to jump in that toilet and flush. I had a flashback to finding out I was pregnant and alone and thinking it was the worst thing that could possibly happen. I was so naïve. Having Cass was the single best thing in my life. Almost losing her then was the absolute worst.

I stayed there, crying quietly into the toilet, wishing he would leave me there.

"Come on," he said, backing up so I could crawl out backward.

I did and rose shakily to my feet, heading to the sink to wash my mouth out.

"Still feel sick?" he asked.

I shook my head. "I don't think so." I looked at him until he came into focus, and then I looked back down at the counter as I felt crying potential coming on again. "Thank you, you didn't have to do this."

"Well, I couldn't let you pass out on the floor."

I nodded and took a chance, meeting his eyes. The distance there hit me to the core. "Thank you." I hoped he could read my worn-out, swollen, red eyes and know that was for everything. Saving Cassidy's life without hesitation. Everything.

His mouth twitched, and he looked away. "No problem."

My heart ached for him. "Ben—"

"Not now," he said, his words clipped. He closed his eyes and let out a slow, controlled breath. "Not yet, okay?"

I blinked back the burn, knowing I had to give him that. "Okay," I whispered.

When he opened his eyes again, the pain there, the tears reddening them, broke my heart into five hundred little pieces. But he opened the door for me anyway.

CHAPTER

18

I woke up to a nurse's voice over the intercom, paging someone named Dr. George. I'd slept off and on curled up on one of the couches, with Ben's jacket as a blanket, and I could feel the weight of my two-hundred-pound eyeballs as I tried to clear them. Sleeping after crying was never pretty with me. And my mouth tasted like rotten dragon dung.

Sherry was asleep in Kevin's lap, as he stared straight ahead at nothing. Mom had left around two in the morning, promising to come back later. Josh was curled up in a chair like a little boy. Ben was gone. My heart fell a little further at that.

"Your boyfriend went to get coffee," Kevin said, his voice flat and free of bite. It worried me a little.

I just looked at him, not trusting that my voice would even work yet. He gently lifted Sherry's head and slid out from under her so he could stand and stretch. His hair stood on end in places, and I noticed his two-day growth was going a little lighter than blond.

"Does Cassidy know?" he asked.

I leaned forward and massaged my temples, since a screaming headache was another joyful by-product of the night before. "Yes."

"What?"

The word bounced around the room, against my ears, against my body. I kept my head down. "Can you give me a few minutes to pull myself together before you lay into me?" I asked. "I can't even think right now."

"That's all I've done is think," he said. "All night. About everything. When did Cass find out?"

"Kevin, ple—"

"When?"

I blew out a breath. "Yesterday."

I waited in that pause, almost hearing the thoughts form in his head.

"You told her." It was a statement, not a question, and it was barely audible.

I shook my head, still holding it down. "She overheard us talking."

"You and Landry?"

I looked up. "No. Me and Holly and Mom. Ben didn't know, either."

"And she left upset?" Kevin said through his teeth, walking closer.

I closed my eyes, or as much as they would close. "Yes. I tried to stop her, to talk to her, but she's stubborn and tempered like you."

It was out of my mouth before I could think about it, and there was no taking it back.

"She's nothing like me," he said, his voice wobbling on the words, and I was hit with the irony of her saying those same words about him.

"Yes, she is," I said, looking up at him. "You raised her, Kevin. How can she not be?"

But he didn't hear me. "She's like him," he said in a whisper. I saw Ben return out of the corner of my eye, holding a cardboard cup carrier, and Kevin turned to follow my gaze. "Yes, him. So many things I see about her now, that I never thought to question."

Sherry stirred on the couch. "Kevin?"

"Like how the hell do you get brown eyes in three generations of blue-eyed people on both sides? Hmm." He walked up close to me and looked down into my face with anger but also an emptiness that I knew was impossible to fill.

"I'm sorry," I said, feeling like it was an echo.

"You're sorry," he repeated, grabbing one of my hands and yanking me up. He turned to Ben. "Does that make *you* feel better? Because she fucked you over, too, evidently."

Ben's jaw tightened. "Look, this isn't the place or the time—"

"Oh, yeah, it is," Kevin said. "How does it feel, Landry?"

"Don't," I said, feeling the hint of warning bells.

"Congratulations, it's a girl!"

"Kevin!" Sherry said, swinging her feet down.

"How does it feel to find out somebody else raised your only child?" Kevin asked, raising his arms in question.

"Stop it!" I yelled, shoving one of his arms down. "You're making it worse. We'll deal with this later; right now it's about that girl in there."

Kevin wheeled around and had my face in his hands before I could even take a breath, backing me up a step. "Exactly," he hissed. "And *that girl in there* is still yours." His mouth trembled with the effort not to cry. "I have nothing. You took the one thing I thought I did right in my life away from me."

I was tired. More than exhausted, I was tired of being the bad guy. I pulled his hands off me and started to say that, when Ben spoke first.

"Excuse me, you have nothing?" Ben said, his voice quiet but firm.

Kevin turned to him, a look of disbelief across his face. "You really don't want to do this right now."

"No, you brought this show," Ben said, setting the tray of steaming cups down. "You want to push Emily around and make a bunch of noise, come on." He stepped up and crossed his arms so there wouldn't be confrontation. "I know you're upset, Lockwood. You have every right to be. But, my God," he said through his teeth as his own emotion came to the surface. "That girl is amazing. And you got to—" Ben stopped as tears sprang to his eyes and his voice failed him. "You got to hold her at night when she had a nightmare, see her take her first steps, teach her to ride a—"

He scrubbed angrily at his face as the flood wouldn't stop once he let it open. I didn't even know I was crying, too, until the drops fell wet on my hand.

"Don't you ever tell me you have nothing," Ben continued. "Because you got it all, buddy. And just because a little DNA got in the way, that doesn't change twenty-one years." He pointed randomly off to the side. "You think she ran off and wrapped her car around a tree because she was *happy*?"

He wiped his eyes again and grabbed one of the cups before he walked off down a hallway to nowhere. I turned around to find my chair and met Josh's gaze. Quiet Josh, who'd sat there all night in complete silence, looked at me like I had personally pulled his life apart. That line was growing.

TIME RAN ON A LONG LOOP CIRCUIT, BEING INSIDE WITH NO windows. I had no sense of day or night, except for when the meal carts came around. Cassidy was moved to a room but still hadn't woken up past stirring, so we took turns sitting with her. Her doctor told us that it was normal that she didn't wake up right away, due to the head trauma. While that made sense, it turned me inside out. She looked so young and fragile, all hooked up to tubes and wrapped up. Her head was bandaged on one side, and her face was swollen and cut up and purple from an apparent face-plant with the steering wheel and much broken glass.

Josh made his stand. Anyone could come and go as they wanted to, but he wasn't leaving her side. I didn't argue with him; I had to respect him for that. I sat on the other side of her, holding her hand, begging her silently to forgive me.

Holly came with fresh clothes for me, having finally heard the news when my mother physically went to her house. Mom and Aunt Bernie came and checked on Cass, checked on me, and watched Kevin and Ben for spontaneous combustion, but the two mostly avoided each other. Ben was the only one who never went in Cassidy's room. He stayed in the waiting room, hour after hour, getting drinks or snacks when people needed them, leafing through every magazine there was, but not saying much.

He never asked for a visit with her. And I was afraid to offer it, for fear that would be the moment she'd wake up. I didn't think that would be the best thing to start her recovery with.

I found it interesting that Kevin finally broke to the hygiene gods and had to leave for a quick shower, whereas neither Ben nor I did. I didn't care if I smelled. I only needed to see her wake up and talk to me. Ben was looking pretty rough, himself, his dark beard mixed with gray making him look ten years older.

Finally, in a prime moment right after Mom and Holly and Aunt Bernie had left, Kevin strolled back in, looking fresh and clean but just as tired, and Josh walked out.

"She's awake," he said.

"Oh my God," I said, jumping to my feet. "I'm coming."

Josh held out a hand. "They're with her right now, checking her over." He ran a hand through his spiky blond hair and then rubbed his eyes. He looked enormously relieved, and let a little smile through. "But she actually talked." He closed his eyes and repeated it again, as if to himself. "She actually talked."

My heart warmed all the way up for him right then. He loved my baby that much. Tears came to my eyes, and I walked up and hugged him. He didn't hug me back right away, just kind of did it halfheartedly, but that was okay. I understood that. I was everyone's Antichrist of the moment, and while it was beginning to wear on me, the only thing that mattered was Cassidy's recovery.

"Thank you, Josh," I said and then let him go. "How long will they be with her, did they say?"

He looked away, looking at everyone else but me. "Um, they said they'd come tell us," he said. "But she actually just asked for her dad."

My chest physically hurt. Like something sat on it. I concentrated on pulling in a slow, deep breath and letting it go. She didn't want to see me yet, and that was okay. It wasn't about my need, it was about hers. I repeated that in my head as I watched Kevin's eyes water up, thinking that eventually I'd buy it.

"Which one," he said bitterly, blinking back the tears.

"Jesus," Ben said, making Kevin wheel around. "Who do you think? She's not gonna ask for me, and she's certainly not gonna call me *Dad*."

"Quit being an ass, Kevin," I said, finding my voice. "Go be what she needs."

His cocky expression faltered, and there for a second was the Kevin I knew. I prayed that version would stay while he talked to her. She didn't need a lecture or a guilt trip about him.

It was fifteen minutes later when Dr. Branson came out and told us that all looked good so far. "Mr. Lockwood, she's asking for you," she said. "And after that, just one at a time please. I don't want to overwhelm her right away."

Kevin swallowed hard and blew out a nervous breath before following her down the hall. I was left with Josh and Ben, and we stood eyeing each other until I turned away. It was my turn to go off alone. I—couldn't stand being in that cramped room another second. I picked a hallway at random and let my feet carry me, refusing to let tears weigh me down again. I was tired of crying. I was tired of being everyone's whipping post. *Yes, I lied,* I thought as I rounded a corner to God only knew where. I made a solo decision at the age of twenty-one, to not voice the possibility that it wasn't Kevin I was pregnant by. I was young and pissed off for being what I thought was used and discarded. I was mad and scared—and heartbroken. And then when I knew it to be fact, I let it be. Because it was too scary not to. Days and weeks and months and years went by, and I buried it more and more. I made what I thought was the best decision at the time. Or maybe just the easiest. Yes. I lied.

"I'm sorry," I said as I found myself staring at a door that said CHAPEL.

"I know," said a familiar voice behind me.

I turned to look into Ben's eyes.

My skin did its familiar tingle it always did in close proximity with Ben, but my brain just wanted to go the other way.

I licked my dry lips and wished Holly would have brought a toothbrush with the clothes that morning. I wasn't up for more beatings. I was thinking I'd been led to this chapel for a reason, for some peace.

"Why'd you follow me?" I asked.

"Make sure you're okay," he said.

"I'm fine," I said, hugging my arms to myself.

He glanced at the sign on the door behind me. "I found this myself, the other day." He gestured with a nod of his head. "Mind if I join you?"

I really wanted to be alone, but it being God's little nook and all, I didn't feel I had a place or the right to say that. "Okay," I said, turning to go in.

The room was dimmer than the hallway, and ten degrees cooler, washing over me with an instant diffuser. I felt calmer, just being there, and I took a seat in a pew to the left, halfway up the aisle. There were only sixteen pews total, eight on each side, split like a real church that had been shrunk.

Ben sat next to me, and I closed my eyes so I wouldn't think about him. I wasn't there for him. I was there to find—something.

It's been a while, I said in my head. I'm sorry for that. I've been busy—no, I've been lazy—It wasn't working.

"I need to talk out loud," I said, pulling the kneeler down and getting on my knees, so I couldn't see him or feel him. "So if you don't want to hear this, you might—"

"I'm fine," he said. "Don't worry about me." He said that with his head bowed, not looking up.

"Okay," I said, unsure.

I faced the front and focused on the simple wooden cross that sat on a table. It had been a long time since I'd touched base with that side of me. I stared at it, knowing there was so much to say, and suddenly none of it seemed worthy. I felt foreign in there, and realized I'd probably felt more in touch with God sitting up on my mother's roof than I did in a church.

I closed my eyes and tried to let it sink in, but I was fighting it. Then I felt pressure on the kneeler pad next to me, and Ben took my hand.

"Our Father, who art in heaven," he began.

I opened my eyes and stared at his profile. His eyes were closed, and he continued with the prayer I knew from childhood. He spoke so calm. So sure. Even with everything he'd been through in his life, with his dad, his childhood. Me.

He finished and stayed where he was, not letting go of my hand. I looked at it, at the cross, and closed my eyes again, wanting what he felt.

"I love you, Em," he said softly.

My eyes flew open.

"I have to start with that," he continued. I looked at the side of his head, because he still wasn't looking at me. "I'm trying with the rest of it."

"I don't have the energy for a fight, Ben," I whispered. "I'm—"

"I don't, either," he said, turning to meet my eyes. He looked as beat up as I felt. "I just wanted you to know—that's all I can give you right now."

He got up and walked slowly out, leaving me there. I knew in my heart he wouldn't be in the waiting room when I got back.

CASSIDY DIDN'T ASK FOR ME, BUT I DIDN'T GIVE HER THE OPTION. I went in after Kevin left her with Josh. She met my eyes and then closed hers and went to sleep. As much as that ripped at my gut, I had to let it be okay. She had to come to me on her own terms. That was her way.

I held her hand as she slept, remembering her tiny little fingers when she was born, the impossibly small fingernails and little creases at the knuckles.

"Mr. Lockwood told her how it really happened," Josh said from his chair on the other side of the room, his voice hushed. I'd thought he was sleeping, too, and his words startled me.

"What?" I asked, looking at her beat-up face, her mouth slightly open. "What do you mean?"

"He told her that you didn't cheat on him, that you didn't do what he did."

My eyes filled with hot, burning tears, and I blinked them back. "He said that?"

Josh nodded. "He said that y'all weren't married yet, and weren't even together anymore when—you know—" He looked so creeped out at the thought of me having sex, it was almost comical.

"Yeah," I said, trying to end his discomfort.

"So anyway, he told her she didn't need to be mad at you, but she's still—I don't know."

"It's okay," I said, looking at her. "She feels betrayed. I get that." He got up and pulled her sheet up a little higher, and he touched her cheek as I watched him care for her. "How are the two of you?" I asked.

He shrugged. "We haven't really had a chance to talk about it, but I'm not giving up."

I smiled. "Good for you."

He looked at me with a surprised expression. "Really?"

I gave a little head shrug. "You're a good man, Josh. She's lucky to have you."

Ben wasn't there when I went back to the waiting area. No one was. Kevin had evidently left for the night, and Josh gave me permission to go home as well. I'd actually laughed out loud when he said that, and the sound was so foreign to me that I had to stop and think the last time I'd heard it.

I decided to take him up on it, thinking Kevin's idea of a shower was probably a good one now that Cassidy was among the conscious. I promised to be back the next morning to let him go do the same, and although he balked at first, he agreed once I pointed out that she was now awake and could smell him.

It was a mild night, chilly but not wet cold like Texas could be, when it goes to your bones, so I grabbed a thick blanket and headed out to the swing in my pajamas. In my red pajamas that Ben had peeled off me the day we made love all over the house.

I hugged them to me at the memory, wondering what he was doing. It had taken every ounce of willpower I had not to stop at his house on the way home. And then again not to leave and go over there after my shower. And then again before I went outside. Every single cell in my body wanted to go talk to him, but I had to let it rest. Just like with Cassidy, I had to let him leave and figure things—and there was another thing she came by honestly I supposed. And with both of them, I felt the empty hole in my middle where my fear festered. The fear that they wouldn't come back. I'd survived Ben's departure before, and could probably do it again, but I didn't want to. Not after rediscovering something so amazing. But Cass—my skin went icy just thinking about that. I didn't think I could survive losing her.

I pulled my fuzzy-socked feet up in the swing with me just in case anything nocturnal decided to crawl on them, and wrapped myself in the blanket. The night sky was clear and full of stars. I remembered sitting out there on lawn chairs when Cassidy was little, trying to count them and laughing as we kept having to start over.

Ben had missed all that. But we'd beaten the what-ifs to death. Things happened as they were supposed to, I had to believe that. And even if that weren't true, there was nothing we could do to change it now. All of us—myself, Cassidy, Kevin, Ben—all we could do was look forward. I covered my face in my hands.

"Shit, that's such a load of crap," I muttered into them.

I heard my gate open, and in the dark, that was a little unsettling even though I was hoping it was Ben. Per my luck on that, it wasn't. It was Kevin.

I had a brief second of self-preservation, where I wondered if he'd brought a weapon or a vial of poison or something, but he just strolled slowly over to where I sat on the swing with his hands in his pockets and leaned his head back to look up at the stars.

"You didn't answer the door; I figured you might be back here," he said. "It's clear, tonight."

I stared up at him. "Are you here to kill me? Because about all I have the strength to do from here is throw this blanket at you."

He shook his head while still gazing upward. "Nah, wouldn't be worth the jail time."

I moved my feet up a little closer to me. "Want to sit down?"

He looked down dubiously, as if maybe it was a trick, then landed heavily on the swing. He didn't say anything for a few minutes, just swayed us gently with his feet. I felt so sorry for him suddenly, thinking of how I'd just gone sick over the possibility of losing Cassidy. To find out she wasn't even mine—

"I'm so sorry, Kevin," I said, and I could tell by his profile that he closed his eyes. "I don't expect you to care that I'm sorry, I'm not saying it for me. I just truly regret—" I had to stop. "No, I don't."

He looked at me, and in the dark I couldn't quite read his eyes.

"I can't say anything that's gonna be right, I'm screwed no matter what I say, so I'm just gonna talk. I'm sorry how things happened, but I don't regret you raising Cassidy. You—you're a fantastic father. She is who she is partly because of you. If I ever see Ben again, I'll tell him I'm sorry that he *didn't* get to raise her, and I do regret that for him, but I don't for you. You did everything right."

He looked away and wiped his eyes, then looked up at the sky again. "Except with you."

"Oh, yeah, you sucked as a husband, but you were an A-plus father."

A laugh broke through his tears, and I dared to laugh with him for the seconds it lasted. "And Josh told me what you said to Cass tonight, Kevin." I nudged him with my foot. "You—were pretty A-plus there, too. You could've made me out to be a scheming troll."

"I think I went in there with that, actually," he said, scrubbing at his eyes again. "But the second I saw her, I broke. I just wanted her to feel like everything would be okay again. It wasn't about me, anymore."

I felt my own tears fall but I wiped them quietly away. It wasn't about me, either.

"She told me I'd always be her dad, no matter what," he said, his voice breaking. "That meant more to me than anything ever has—or ever will."

My own flood started again. "Maybe in a backassward way, this can help y'all get close again."

"Don't push it."

I chuckled. "Sorry."

He looked my way. "What do you mean *if* you ever get to see him again?"

I gave a head shrug. "I don't know if he can forgive me. And I can't blame him for that any more than I can blame you."

Kevin sighed heavily. "I probably didn't help that."

"I doubt it was anything he wasn't already thinking."

"But if you didn't know," he said, the tone in his voice testing me, "and he left town, how could you have done anything differently?"

"Well, for starters, I'm sure he's probably thinking I should have said something since he's been back," I said. "Other than that—there are things I could have done."

"Like leaving me?" he said, turning toward me.

I paused, thinking out my words. "I could have hurt you like that." I shook my head. "I could have tried to track him down, and I know that's what he's thinking. But honestly, you and I were making a life by then." I looked at him. "I made a choice. Was it wrong?"

His head moved slowly back and forth. "Did you ever love me, Emily? I mean, really? Or was I just convenient?"

My stomach contracted. "Of course I did. We were a family, Kevin. I didn't marry you to get a father, I married you because I believed you *were* the father." Sort of. It was enough of the truth to put his heart at ease, and I needed to do that for him.

"And if he would have never left?"

Oh, God, don't ask me that.

"Never mind, don't answer that," he said, as if reading my mind. "I'm gonna go." He stood up slowly so that the swing didn't lurch.

I pushed the blanket behind me and stood as well, and before I could think better of it or give him a chance to back up, I wound my arms under his jacket and hugged him to me. It was foreign and familiar at the same time. I felt him catch a breath in surprise, then after a second or two his arms came up. One around my back, one hand cradled my head, and I felt him lay his cheek against my head as he held me. It had been years since I'd been in Kevin's arms, and while it was comfortable, it wasn't right. It wasn't Ben.

He pulled back and looked down into my face. "I'm gonna marry Sherry," he said.

I smiled. "Really?"

"And I'm gonna be faithful."

I bit my lip. "Okay."

"No, I'm serious," he said. "When Cass told me she didn't think people could be faithful, it hit something with me. I have to show her that I can."

That reminded me. "Did you know that Cass and Josh were engaged?"

He frowned. "They are?"

"They were. She broke it off that night. There's a ring and everything."

"Well, he's there—"

"Because he's determined to get her back," I said, realizing I sounded like a cheerleader for Josh.

"I thought you weren't crazy about him," Kevin said.

"I wasn't," I said, crossing my arms for warmth. "But the last few days, he's surprised me."

"We'll see," he said, sounding like the old Kevin.

"Kev."

He stopped himself and ran a hand over his face. "Okay. I'll give him a chance." He walked slowly around the swing toward the gate, and stopped halfway there, gazing up at the stars again. "I can't speak for what goes on in Landry's head. But for what it's worth," he said, turning his body partially back to me, "he's a moron if he walks away from you a second time."

I watched his figure retreat into darkness and heard the gate click closed, then sat back down and pulled the blanket around me. I longed for Ben, ached for Cassidy, and sent a small prayer of thanks up for at least Kevin's—something. I don't know if it was forgiveness. Maybe just acceptance. Something other than hatred. He had hugged me back at least.

And he was vowing monogamy with Sherry. That had to be a plus to come out of this, right? Yeah, don't push it.

CHAPTER

19

I walked through Mom's front door the next morning, determined to have a good outlook. Josh and Kevin were speaking to me, so there was improvement, but the two people that I needed the most were still on the fence. Or maybe not even on it. They might have been skipping on the other side of it for all I knew.

First thing I'd noticed was the absence of Ben's truck, but that was okay. He deserved a day off. Sounded reasonable.

"Hey, we're almost ready," Mom said, emerging from the hall. "Come get you some coffee and sit a second."

Mom looked ready to me. "*We* meaning Aunt Bernie?"

She winked at me. "Eye shadow."

"Ah."

"So, how was Cassidy last night?" she asked.

I tilted my head. "Ignoring me, but I think she had a good talk with Kevin."

"Really?"

"Yeah, he came over last night," I said, climbing onto a stool and letting my mother fix me a cup like I was little. "Seems he doesn't wish me dead."

"Well," she said, giving me a look. "It's not like he's all purity and light."

I stirred the creamer in. "No, but even he didn't deserve this, Mom. He loves her."

"I know he does, honey." She studied me a second. "What about our Ben?"

The concrete in my chest shifted a little. "I don't know. Trying not to think about that. Next?"

She patted my hand. "The house is being shown this afternoon."

I felt a weird little pang of sadness. "Really? By who?"

"I have no idea," she said. "I'm just glad it's getting closer to being ready."

"You anxious to hit the road?" I asked, feeling a silly separation anxiety over the thought of her leaving.

Her expression changed. She looked conflicted. "I was. At first."

I leaned forward, my elbows on the bar. "Change of heart?"

She shook her head. "No, not really. I still want out from under this wooly mammoth," she said with a chuckle. "I'm just not all up on the *leaving* part. Not now, after Cass's accident."

"She'll be fine, Mom."

"I know, but I just—you know there's still furniture that has to be moved—maybe Ben—oops, sorry."

I smiled. "It's okay."

"Anyway, there's still things to do. And I don't want to leave

Cass right now. I don't know," she said then, in her *I'm done* voice, popping her hands on the bar. "Spending time with that girl has been a blast, too. I'm not ready to leave that, either. She's been a big help. She got you those two boxes of books, right?"

"Yeah," I said, rubbing my face that I didn't bother fixing. I didn't see much point. "They're still in my car, actually."

"Probably stay there till you sell it and they'll go in the next one."

I chuckled. "Probably."

"Girl, those have been here since you moved back in. Sell them or something, it's deadweight."

"I know," I said.

"They've been all over this house," she said, washing her cup out. "I think I finally moved them out of your room when your Uncle Tommy needed a place to sleep for a couple of weeks. Moved them to the hall closet, then I needed that for something and I moved them to your dad's office for a while." She shook her head. "I don't even know how they made it downstairs to that closet."

"Dad's office?" I asked, as memory dawned. "They were in Dad's office?"

"For a while," she said, looking at me funny. "Why?"

I got goose bumps. "Oh, my—hang on." I was off that stool and out the front door in seconds, hitting the remote on my keys for the back trunk. "Damn it," I muttered when of course it didn't work. I opened it with the key and stared at the boxes.

Pulling one open, I was greeted with multiple titles of all genres and colors and authors.

"What are you doing?" Mom asked, coming down the front porch steps, looking at me like I was crazy.

"I don't know," I said. I also didn't know how I would explain it, but I couldn't worry about that yet.

I pulled books out, three and four at a time, and set them on the driveway, going back for more. Some I hadn't seen since I was a teenager, since I probably boxed them up to move *away* from home and they never got unpacked.

"Emily, have you lost your senses, girl?" my mother asked me. She looked around. "Mr. LeBoeuf is gonna start talking stories if you keep this up."

"Let him talk, he needs entertainment," I said, emptying one box completely. "Hmm. Okay, well maybe not."

"Maybe not, what?"

"Nothing," I said. "Let me look in here."

"Lordy, can I put these back in?" she said, gesturing to the empty box and the pile on the ground.

"Sure," I said. "Did Cass look through these?"

"I doubt it," she said. "We opened them, and I recognized them right off. I've shuffled them around enough, I ought to."

Three layers down, and my fingers hit metal.

"Oh my God."

"What?" Mom said, looking alarmed.

I looked at her, feeling tears come again. I swear, I was going to dehydrate. I dug down to wrap my hands around the edges and pulled it up out of the books, sending them tottering askew. I didn't care. It was the box.

Mom and I both looked down at it. "What's that?"

My chin quivered. *Your house's final gift to you.* "It's Dad's box."

Her eyes shot up to mine. "Dad's—what?"

I just nodded.

She shook her head. "But—why would—how do you know that?"

"I just do," I said. "Come on."

I left everything there in the driveway and carried the box in the house, Mom following on my heels like a confused puppy.

"This makes no sense, Emmie," she said as I laid it on the bar. "Why would he put it in a box of your books?"

"Because they were in his office," I said. "And Uncle Tommy saw him take it out of the real hiding place behind the poster, so he hid it temporarily so Tommy wouldn't come steal from it. And then he died."

Mom stared at me like I'd just spoken in tongues. "You need to take a nerve pill."

"I can't explain it all right now, Mom. But it's true, so open it."

She shook her head, looking frazzled and a little annoyed. Until she flipped the latch and lifted the lid, the hinges crackling with years of not moving.

It was exactly how I'd seen it in my vision. A stack of money, and a stack of scribbled notes on various slips of colored paper. She might have questioned the origin of the money, but there was no mistaking her own handwriting. Her hands shook a little as she touched one and picked it up.

"What does it say?" I breathed.

I heard her breathing get a little faster, and she sniffled and laughed before dabbing at her eyes. She picked up another one, and another. "It's all the little notes I'd leave for him now and then. *X marks the spot*—" She laughed again. I chuckled to myself, as I couldn't tell her I knew what that meant.

"And this—" She picked up a small flip notebook, with listed items, clearly in my dad's handwriting. "Oh, sweet lord," she whispered. "Charles."

"What?"

I walked around to read it with her. It was a ledger of sorts, dated with dollar amounts added and taken away, over the decades, with little comments next to them.

One day we'll see the pyramids!

Skipped coffee with the guys for one month

For The Grand Canyon

Minused for Tommy . . . will repay

There were years and years and years of them, and way too many Tommys.

The last one showed the $500 withdrawal, on May 7, 1998, with a balance of $11,450.

I picked up the bundle of green. "Oh my God."

Mom was full-out crying by then, and I put an arm around her. "He gave Tommy money the night he died."

"I'm guessing he never repaid it."

"Of course not," she said, sniffing. "He never did. Then he went and died the next year, the mooch."

I laughed, and she did, too, in spite of the tears still flowing. The knocker banged, and we looked up to see Holly come in.

"Hey," she said. "What's—what's the matter? What—is Cass okay?" she asked, her face going scarlet with worry.

"Yes—Cassidy's awake," I said, calming that fear. "We're going over there in a minute; what are you doing?"

"Coming to see if Mom wanted to go up there with me, and I saw your car."

I smiled at her. "Come see this."

She set her purse down and looked over my shoulder. "Holy shit, where did all that money come from?"

"Dad's box," I said.

She head-jerked at me. "Seriously? This is the box? There's really a box?"

"I told you," Mom said, wiping her face. "I knew there would be."

"Where was it?" Holly asked.

"How did you know where it was?" Mom asked then, turning to me. "How did you know it was in your books?"

"What?" Holly exclaimed. "Somebody tell me!"

I bit my lip. "I dreamed it."

Mom gave me a raised eyebrow. "Emily Ann, don't you lie to me."

"I'm not lying," I said, and decided to deflect. "Mom, look at this." I picked up the money again. "You can go anywhere you want now." I lowered my voice to a whisper. "You don't have to ride around in a big blue gas guzzler to travel. You can go somewhere amazing."

Mom touched the money and smiled as tears rolled down her face. She shook her head slowly. "It wasn't about the places, honey. It was about seeing them with your dad. Without him, they're just thumbtacks on a map."

"I can't believe he saved all that," Holly said.

I thought about how much more there would have been if Uncle Tommy hadn't mooched it. But still, over eleven grand was nothing to sneeze at.

"Jesus, Charles," my mom said. "What I could have done with that kind of money."

"It wasn't there for that, Mom, he wanted to take you somewhere special."

"That's pretty damn special," Holly said.

"Have you priced trips for two to Egypt?" I said.

"Not lately," she countered.

"Girls," Mom interjected. "It doesn't matter." She picked up the bundle of money and counted off a few thousand. She put that back in the box with the notes, and put the rest of the bulk in her purse like it was grocery money. "But I know a little girl with that same wanderlust that still has her special guy to share it with."

CASSIDY WAS INCLINED A LITTLE IN THE BED WHEN I WENT IN, and her face—the part that wasn't black or purple—wasn't as pale as before. She had a cup with a straw that she was sipping from. She looked up when I came in, and although she averted her eyes to the muted TV attached to the ceiling, at least she didn't just close them and go to sleep.

Josh looked up from the newspaper he was reading.

"Hey, I'm glad you're here," he said. "Mind hanging for a little bit while I run home and change clothes?"

We'd already had that conversation, so I knew it was a show for her benefit, and the look he ignored from her would have disintegrated a lesser man.

"I'll be back in a few, baby," he said, kissing her hand.

"Yeah," she said, her voice scratchy, but the sarcasm came through just fine.

He smiled at me on his way out, and I winked at him.

"Subtle," she rasped.

I didn't say anything as I sat down on a tall-backed stool I assumed was for the doctor. "He's a good guy, Cass."

She coughed and gripped the railing as the pain from that ripped through her. "Now I must be dying," she said through her teeth.

"No, we've just had some conversations since you decided to drive like an idiot down a dark road."

She closed her eyes. "Can we save this for another day?"

"No, I don't think so," I said. Her attitude had sucked the coddling right out of me. "You want to be upset with me, fine. But feeling sorry for yourself is beneath you. Going off like that, hurting a guy who loves you unconditionally, risking your life, and terrifying everyone who loves you—and then being a jerk about it afterward? That's not who I raised."

"Who did you raise, Mom? Kevin's kid or Ben's?"

"Did you suffer?" I asked, leaning toward her. "Was there ever a time that you didn't feel absolutely over-the-top loved?"

The anger in her eyes fizzled a bit.

"We were once young, too, Cass. We haven't always had the answers, sometimes we've had to wing it. I was your age when I got pregnant. How smart would you be?"

She focused on the cup in her hand and played with the straw. I decided to go for broke and talk to her woman to woman. "Ben was my best friend. Unlike anything I've ever known. And he picked me up every time Kevin cheated on me, and finally I was done with it. It was a couple of weeks later that Ben and I finally crossed that line. And changed everything."

"But he didn't stick around?"

I licked my lips and took a cleansing breath. "He saw your dad beg me to come back to him, and being young and impulsive, he took off, thinking I'd say yes. He didn't stick around to hear the no."

Her eyebrows knitted together over her nose. "You told Dad no?"

"Yes, I did. And then I found out about you. And it was like a Lifetime movie—I knew it could be either one of them, but Ben was gone without explanation, and I was scared, and then your dad was there every day, winning me back. Making me promises." I looked her dead-on. "I wanted to believe him. And I buried my head in the sand about who made you."

"Until I was born."

I nodded slowly. "There was no doubt," I said softly. "But Kevin was in love with you, and I couldn't take that away." I took her hand, and the fact that she didn't pull it away gave me courage. "Baby, I'm not justifying what I did. I probably did everything all wrong, but you've had a great dad that loves you over the moon and back."

"I know." She was quiet for a moment, appearing to process everything. "So that's why you freaked out when Ben showed up back in town?"

I sighed. "Just a little."

Her eyes teared up. "Josh asked me to marry him."

"I know."

"How do I know it's right?" she asked. "You and Dad weren't right. He wasn't even Dad."

"Yes, he was," I said. "He earned that title, Cass. And as far as being right goes?" I gestured around the room. "Who's been here? Josh hasn't left your side in three days, he's barely eaten. He's the real deal, honey. If that doesn't tell you something, then I don't know what you want. You need to make that right."

She hit the channels on the remote, sending the TV into a silent surfing frenzy. "So does everyone know now?" she asked.

I inhaled deeply and let it go. "Pretty much. Ben giving you blood because *we* didn't qualify was quite the train wreck."

She frowned. "That's how Dad found out?"

"That's how they both found out. With me standing in between them. It wasn't my finest moment."

"I'm sorry," she said softly.

"It's okay."

"No—I mean, I'm sorry, Mom," she said, two big tears spilling from her eyes. "I'm sorry I caused all this mess."

I squeezed her hand. "You didn't cause it, doodlebug. I kept this secret. The chain of events to unravel it kicked into gear the day Ben came back into town. It was just a matter of time."

"What about Ben?" I blinked and she looked down. "What does he think about it?"

I fought the tremble in my mouth. "He's—pretty devastated. But he's so proud of you."

"Is he still here?"

I shook my head. "He left last night. He needed to get things sorted out, I think." *Or get the hell away from me.* I pushed a small smile. "Like somebody else I know."

"Is he mad at you?"

I chuckled. "Oh, yeah. But mostly he's just hurt." The burn filled my eyes again. "Overwhelmed that he missed your whole life and didn't even know it."

"You love him again, don't you?" she asked. I met her eyes and blinked my tears free. "I've never seen you like this with anyone else."

I nodded. "I do," I said, hearing the shake in my voice and hating it. I cleared my throat. "But it doesn't matter, baby girl. What matters right now is getting you well and out of here."

"Don't change the subject," she said.

I swiped fingers under my eyes and blew out a breath. "Ben is a point I can't control or fix. You are my priority right now."

"And I'll be okay," she said. "He loves you, too, Mom." I closed my eyes, remembering those last words he said to me. "If Ben's the real deal for *you*," she began, "you need to go make it right."

I had to give myself a couple of seconds on that one. "I hate it when you use my words."

"I know," she said as I got up and readjusted my purse on my shoulder. "Where are you going?" she asked. "Josh clearly left you to babysit. And when do I get more than one visitor?"

"When you get out of ICU," I said. "And Nana has something to talk to you about."

"Nana's here?"

I went outside to get Mom, and she walked nonchalantly to the hallway door. "Bernie doesn't know about the money, so don't say anything," she said under her breath to me as she clutched her purse.

I raised an eyebrow. "Why?"

"I just don't want her knowing I have that kind of money," she said. "She tends to want to spend whatever's around."

I looked past her to where Aunt Bernie and Holly were chatting in the waiting area, and Holly looked as if she wished for UFOs to beam her up.

"Okay," I said, shrugging. "But tell me you aren't just going to hand her that cash, to keep around *here*?" I gestured around us.

"No, and thank you for thinking I'm that brainless," she said, giving me a look. "I'm going to the bank from here. Putting it in a little savings account for her. Just want to show it to her first."

I hugged my mom. "You're amazing, you know that?"

"Yeah, I know that."

It was the next night before Cassidy was moved to a regular room, and another week and a half before she was released. Normally, she would have walked her muscles stronger after the surgery, being dragged from bed at crazy times of night to shuffle around the nurses' station. Having only one good leg pushed out the healing.

She didn't argue too much when I insisted she stay with me for a couple of weeks. Not because I was that awesome, but because I had the only house with one floor. Her apartment, Josh's apartment—everything was stair-challenged for her, so I got her old room fluffed and cleaned up. And by that, I mean I actually did it myself, instead of paying someone else to do it.

I had nothing else to do every night when I'd get home from the hospital. I had no active clients since I'd referred them all to other Realtors. All, meaning three. And I had no other kind of life other than going to Mom's to play Scrabble with her and Aunt Bernie.

And that was just sad.

I couldn't bring myself to go "make it right" with Ben. I had pursued him enough, and then slammed him with the shock of a lifetime. He could either make up his mind to forgive me or decide it was too much. However he played it, it had to be his decision.

I was so busy making sure that Cassidy was taken care of and had everything she needed to heal properly that I didn't have time to sit and ponder the what-ifs. Or whether he knew that it had been exactly twenty days since he left me in that little chapel.

But at night, lying alone in my bed, I'd look at his pillow and picture him sleeping. Every morning was a weird mixture of feeling a little bit emptier and a little bit stronger. He'd left me before. I could ride it out again.

I had just helped Cassidy from her room to the couch one morning, with pillows, a steaming mug of coffee, and the remote, when my doorbell rang. I opened it, already knowing it was Josh, coming to take care of his woman. I had to hand it to him, he was dedicated. Only problem was he kept bringing their things over and leaving them there so she'd feel at home. Her movie collection. Her favorite pillows. His favorite video game and headphones. I was slowly becoming their vacation house.

He waved on his way in but pointed behind him. "Your mom's here," he said.

I waited as she ambled up the sidewalk. "Hey," I said. "What's up?"

"I assume you have coffee?" she asked, pushing the arms of her royal blue velour jogging suit up.

"Of course," I said. "What's with the outfit?"

"Bernie bought it for me."

"Ah, that explains it."

She gestured the same to me as she came in and I shut the door. "What's with yours?"

I had on ratty blue flannel pajamas with two buttons missing and a tank top underneath. "I'm comfortable."

We poured our cups, getting ready to go out in the backyard. I needed some of the sunshine I'd heard rumors about, something to make the yuck go away.

"I don't get a hello?" Cassidy said to Mom, feigning hurt feelings.

Mom waved. "Hello!"

The two of them had sat nearly every night poring over the internet travel sites, as Mom helped her plan the perfect honeymoon trip for her and Josh. She'd also brought the telescope. Presumably for Cassidy, but we'd have to see.

"We'll be in the back for a while," I said.

"Show him your notes," Mom said over her shoulder, and Cass held up her travel spiral notebook victoriously.

"I miss the swing," she said. "I want to come, too."

"Maybe later, I'll put a lawn chair out there for you," I said. "Something a little more stable than the swing."

"Deal," she said.

"I'll bring ours," Josh said.

I put on a smile. "Fabulous."

Mom and I breathed in deep as we walked out, the air fresh and crisp and remarkably dry under a perfect sky. The swing swayed gently under our feet as the coffee warmed our insides.

"Has Kevin been coming by still?"

"Yeah," I said. "Every couple of days, he comes by and walks around the block with her." I laughed. "Takes about an hour to do that at her pace, so they've been talking."

"I'm so glad."

"Me, too."

"And Ben?"

I felt myself wilt a little. "What about him?"

She nudged me. "You know what about him. Don't play dumb with me."

I shrugged. "There's nothing to tell, Mom. I haven't seen him."

There was a pause, and then she asked, "Has Cassidy said anything about him?"

"She's asked some questions here and there," I said, tracing the rim of my cup with my finger. "Mostly, I've told her she can ask him anything she wants to know, which I'm hoping is true. She said she would kind of like to know him better. She has a cousin, you know. Bobby's son."

"Holy crap, I didn't think about that," she said, looking at me. "Did she know him?"

I shook my head. "They put him in private school."

"You know those new condo places they built last year?" Mom asked. "Overlooking the river?"

I got whiplash from the subject change. "Yeah."

She took a sip of coffee. "I went and talked to the office people there today."

I looked at her in surprise. "For?"

"Me to lease one."

That was the second time she had rendered me speechless.

"Um—"

She waved a hand. "I know. I know what I said—all the traveling, blah, blah, blah. But you know what?" she said, scrunching up her nose. "Turns out I'm having more fun planning Cassidy's trips than my own."

"But—that won't be forever, Mom."

"I know," she said. "But it got me thinking about doing that for other people."

"Oh, lord." I had to laugh. "I thought you wanted to do something with cooking."

"I could combine it," she said. "And I don't want that big house anymore, but just a little place I wouldn't have to keep up much with would be okay."

"And—Aunt Bernie?"

She shrugged and took another sip. "I could go for quick trips when she's nearby, and then come back." She turned to face me. "Cassidy's little doo-ditty showed me what's important. I want to be around for my family."

"Have you told Aunt Bernie?"

"Yep," she said. "She's gonna leave in a day or two and come back in a couple of months. I'll probably be settled and ready for a little road trip by then."

I looked in her wise eyes and gave her a smile. "Okay then. My mom's getting a condo."

"Is that embarrassing?"

"Not at all," I said with a shake of my head. "I'll take that over Big Blue any day."

She laughed, and then the sound of the gate latch shutting caught both of our attention and we turned. Two seconds later, I forgot all about condos.

CHAPTER

20

BEN STROLLED SLOWLY AROUND THE HEDGE, STOPPING WHEN he saw us.

Lots of things stopped on me, too. My feet, for instance, lost their blood supply in seconds. *Protecting the heart.*

"Hey," he said, his voice sending my skin on a little ride.

"Hey."

He pointed behind him at the gate. "Josh said you were back here." He glanced at the back door window. "I didn't want to go through the house."

I got to my feet, so happy that I could stand on them and not fall over.

He crossed his arms. "Morning, Mrs. Lattimer," he said with a warm smile.

"Good morning, Ben," she said, her voice full of smiles and innuendo and I wanted to shove her off the swing for it. "Missed you, lately."

He nodded but didn't address that. Instead, he returned his gaze to me. "Is it a bad time?"

"No!" Mom said, jumping off that swing like she was a spry little kid. "I was just thinking I needed to go whip up something to eat."

"Really?" I said.

"Sure was," she said, lifting her chin. "My Cass loves waffles."

"You're gonna make waffles?"

"I'm gonna make whatever I can find in your kitchen," she said with a haughty look. She winked at me though before she went through the back door.

And then we were alone. Ben in his standard jeans and shirt over a T-shirt. Me in pajamas. Again. Much crappier ones. But the wiggle in my belly was not about my attire. The more disturbing issue at hand was the intensity in his gaze. He didn't blink. He didn't move. And all I could do was grip my cup with all I had and hold my head up high. If he was coming to tell me good-bye, then that was his prerogative. I would not cry. I would not crumble in front of him.

"How is she doing?" he asked, his voice quiet. He walked a few steps and stopped again.

I nodded. "She's getting better every day. It's just slow going."

We looked at each other until I thought my skin would catch fire. Something had to give, or start, or end.

"Ben—"

He closed his eyes as if he dreaded speaking. When he opened them again, I saw the struggle. He took another couple of steps, bringing him just out of touching reach. I focused on his hands, the rough callouses and skin that I remembered felt like heaven on my face.

"Were you ever gonna tell me?" he said.

My breath left me. I didn't have an answer for that. "I was about to tell you when the police called me," I said.

He shook his head slowly. "If that hadn't happened. If she'd never overheard it, if none of that ever went down?" he said, nailing me down. "Would you have ever told me that I had a daughter?" he repeated.

I looked at him with my chin up, not letting myself falter. "I don't know, Ben." His expression of hurt pained me, but I wasn't going to lie anymore. "I'm sorry," I said. "I didn't know how to go there. How to tell you without Cass or Kevin knowing. How to tell her without Kevin or you finding out. There wasn't a solution that didn't hurt someone."

He walked up closer, inches from me. His eyes looked raw, like he hadn't been sleeping. "I know I was gone. I know—you thought I left you—and so I'm not dogging you for giving up on me," he said, his voice cracking a little. "But do you know what it would have meant—" He stopped and angry tears filled his eyes. "To my mother?"

I shut my eyes to the pain in his face.

"She didn't go anywhere," he said, pointing behind him. "She was right there, in my house. My brother was right across town."

I nodded, my eyes still closed as tears leaked out beneath them.

"I was wrong for that, Ben," I said. I opened my eyes and the tears fell hot down my cheeks. "I'm sorry. I'm so—so sorry." Seemed like I was saying that a lot.

He ran a sleeve across his eyes. "So am I."

So it was good-bye, then. Okay.

He turned around and let out a ragged sigh as he walked back around the side of the house and through the gate, clicking it shut. I stood there, feeling the burn and the horrible, stirred-up hole of acid in the pit of my stomach. Okay, he'd seen me cry, after all, but I hadn't crumbled.

I couldn't make my feet move, however. All I could do was stare at the place he'd been standing, and cry softly for the only man I'd ever truly given my heart and soul to.

Finally, I turned around and walked in the house. Josh and Cass were involved in a show, but Mom turned from the open refrigerator when she heard the door. Her face fell when she looked at me, and she shut the fridge and came over to wrap me up in a big hug.

"What did he say, honey?"

"Not much," I said, sniffling. "Basically that I'm a big, fat liar."

"He said that?"

"No, but it all meant the same thing."

She chuckled silently and rubbed my back.

"I'm sorry, baby."

I pulled back and went for a paper towel to mop up the mess that was my face.

"It's okay," I said. "I think I already knew it was done for, I just—still had that grain of hope, I guess." I wiped my face and sucked in a fast breath to cleanse everything from my head. "Okay, enough of this. Do we have waffle stuff?"

She paused and then went with it. "You barely even have cereal."

"Kinda what I thought," I said. "Let me go throw some clothes on and put a bag over my head, and I'll make a quick run to the store."

"I can go, Emmie."

I shook my head. "I'm better when I'm moving."

She nodded and winked and gave my hand a squeeze. "Okay then. Get moving."

I passed behind the couch on my way to my bedroom. Behind where Cassidy and Josh were heavy into a discussion about music videos.

"Mom?" she said.

"Yeah?" I responded, pretending to pick up an imaginary something off the floor.

"Ben came by?"

I chewed at my lip and turned to her as she looked at me from her awkward angle. There was an odd expression of curiosity there. Or hope.

"Yes."

Her eyes registered my appearance. "I guess it didn't go well."

I linked fingers with her over the couch. "He asked how you were doing, doodlebug. Feel free to reach out on that anytime you want."

She raised an eyebrow. "That's not what I asked."

I squeezed her finger and smiled. "I know."

It only took me a few minutes to wash my face, slap on a little powder, throw a sweatshirt and jeans on, and twist my hair up in a clip. I smiled in the mirror before I left the bathroom, insistent on not letting the knife in my gut get me down. I was better than that. I had done the best I could do at the time, and the best I could do since. That probably wasn't true, and most likely I could have made some better choices, but it was what it was. I took a deep breath and decided that I was clichéd out.

"Back in a bit," I called over my shoulder as I opened the front door. But my words were cut as short as my steps as the door shut behind me and I found myself staring into Ben Landry's face again.

OR NOT ACTUALLY UP IN HIS FACE. MORE LIKE ACROSS THE yard. But the shock value of him still being there, and looking at me, and—still being there! He might as well have been two inches away.

After the stutter step, and the funky little noise that came out of my throat, I made my way around the porch and through the yard toward where he stood leaning against his truck with his arms crossed. His eyes never left me, but I couldn't read them. I stopped about a foot away, thinking it was a reasonable personal space and yet he could still touch me if he wanted. If *he* wanted.

"I thought you left," I said. My voice didn't sound right. I crossed my arms, too, so we could match.

"I thought you'd be eating waffles," he said. His eyes looked so tired, I wondered if his staying was more from being too exhausted to make it inside his truck.

"Going to—get the stuff," I said, pointing toward my car. That he was parked behind.

He nodded, and then took a long, deep breath.

"I couldn't leave," he said, the words barely a whisper. I didn't dare breathe, waiting for the why and the whatever came next. "I got in and out twice already. But seeing you—" A look of almost unbearable sadness came over his face. "And knowing she's right in there—I couldn't drive away."

Everything in my body wanted to close the gap and touch

him, go into his arms, bury my face in the warmth, and wrap myself around him. I crossed my arms tighter to avoid the urge.

"You're welcome to go talk to her," I said, thinking it easier to just make it about Cassidy. "She's been wanting to talk to you, too."

His eyes woke up for the first time since he'd been there. "She has?"

I gave a little smile and nodded. "Yeah. She liked you already, Ben. Now she wants to get to know you a little." I looked down at a rock stuck in the grass, and I toed it with my sneaker. "That's up to you, though."

He looked at the front door like it had gold behind it. And I guess it did.

I readjusted my bag. "If you're gonna do it now, though, can you move your truck? I need to go get that waffle mix or my mother will—"

My words died on my lips as his hand landed warm against the side of my neck, gently drawing me closer to him. I looked into his eyes for answers but only got questions.

"I don't know, Emily," he whispered, as if reading my mind. "I don't know what to do, or how this will work. Or if it will." His other hand tucked a fallen lock of hair behind my ear, and I thought my ear might catch fire. "But I know I can't go the rest of my life and not try to know my daughter." His eyes pierced mine. "And there's no way I can walk away from you again."

Rather than try to talk, or ask anything that could spoil the magic of that statement, I took the gamble and moved forward, burying my face in his shirt. I wound my arms around his back, and he responded by pulling me to him so tightly it nearly squeezed the breath out of me. I didn't care. Breathing was over-rated.

"I can't promise you this is going to be easy, Em," he said, his words warm in my hair. "It's gonna take me some time."

"I'm not going anywhere," I said against the base of his throat.

He kissed the top of my head, and that was like a magnet for me. I lifted my face and found his lips and that was all I needed.

AUNT BERNIE LEFT IN A BLAZE OF BLUE, WITH MUCH FUSSING and weeping and promises to be back in a couple of months to steal Mom from her hip new condo and take her on the ride of her life. Holly and I put Cass in the car and brought her over for the big farewell. Josh, too. And Ben, too. He actually carried her from the car to a lawn chair. They were connecting. Slowly.

Rather than move Cass more, the guys found additional lawn chairs in Mom's garage, and decided to have a yard party right there on the front lawn. Holly left to get her big cooler and some ice, and Mom got distracted by too many fallen sticks in the yard and had to go gathering.

I had something to do. I excused myself for the bathroom and headed to the stairs. Tandy met me and acted as if she wanted to follow me. I felt sorry for her that second and knelt to pet her, which surprisingly she let me do.

"You're probably confused, huh?" I said, scratching her chest. "Be glad you get a condo, girl. You just got a reprieve."

I took a deep breath and headed upstairs. The room that I had shunned for a while was calling to me. Not really—not in the way that various parts of my mother's house had called to me in the past month or two. It was just something I wanted to touch base with.

I walked in the now totally empty room and sat on the window seat, moving the blinds so I could see out. I felt a sense of sadness, knowing I would soon not be able to do that anymore. Would the new owners go out on the roof to look at the stars? More than likely, they'd use a chair in the backyard.

I pulled my knees up to me and thought about everything I'd seen in the past two months. Everywhere I'd been. All the direct results of what that house tried so hard to show me.

"Thank you," I whispered, feeling a little silly about it but knowing it was necessary somehow. I closed my eyes. "So much. You changed our lives."

"Whatcha doing up here, honey?" my mother asked, breaking my reverie as she entered the room.

I smiled at her and shrugged, trying to shake off the weirdness I'd just felt. "Just thinking back, I guess."

"I've been doing a lot of that, myself," she said. "Hard not to after being here so long. Raising a family."

"Seems like our whole lives were here inside this house. Even after Holly and I left, like we were still here."

"Yes, they were," she said, looking around from the walls to the ceiling. "Lots of memories in these walls." She leaned over and hugged my neck. "Sometimes I wonder what they'd say if they could tell all the secrets they absorb," she said on a chuckle.

I looked up at her and then let my eyes travel the room.

"You'd be surprised."

TURN THE PAGE FOR A PREVIEW OF
SHARLA LOVELACE'S PREVIOUS NOVEL . . .

The Reason Is You

CHAPTER

1

STARTING OVER SUCKS, BUT AT FORTY IT SUCKS THE LIFE OUT OF you. This thought squeezed my brain on the six-hour drive to Bethany from Dallas. I second-guessed my decision for the ninety-ninth time, eyeing every exit ramp as a potential escape hatch. As we got closer to the dark clouds looming above my hometown, in a Ford Escort with no air-conditioning and my sixteen-year-old daughter hanging her naked legs out the window to dry her pretty little coral toes, I felt the options slipping. One by one.

Not that I wasn't grateful to have a destination. My dad loves me, and he's never judged. But this time was no visit. It was the real deal, with bath towels and Tupperware and everything that would fit in a U-Haul trailer. My head started to bang out a rhythm just thinking about it, but I knew it was the smart thing to do. I'd tried everything after losing my job, and despite the number of times I pushed reality aside, it kept waving at me.

I had Riley to think about. I had to keep a roof over her head, and I couldn't afford to be choosy on what roof that was. We would be okay. I glanced over at her, eyes closed, jamming to whatever her iPod was pumping into her head, and I prayed she would be okay. That she wouldn't be tainted by association with me.

"So, when do we get to Podunk?" she said after we drove through Restin, the nearest big town. Not big like high-rises. Big like it has a Walmart.

I cut my eyes her way. "Wow, that's nice, Riley. Good attitude."

"Well?" she whined, holding her cell up to the window. "I barely get a signal when we go to Pop's. It's like the world falls into hell at the city limit."

"Sorry. Make do."

She rolled her eyes with a smirk, then pulled her dark hair down from its ponytail and fluffed it out before tying it right back up again.

"It's so sticky," she muttered.

I scooped my own hair back. "Rain's in the air," I said. "Get used to it."

The scenery turned from flat and drab to rolling hills of pine trees and underbrush. I knew we were close. I knew my dad had probably adjusted and readjusted the furniture on the wraparound porch. Probably checked out my old bedroom and the extra bedroom just one more time. It was one in the afternoon, and he most likely had dinner planned for that night and the next two.

The sign came closer as we topped a hill, barely visible under the neglected tree branches. The paint was worn off to nothing, and the words were just a darker shade of old.

Riley squinted as we approached.

"Never noticed that sign before. What does it say?"

"Welcome to hell."

That won me a fun look. On the downside of the hill, the town came into view, but not before a few straggling old houses made their unfortunate presence known. Riley turned in her seat as we passed an old wooden house with an iron rooster on top and three broken-down trucks out front.

"Was that a toilet in their front yard?"

"Uh—yeah, I think so," I said.

"It said FOR SALE."

I looked over at her. "You in the market?"

"Somebody's actually going to buy a used toilet?"

I bit my lip to keep from smiling. "Makes a dandy barbecue grill, I've heard."

She rubbed a hand over her eyes and slumped in the seat. "Oh God."

"Yeah, good luck with that."

We drove past the embarrassment, into the timeworn little town of Bethany. Past the different levels of new, getting progressively older as we reached the center and drove halfway around the circle before we veered off to the right. Past the old market and then past the Bait-n-Feed. I eased to a halt at the stop sign, and stared ahead. It was the last one.

Riley pulled her feet in, and I felt her eyes on me.

"So—" she said, letting the word hang.

I tugged at my bottom lip with my fingers. "What?"

"Just wondering how long we're gonna sit here?"

I took a slow breath and let it out. "Just thinking."

"About it being final?"

I stared at the blue eyes so much like mine. Damn, that kid could hit a nerve when she wanted to.

"It's not for a weekend this time, Mom," she continued, her voice smaller. "When we get to Pop's, that's it."

My eyes burned and I had to look away. I grabbed my lipstick from my purse and blindly swiped some on as I contemplated being Worst Mom of the Year.

THE HOUSE WAITED AS WE ROUNDED THE GRAVEL DRIVEWAY, like it knew we were coming. Faded and solid, with memories soaked into the solid oak beams, it was home. I wanted so badly to give Riley that feeling. All I'd managed so far was three apartments with thin walls and a key to the pool gate.

True to my guess, my father sat in one of the porch chairs, nursing an orange soda. His blue fishing hat looked newer than usual, but the blue coverall jumpsuit and ragged work boots were the same.

Riley stretched her way lazily out of the car and met my dad halfway up the steps.

"Hey, Pop," she said, winding her arms around his neck.

He did his little growl that used to make her giggle when she was little, and lifted her off the ground. Barely.

"You're getting tall."

"I put an extra inch on this morning, just for you," she said as she tugged on his short white beard.

I gave the trailer a look and then decided to come back later for all that. Pretend it was temporary for a few more minutes. Instead, I let my dad suck me in for a giant hug. I closed my eyes and breathed in the smell of tobacco and Steen's pure cane syrup that I would know in my sleep if I was struck deaf and blind.

"How was your trip?"

"Peachy."

My voice was muffled into his chest, but the answer didn't matter.

"Just glad y'all are here and made it safe before the rain hits."

I couldn't tell him that I knew we would. The rain always waited for me. I looked around. The only new addition was a weather vane in the form of a B-52 bomber plane, metal propellers and all, flying above the house, giving sound to the breeze as the little blades caught it.

"Everything's pretty much the same."

"Just older and creakier, like me," he said, laughing.

We shuffled into the house, and I braced myself for the horse that bounded across the worn hardwood floor.

"Bojangles!" Riley exclaimed, hitting her knees like a little kid.

But the five-ton black Rottweiler only had eyes for me. For some damn reason, that beast loved me and felt the need to share the joy every year when we came. His big feet landed on me with the momentum of a subway train, and down I went.

"Bojangles," I grunted.

"Sit!" Dad said.

Bojangles sat.

"Can you get him off me first?" I asked through my teeth.

Riley giggled and pulled him off, jogging to the kitchen with Bojangles at her heels to get a treat. After all, he'd performed so well. Dad helped me up and looked over his shoulder.

"She seems okay."

"She's used to disappointment, Dad, she rolls with it."

He winked at me. "Come on."

I heard the back door screen bang and knew they had headed out for a rendezvous. The dog might love me, but he knew who to hit up for the party. With the exception of one unfortunate goldfish, he was the closest thing Riley'd ever had to a pet.

"At least it's summer. She has some time to get settled in and meet people."

I looked away. "Yeah."

"Quit worrying."

"Yeah," I repeated.

"It'll be fine, Dani," he said, touching my arm so that I turned back. "She's tough."

"Tougher than me."

"Tougher than you used to be. But you're a different person now."

I smiled and looked around me. At the room that never changed, the furniture that never moved, everything still in its place. The same pictures adorning the wall, the same clock ticking in the corner over the rarely used fireplace. The same soft rug on the floor. Everything freshly dusted.

I felt like that room. All the same but freshly dusted.

"You'll be fine once you start working and get your feet under you."

He headed to the kitchen and came back with two waters, handing me one. He started to say something, when I heard Riley outside.

"Hang on." I held up a finger as the back of my neck tingled and I leaned out on the porch.

I walked around to the side steps and stopped cold. Leaning casually against my car, in his usual all black and sunglasses, arms folded across his chest, was Alex.

Sweet God.

. . .

I was sixteen when I met Alex. He appeared at my car as I left a party I'd only been invited to as entertainment. I was drunk and hysterical and attempting to open my car door with a house key, and he charmed me with his arrogant good looks and convinced me to walk home instead. We took the long way by a diner and he sat with me as I bought a hot chocolate and a muffin.

He was old, I thought at the time. Thirty-one, he told me. Almost twice my age, but he had that sexy, confident, hot-as-hell older-guy thing going for him. He laughed at my bumbled attempt at flirting and told me to drink my hot chocolate. I was too buzzed to notice the other patrons that cut their eyes my way and whispered about *that loony Dani Shane talking to herself again.* Or maybe I was just hardened to being the town joke.

Call him my guardian angel, or whatever, but he probably saved my life that night. And unlike the others, he didn't move on. He became my only friend. I won't deny that my hormone-ridden brain played out more than a few fantasies involving Alex. He was hot for a dead guy, and funny, too. It was easy with him. Instant. Like I'd known him all my life.

When I left for college at nineteen, he left a white rose on my windshield, and that was the end of it. At the time I thought I'd at least see him when I came home to visit, but no. He was done with me.

Until that moment, when he chose to chat it up with Riley as a grand entrance.

With Riley.

My head said to walk forward, but my feet went numb. Then he looked my direction, and suddenly I was head-to-toe buzz with blood rushing in my ears. I took a deep breath and attempted normal as I made it down the steps without tripping.

Riley saw Alex. Riley wasn't supposed to see people like Alex.

She had her usual folded-arms-with-one-hip-jutted stance, looking annoyed as hell, while Bojangles circled the yard in a frenzy with his nose to the ground. Alex slowly took off his glasses and locked his blue eyes in on mine with that arrogant little smile of his. I felt heat radiate from every pore.

"Dani," he said, low and smooth, and all the breath left me. "My God, look at you."

I opened my mouth to say the same thing, that after twenty-plus years he still looked exactly the same, hot enough to melt my shoes. But then the mommy gene stood up and waved and I remembered Riley was there.

He laughed, a deep throaty sound, as he pointed at Riley.

"I knew it had to be."

A nervous noise squawked from my mouth. Nothing profound like I always imagined it would be.

"The eyes were the first clue," he said with a wink.

Riley frowned, her expression a mix of disgust and wariness.

"God, you know this perv? He was here on the car watching me and won't tell me who the hell he is."

He smirked. "The sweet, gentle nature was the clincher."

I couldn't quit staring. Alex—right there in front of me. My whole past poured down over me in a whoosh, as I locked eyes with the one person that had made it all bearable.

"Mom!"

Riley's voice jolted me back and I jerked her direction. "What?"

Her face screwed up in disgust as she studied me. "Ew."

"What?" My eyes widened as I imagined boogers on my face or something.

"God, Mom, could you be more obvious?" she said under her breath as she looked from me to Alex. "What, did y'all date or something?"

Alex laughed, and I felt my jaw drop a little, and I briefly wondered if my deodorant would hold up to the nervous breakdown coming on.

"Not exactly, sweetheart," he said, his gaze hardwired into mine.

The disgust came back again, as I knew it would.

"I'm not your *sweetheart*, and you can do googly eyes with my mom all you want but stay away from me." She turned to go and then threw back over her shoulder, "By the way, it's summer. The all-black thing is a little Goth."

I stared after her, trying to process it, then closed my eyes and willed it all away. I had never once had a three-way conversation with Alex. No one had ever seen him but me. That whole circus act with Riley had my brain on meltdown.

"Surprise."

His voice was soft and low and when my eyes popped open, his expression had gone just as soft.

"What?"

"Apple doesn't fall far from the tree."